AN ANCIENT DESIRE... A FUTURE PASSION

"She failed," he said with satisfaction.

"Who failed?"

"Your damnable ancestress. She tried to make sure women would never want men again, but it didn't work."

Then he drew her against him and lowered his face to hers once more, but this time his mouth brushed against hers, moving softly, teasing her lips open.

Amala heard the echo of his last words as her world spun about her. Her whole body came alive with sensations. His tongue began to probe hers, and she stiffened and tried to draw away from the strangeness. But he wrapped a hand around the back of her head and held her in place until she no longer wanted to get away. She didn't even know she'd moved her own hand until she felt her fingers threading their way through his hair. From somewhere deep inside her, a moan pushed its way into her throat.

Other *Leisure* and *Love Spell* books by
Saranne Dawson:
SPELL BOUND
CRYSTAL ENCHANTMENT
STAR-CROSSED
ON WINGS OF LOVE
AWAKENINGS
HEART OF THE WOLF
THE ENCHANTED LAND
GREENFIRE

LOVE SPELL 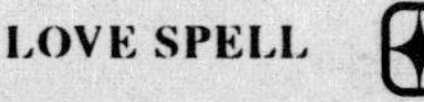 NEW YORK CITY

LOVE SPELL®

June 1997

Published by

Dorchester Publishing Co., Inc.
276 Fifth Avenue
New York, NY 10001

Printed in the United States of America.

Prologue

THE BOATS MOVED SLOWLY TOWARD THE MIST, TRAVelling in a wide, loose line. Most were smallish craft, but here and there amidst them were the large, elegant boats belonging to Great Families. A few of these were towing heavily laden barges, which slowed their progress considerably.

One by one, they were swallowed up by the thick, gray-white mist, and on board the occupants hastily donned waterproof cloaks to protect themselves from the sudden, penetrating dampness and chill. They moved now in almost total blindness because not even the strong beams of light from the large boats could pierce the gloom for more than a few meters.

No voices broke the eerie silence except for

the occasional cries of young children and babies—and those were hastily hushed. The only other sounds were the low-pitched hums of electric motors and the soft splashing of their passage.

Three kilometers behind them, small, swift boats knifed through the water, then veered sharply away from the mist at the last possible second. Aboard those boats there were curses and shouts of outrage, but the occupants of the lead boats were too far into the sound-dampening mist to hear those cries.

They moved ever more deeply into the gloom. Cloaked figures stood motionless on the decks, arms clutching babies or flung protectively around the shoulders of older children. On the bridges, inexperienced captains kept their eyes on the navigational equipment, steering due west.

The tension was palpable, binding together the entire fleet. Today was Freedom Day, a day planned for nearly a generation. Among them were those who had grave doubts, but there were none who had not come willingly. What must be now would be. There could be no turning back. Year by year, as the plans were formulated and then executed, more had been drawn in. From the Great Families to the lowliest, all had been galvanized into action by the promise of a new life—surely a better life.

Then the mist vanished abruptly. One moment they were still deep within its damp embrace, and the next moment the sun shone warmly once more. All eyes stared straight ahead where the island rose to welcome them.

The boats poured into the small natural harbor, jockeying for position at the long wharves. The small crafts clustered together at one end, making space for the larger ones that were just now emerging from the opaque mist. By the time the first of these grand boats had made its way in stately fashion to its pier, the occupants of the smaller crafts had disembarked and were standing in quiet groups on the shore. All eyes sought out the last of the Great Families' boats, then locked onto the small, erect figure standing in the bow.

The breeze caught her long, pale hair and whipped it about her face for a moment before she reached up with a bejeweled hand to brush it from her eyes. All of them took note of the heavy, ornate Family ring on her right hand—and the absence of bracelets on her wrists. Many of them then looked down at their own empty wrists and now realized the full enormity of what they had done.

As the woman with the golden hair stepped off her boat, a few mothers reached out to clutch their sons, then slowly let them go again. Already, the painful process of separation was beginning.

The golden-haired one walked toward them, small of stature but powerful to the very tips of her soft leather shoes. Every woman present drew strength from her—a sorely needed strength.

"It is done," she said in a low voice that nonetheless carried to all of the scattered assemblage. "We must give thanks to Aleala."

Her remarkably deep blue eyes lifted to the great mountain behind them, and all other eyes followed. The peak rose precipitously from the lush green land, its crest shrouded in the same strange mist that now obscured the land from which they had come.

Leaving their possessions on the shore, the women moved toward the mountain, walking in silence as they followed the ancient, worn path. The climb grew ever steeper, but none of them faltered, not even the elderly or those carrying infants. Aleala drew them upward, giving them strength, singing her sweet, soft encouragement in a music felt rather than heard.

At the broad place just below the crest, once more enshrouded in the mist, they all knelt in a reverent silence.

The next two weeks saw a frenzy of activity as they made temporary dwellings into permanent homes and began to erect new homes—inexpertly, but in the end satisfactorily. The rich land was quickly prepared for planting, often by women who had never before tilled the soil. Soft hands and scented bodies gave way to calluses and sweat. Committees met far into the night as the women wielded a welcome new control over their destinies.

It was a time of heady excitement that dissipated any lingering doubts. Freedom was tasted and found to be an incomparable elixir. The greatest worked with the lowliest and discovered the joys of a sisterhood that knew no class distinction. If at night there were still occasional tears and fears, they were quickly banished with each new day's labors and promises.

At the end of the first week, the women who had been assigned to keep watch from the slopes of the mountain were reassigned to other tasks. No boats had come through the everpresent mist, although they all knew that furious assaults must have been made and were probably still being made. Aleala was keeping her promise of protection.

The Council members in particular breathed far more easily now, because they had been forced to decide what should be done if any men somehow made it through the mist. Brutality and death were what they had left behind them, and they had cringed at the prospect of bringing it to this haven of peace and gentleness.

Then, as the second week drew to a close, the tension in the settlement began to grow once more. The male children—all of them under 12—had already begun to whimper with sickness. Only the very youngest remained healthy. But it had been necessary to bring them; the men would need time to prepare for their care.

At dawn, exactly two weeks after their arrival, the entire community once more assembled at the harbor. The sick children were wrapped in heavy cloaks and brought aboard the Great Family boats which moved quickly away from the docks. With one exception, the women aboard were older women without young children.

The woman with the golden hair stood as she had before in the bow of her elegant boat. Her right hand with its great ring rested lightly on the shoulder of her son. He was nearly 12 and tall for his age, almost as tall as she. His face was rather pale, although he'd been less weakened than most of the others. He had, she thought, his father's enormous strength as well as his iron will.

"Why aren't the other mothers going home?" he asked in a voice that even in adolescence was developing a ring of authority.

She didn't look at him. "None of us is going home, Sherad. The island is our home now."

He drew slightly away from her, frowning in obvious confusion. "But you can't stay here. Father won't permit it."

A bitter smile curved her full lips. "Your father no longer has any say in what I do."

The boy was silent as they moved into the mist. Something in his mother's voice had frightened him, although he was certain that she couldn't be speaking the truth. When he spoke again, he strove hard for a tone of certainty.

"Father will come get you."

She shook her golden head, half-covered now by the cowl of a heavy cloak. "He cannot come after me, although I've no doubt that he's tried.

No man can come through the mist. Aleala has decreed it."

There was the smallest catch in her voice as she prayed silently that he hadn't lost his life in that attempt. Then the momentary weakness passed, and she resumed speaking in a normal tone.

"That's why the boys must return. You see how they all grow ill. This is a place for women."

"But Father told me that men used to come here," the boy persisted.

"Yes, they did, but that was long ago, before Aleala turned her back on them."

"Father said that Aleala is unimportant—irrelevant." He pronounced the word carefully, emphasizing the recent addition to his vocabulary.

"I doubt that he believes that now," his mother replied with the dry humor that could surface occasionally.

"But when *are* you coming home?" the boy asked, his voice slightly tremulous, as though he might already have guessed the answer.

She turned to look him straight in the eyes, silently searching that young, still-innocent face that was a remarkable blending of both his parents.

What a good child he is, she thought with a fathomless sadness, but in a very short time . . . She'd seen the signs already—the occasional outbursts of male arrogance and even a certain contempt toward her. In a few more months, on his twelfth birthday, he would have been taken from her in any event and sent away to school to learn to be a warrior.

"Never," she pronounced firmly, her gaze remaining locked upon his in one final effort to make him understand. "We will never return."

"But why?" he asked petulantly. "Why do you do this?"

"Because your father—and all the other men—refuse to give up making war. Because we no longer wish to raise sons and send them off to be killed."

There was far more to it than that, but she knew he could never understand. How could she explain to him the injustice of the iron laws that bound women's destinies to men's, that gave them no freedom and no choice—not even the choice of a mate or the number of children to bear? A girl even younger than he was could have understood, but he was male and such comprehension was beyond him.

How many times, she wondered, had she tried to make Jorlan understand? How many ways? How long had she continued to believe that one day she would find the right words, the right way to make him see what he would not see? Once or twice, sated from lovemaking, he had actually listened to her—or so she'd believed at the time. But in the cold light of day, nothing had changed.

"What's wrong with war?" the boy blurted out suddenly. "Father is a great warrior, the greatest who ever lived."

"Yes, he is." She nodded sadly, then murmured almost to herself, "And so will you be one day. I've no doubt of that. But I won't have to watch it."

Before either of them could speak again, the mists parted. Far out at the horizon, the land they had left behind rose in a dark smudge against the red-gold of the dawn. And between them and that land—a little more than a kilometer away—a flotilla of boats waited.

This was the dangerous part; they all knew that. If the men could seize them before they could retreat into the mist, they would never see the island again. Each of the women present reached nervously into the pocket of her cloak and touched a tiny capsule, knowing that if the men attacked they must swallow the poison quickly. The men had been told of the capsules, and the women could only hope that no assault would be made.

The waiting boats began to approach them slowly and cautiously. The women herded the boys into small dinghies and prepared to lower them over the sides. The golden-haired woman dropped her hand from her son's shoulder, then said in a tight, choked voice, "Go!"

He stared at her for a moment with an expression that was part perplexity, part annoyance—then did as told. She watched him until he was safely in the water, and then she searched the waiting boats that remained at a discreet distance.

She saw Jorlan almost immediately, his long,

powerful legs braced against the roll of the craft as he lifted the megaphone to his mouth.

"You won't get away with this, Amala! We'll find a way through sooner or later!"

She smiled bitterly. For the first time, she had nothing to fear from him. For the first time in her life, her own thoughts and feelings could take precedence over those of a man. The rush of pleasure that accompanied that knowledge very nearly eliminated the pain of separation from her son.

Jorlan was too far away for Amala to see him clearly, but her mind's eye saw that strong, handsome face and she actually felt the touch of those midnight eyes upon her.

For one wild, irrational moment, she actually wanted to go back, to feel his powerful arms around her once more, to lay with him in their marriage bed, to feel the driving force of his need for her.

Then she willed the memories away. What was it in women that could make them willingly accept slavery in exchange for a few moments' pleasure in the arms of a man? Once more, she told herself firmly that they all must expunge any desire for a man, now and forevermore.

She hadn't intended to speak to him, but now she picked up a megaphone and raised it to her lips.

"You'll never find a way through, Jorlan. Aleala will protect us. And we will never return. If you wish our people to survive, you will do as you've been instructed."

"You'll pay for this, Amala!" he shouted across the waters, his voice nearly choked with helpless rage.

She lowered the megaphone and turned away as the boats glided back into the safety of the mist.

"We have paid," she said softly and sadly.

CHAPTER ONE

JORLAN STRODE INTO THE SMALL THEATER. HIS dark eyes were already locked onto the huge, high-resolution viewing screen. Disappointment knifed through him when he saw only the everpresent, shifting patterns of the mist.

One of the small group of men present turned from the screen and saw him standing there, scowling at the empty screen. He smiled and raised a hand in greeting.

"Jorlan! Congratulations and welcome home! I'd have thought you'd still be celebrating your victory on Bethusa."

Jorlan clasped the man's arm in a welcoming grip. "I cut the celebration short. There's too much to do here."

It was a small lie. The truth was that he'd cut short his celebration because he was bored. The world of pleasure had lost its appeal very quickly this time. An image of the silver-haired, sloe-eyed Asroth flicked through his mind and vanished quickly. He turned again to the screen.

"Have I missed the dancing?"

"No, they should be coming along soon."

"Has Amala been with them much lately?" he inquired with careful casualness.

"The undisputed star of the show," the other man acknowledged as he exchanged knowing glances with the others present.

Everyone knew about Jorlan's obsession with the golden-haired woman. A few superstitious old men even claimed to see a mystical significance in the fact that after four generations there were once more a Jorlan and an Amala among them. Most of them, however, believed that the women were just playing games with them, seizing upon the appearance of a second Jorlan to torment them with another Amala, but none of them could deny the unsettling likenesses of each to their famous forebears.

Jorlan settled his long frame into a chair. His right hand tapped restlessly against the padded arm, the soft light glinting off his Family ring. He continued to stare at the screen with an impatient frown.

The other man settled back with a smile. It was well-known that patience was not Jorlan's strongest suit. If will alone could have commanded Amala's appearance, she would already be there on the screen, weaving among the scattered boulders in the sensuous dances they had all come to know so well. But will alone could no longer command the women of Volas; that time had ended more than 100 years ago.

Then murmurs of satisfaction rose throughout the room as indistinct figures appeared at the edge of the screen, moving slowly toward the center. Jorlan leaned forward with intense concentration as one figure separated herself from the group. Pale hair caught the breeze as she flung aside her hooded cloak and then bowed her head in a moment of prayer.

Jorlan grunted his dissatisfaction as he saw that she continued to wear the same shapeless costume. The top was loose with long, flowing sleeves, and the bottom consisted of baggy pants that ended in ties just above the ankles. Pants on a woman! Ever since they'd finally found a way to spy on them, the men had been loudly voicing their disapproval of that masculine attire. They were all long since convinced that it was just one more act of defiance—though of course the women had no way of knowing they were being observed.

For some years, they'd all had short hair, too—yet another blasphemy—but recently some of them, Amala included, had let their hair grow long again. No one, however, pretended to see any significance in that change, since women's tastes were known to be fickle. Tomorrow they might decide to shave their heads.

Amala moved to the center of the circle, as she always did when she was among the dancers. As Jorlan's companion had said, she was the undisputed star of the show, the most athletic and graceful among them. The others blurred into the background as she began the swaying, sinuous movements of the age-old dance.

Raw hunger coursed through Jorlan's veins, a hunger that should by all rights have been well-sated by his stopover amidst the pleasures of Bethusa. But neither Asroth, for all her skills, nor any other woman had ever been able to prevent the return of that hunger every time he saw Amala.

She had become a symbol to him, an image he carried with him as he ventured into intergalactic battles. In defiance of all logic—and Jorlan was a very logical man—he continued to believe that she would one day be his ultimate conquest.

In the years since the women had deserted them, the men of Volas had conquered their own world and then carried their supremacy into space. They were masters of entire star systems and rulers of many worlds, but their women remained beyond their grasp, safe on their damned island.

Jorlan remained utterly still, his big, hard body tensed and his eyes riveted on the screen. His long fingers gripped the armrests, and small muscles bunched beneath his curly black beard. Others drifted into the room, keeping their distance from him as they exchanged knowing smiles.

On the screen Amala continued to dance, displaying the remarkable agility that had marked her as a star performer years ago. It was difficult to judge accurately either her height or her figure, but Jorlan could see that she was slightly smaller than average, and certain movements hinted at a well-rounded figure.

Then the dancing ceased. The others made their final obeisance to their goddess and disappeared from the screen, but Amala remained, as she'd done on several other occasions when he'd been here watching her.

She walked over to the edge of the camera's range and picked up her cloak, then drew it about her as she walked slowly back to the center of the screen. Jorlan's breath caught in his throat as she turned to face that unseen camera—and him.

In order to filter out the worst of the mist, the camera unfortunately was black-and-white. That robbed him of the full impact of that gaze that seemed to be staring directly at him, but knowing that the original Amala had had the remarkable blue eyes of her family, he was sure hers were the same.

She remained quite still for a few moments, staring into a camera she couldn't possibly know existed and at a man who could be no more than a name on a list to her. But Jorlan was certain that she *did* know he was there watching her.

There was defiance in every fiber of her being—in her stance, in the slight uplift of her chin, in one fine, raised brow. As always, he found that masculine quality in a beautiful and delicate woman very unsettling. Furthermore, it was an exact copy of the expression he'd seen in a portrait of her infamous ancestress.

Finally, with an arrogant toss of her golden mane, she wrapped the cloak more tightly about herself and walked quickly away, leaving the screen empty once more.

The total silence of the theater was now broken with rather overly loud conversation and slightly uneasy chuckles, demonstrating that Jorlan had not been the only one affected by that vision. But reality returned much more slowly to Jorlan, and with it came that powerful and bitter sense of loss.

The next morning Jorlan found Amala still there, hovering about the edges of his consciousness, taunting him with her nearness—and her distance. If he hadn't been expecting company, he would have been waging an inner battle over another trip to the observatory.

Jorlan was uncomfortably aware of his obsession with Amala. While it was certainly true that most of them were obsessed, to one degree or another, with the women, he doubted that his own feelings fell within normal bounds. So, through the exercise of self-discipline that is second nature to any warrior, he permitted himself to watch her only occasionally.

If Jorlan had been asked to explain the emotions that Amala aroused in him, he would have been completely at a loss. It wasn't likely that anyone *would* ask, of course, since feelings were not a matter for discussion among the men.

Certainly, it wasn't love. That word had ceased to exist among them, if indeed it had ever existed. Most of the men, Jorlan included, had come to believe that love was a weakness—the weakness that had permitted the women's treachery.

Neither was it strictly lust, a word that definitely *did* exist among them. Jorlan was thoroughly acquainted with lust. He'd satisfied that urge with Asroth and her compatriots on Bethusa many times. Lust was a natural part of life, like breathing, eating and war.

If he'd been forced to explain his feelings for Amala, he would undoubtedly have described them in terms of a challenge—that which he could not have, and therefore that which he wanted above all else. Added to that was the coincidence of there once again being a Jorlan in his family and an Amala in hers. The breeding process was controlled by the women, as was the naming of female children, but the naming of male offspring was left to the men.

Jorlan had known for many years that there was an Amala among them. Young girls came to the mountain for the first time at the age of 12, so he'd gone many times to the observatory during that year—his nineteenth. And he'd watched each new dancer, seeking the family traits that she might or might not possess.

But as fortune would have it, he hadn't been

there when Amala had first come to the mountain. Instead, he'd been off in the Tarla system, apprenticed to a starship and immersed in the first of his many battles.

He had returned, flushed with victory, to learn from his father that a girl had appeared who bore a startling resemblance to the reviled Amala. By this time, Jorlan was sporting the trademark beard of the warrior and needed only to lift his eyes to the portrait of his own famous ancestor to know that he likewise appeared to be a reincarnation.

Jorlan could still recall with perfect clarity the first time he'd seen her, sylph-like and astonishingly beautiful even at 12 as she practiced the intricate dances under the watchful eyes of the older women. She was still only a child, but the promise of the woman to come was already there. Although he could not have put it into any words, Jorlan knew that he had met his destiny.

He was now 34, while she was 27—and neither of them had yet shown up on the birth lists as parents. Normally, parenthood was conferred at a much earlier age. Moreover, both of them were members of Great Families whose heritage must be preserved.

His Feloth servant brought his breakfast to the sun-drenched terrace behind his mountain home, then padded quietly away, dropping into a hunched, rolling gait as soon as her duty to her master was discharged. As he ate, Jorlan's mind drifted back to the original Jorlan and Amala, their common ancestors. The first Jorlan was regarded by all as their greatest warrior—the man who had completed the conquest of their home world and then survived to take part in the dawning of the Space Age that had provided new opportunities for conquest.

Much had been written about him, of course, and from earliest childhood, Jorlan had repeatedly been made aware of the enormous responsibilities of that name. He took considerable pleasure in the fact that, thus far, he had distinguished himself in battle, although he felt that no opportunity had yet presented itself for him to equal his illustrious ancestor or surpass him.

The original Amala was a subject he and most of the other men found difficult to contemplate. He'd often stared at her portrait and wondered how such a delicate beauty could have wreaked such havoc upon them. She hadn't accomplished it alone, but her helpers had all been women, too.

Somehow over the years, what had apparently begun as a small, secret conspiracy among disgruntled women of Great Families—undoubtedly nothing more than a game played by women with too much time on their hands—had grown until it had finally drawn in every woman of their race.

But while others before her had schemed and laid plans, it was Amala who had carried them to fruition. All agreed that it was she who had transformed a minor rebellion into an outright revolution. Still, she'd managed it only because of a most unfortunate chain of circumstances.

First of all, computers had been developed, chiefly to facilitate warfare, and terminals linked the leaders with each other and with the great central library.

At the same time, those leaders—Jorlan certainly among them—spent less and less time at home as the battles raged between their race and the others with whom they shared their small world.

Somehow, Amala had learned to operate the computer. Some historians suggested that Jorlan, whose indulgence toward Amala was well-known, had actually taught her, but however it came about, Amala suddenly had at her fingertips all the exploding knowledge of a world newly awash in technology. Like the other women of Great Families, she had been given only a rudimentary education and then encouraged in the arts.

Most astonishingly of all, she had actually understood the information she called forth from the computer, information that had provided the last vital link in a chain of treachery.

She had learned the technique of artificial insemination. The procedure had been developed several decades earlier to produce high-quality livestock. Then, as wars raged and young men's lives were lost, it became common practice for male members of Great Families to donate sperm that was frozen against the possibility of an untimely death without an heir.

The process was not really complicated, and Amala was helped further by the fact that she, like many women of her class, volunteered in the busy hospitals. The computer taught her all she needed to know about the technique, and her access to the hospitals and their laboratories enabled her to steal the necessary equipment.

Finally, with the means at hand to perpetuate their race, the women went stealthily about their tasks of stealing and hoarding all the other supplies they required for permanent residence on the island. Their comings and goings from the island were not closely watched because the men had far more important things on their minds, and the general absence of younger and more vigilant men from the city made their treachery that much easier.

Two generations earlier, following a volcanic eruption, the island had been closed to men. Some lives were lost before it was realized that the mist that had always encircled the holy island had become lethal for males. For untold ages before that, both men and women had worshipped on the island, but by the time of the women's betrayal, the men had lost interest in the ancient goddess, choosing instead to worship the twin gods of technology and war.

Once the island was closed to men, some of them had suggested that the women should be denied access, too, but the women clung to their worship of the old goddess. The men were too preoccupied with conquest to make an issue of this female foolishness, and perhaps they were even a bit reluctant to refuse the women their goddess; warriors could be a superstitious lot.

In any event, nothing was done—and the women carried out their nefarious plot. Jorlan still found it nearly impossible to contemplate the enormity of their betrayal and the sheer audacity of their action, but the warrior in him was forced, very reluctantly, to admire their astounding victory.

His furry servant came to carry off the remnants of his meal, and Jorlan switched once more to thoughts of the present Amala. Was it possible that she might have inherited more than beauty from her diabolical ancestress? Was she in fact a reincarnation of that other Amala? Jorlan was no mystic and in fact had no use for religion or mysticism in any form, but he knew that his own resemblance to his famous forebear was far more than skin deep. Was it the same with her?

That possibility lay at the very core of his obsession with her. If it were true, then he wanted the opportunity to rectify the mistake made by the first Jorlan. The one blemish on the great Jorlan's record was that he had permitted his wife to get out of hand—an understandable mistake, given the pressures on him at the time, but a disastrous one, nonetheless.

Only within Jorlan's family was there any real tendency to blame his illustrious namesake for the women's treachery, but that was due in large part to the diaries the family had kept secret all these years.

As a young man, the present Jorlan had pored over these secret writings and, as had those before him, was astounded to find that the great hero had had feet of clay. Amala had been his one weakness, a weakness whose full extent had been carefully concealed from all but family.

The present Jorlan could have excused the earlier writings as the battlefield ramblings of a young and hot-blooded man, but no such excuse could be made for the agonized outpourings of the much older Jorlan who wrote that he would have gladly given up all his glorious victories for the return of his beloved Amala. To the last days of his long and illustrious life, he had mourned that loss. The story in the family was that he had died proclaiming his love for her.

Jorlan was always uncomfortable with these thoughts, although the disquieting fascination they held for him invariably brought them to mind. Those writings had provided a glimpse of something he couldn't understand—and perhaps didn't want to understand. Weakness of any kind was something all warriors abhorred, and yet the greatest of them all perhaps had been among the weakest.

It was for this reason that Jorlan subscribed to the rather common belief among them that they might just be better off in their present situation, however inconvenient it might be in some respects. After all, they still had their sons, the Feloths made adequate servants, and they could still enjoy the pleasures of women—even if they were forced to seek out those pleasures among women of lesser races.

Yet, when he went to the observatory and watched Amala—so close but so damnably beyond his reach—dark thoughts whispered through his brain, raw hunger gnawed at his peace of mind, and his dreams were tormented for many nights thereafter.

Those thoughts returned now in the bright light of day as he sat on his mountaintop terrace, reliving those moments when she'd stood there, staring out at him through the camera's lens—beautiful, desirable and defiant.

Then, with considerable relief, he heard the whine of the arriving airsleds and went forth to greet his friends. Amala slipped into a dim corner of his mind to become nothing more than a nagging reminder of a challenge not yet met.

A difficult rock climb was scheduled for this day. It was an ancient sport still practiced by only a small group of men, as others sought out more sophisticated sports and entertainment.

After greeting his two friends, Jorlan climbed into his own airsled and they were quickly airborne, gliding over treetops to the dusky mountain range at the horizon. Beneath them, the untouched land was a patchwork of greens, interspersed here and there with the pale gold of the rare kodan tree, whose delicate foliage never failed to remind him of Amala's hair.

These were Jorlan's ancestral lands, and although his official residence was hundreds of miles away in a great compound that also housed other members of his extended family, it was here in this rugged mountain country that he spent most of his time on Volas.

The sleds passed in near-silence over a broad clearing that was covered with the blue-green grasses common to the region, and the man in the sled nearest to him called out suddenly. Jorlan looked down and saw the small herd of carelas grazing placidly amidst the long grasses. They were rare and elusive and he knew that his friend enjoyed hunting them, but Jorlan would permit no hunting here.

At the age of 12, he had killed his first—and last—carela. The sight of the dead animal, devoid of all its remarkable beauty and grace, had sickened him, and not even his father's rough teasing could persuade him to hunt again. As soon as his father had died and he had become head of his family, he had issued an order banning all hunting here.

The trio brought their sleds to a graceful landing in a small clearing at the base of the craggy mountains, then alighted and buckled on the anti-grav belts that would protect them from any falls. Following the untimely death some years ago of a much-decorated warrior, the Council had decreed that henceforth all climbers must be protected in this manner. They could not afford to lose good men to such foolishness, since the women kept the population under control at barely more than replacement levels.

The climb began, deceptively easy at first. They went hand over hand, with every centimeter fought for and gained by skill alone. All three men were expert climbers, and they proceeded in a loose line, with one moving slightly ahead and then another. The winner would be the man who reached the top first only if he hadn't been forced to resort to use of the anti-grav belt. This was a test of skill and caution, not one of speed.

About halfway up the rock face they managed to find narrow ledges that provided a respite from their labors. Jorlan crouched next to his oldest and best friend, Zakton, a tall, fair-haired man with the piercing blue eyes that were the trademark of his family. He was also—though neither had ever laid eyes upon the other—Amala's brother. Their other friend was some distance away on another ledge, invisible at the moment except for the curling wisps of smoke from his pipe.

"Have you been to the observatory yet?" Zakton asked, glancing at Jorlan.

Jorlan nodded mutely. He knew that Zakton was well aware of his obsession with Amala, although he had never spoken of it directly.

"Did you see her?"

Once again, Jorlan nodded without speaking. That damnable image was creeping out of its corner into his mind's eye.

"I understand that she's there every day

now," Zakton went on, "although no one knows why. She's never been a regular before."

Jorlan turned briefly to stare at his companion, a slight frown knitting his heavy black brows. It *was* unusual for her to be there on a regular basis. Some women did come nearly every day, presumably out of piety, but Amala's appearances were relatively rare despite her skills as a dancer.

A silence hung between the two of them, a silence filled with an unspoken question. Could that mean she was pregnant? For years there had been speculation among them that pregnant women came to the mountain on a daily basis. Certainly they did so once their conditions became obvious. Presumably, this ensured Aleala's blessings upon the child.

Jorlan stared off into space, his frown deepening. Could she be pregnant—and could it be his? His gut twisted in a silent, bitter rage that he should be forced to sit here speculating about such a thing, instead of knowing beyond question that his child was being borne by a woman he had chosen and banded.

Most men seemed to have long since accepted the way of it now, but Jorlan knew he never would. He didn't want to learn that he had fathered a son only when the birth lists arrived. He didn't much care if it were a girl, and in any event he would never see her.

Without conscious intent, he made a sound of disgust.

"It would make sense," Zakton continued. "She's twenty-seven now—almost twenty-eight, actually."

There was a hint of wistfulness in Zakton's voice, something Jorlan had heard before but had never acknowledged. He didn't really understand it, but then he himself had no sisters. There had been one, born three years after him, but she'd died at the age of four months.

That recollection made him suddenly fearful. What if Amala were pregnant with his son and that child died, too? They knew nothing about the state of medicine on the island, although it stood to reason that they had regressed from the time of their arrival. Old records indicated that there were many medicinal herbs on the island, but Jorlan certainly didn't put any faith in them.

On the other hand, the mortality rate didn't appear to be high, although the women simply might not be reporting miscarriages and stillbirths.

He cursed vehemently at his helplessness and drew a sharp glance from Zakton. "She could be pregnant with my son," he muttered by way of explanation, "and who knows what kind of primitive medicine they practice out there?"

"It could be," Zakton acknowledged, knowing full well how Jorlan chafed at his failure to be given a son and heir. He himself had a five-year-old son, whose mother had died without Zakton's ever having seen her.

Zakton cast a sympathetic glance at his old friend, who moodily crouched beside him. Recently Zakton had begun to wonder if Jorlan's failure to become a father was the result of deliberate actions on the part of the women. Just as the name Amala was reviled among the men, Jorlan's name might well be anathema to the women, and they knew that he was the last direct descendant of the first Jorlan.

On the other hand, it was entirely possible, to Zakton's way of thinking, that his sister had chosen Jorlan to father her children and was simply making him wait to exact her own revenge. They had no idea how the women chose the men who fathered their children, but it was not beyond the realm of possibility that his sister had the family trait of well-developed irony.

In his own way, Zakton too was obsessed with Amala. He'd always been intrigued by their infamous forebear, and when he'd first seen his sister, he'd been awestruck by the resemblance.

Zakton smiled to himself as he thought about a union between these two—a real union rather than the spurious kind that now produced their children. Jorlan had certainly inherited many of the traits of his ancestor, and if Amala were anything at all like the first Amala . . .

Jorlan got up abruptly and announced that it was time to continue their climb. After calling out to their unseen companion, the men once more began their tortuous ascent. The other two men noted that Jorlan's attention to the climb had obviously faltered, since he was forced to resort twice to the use of his anti-grav belt.

Finally, with shouts of triumph and some

good-natured teasing, they reached their destination. The mountain they had chosen was the tallest in the range, and from its flat, narrow summit they could see all the way to the seacoast. Far out at the limits of their vision, the blue-green waters faded almost imperceptibly to a milky-white line between sea and sky. Forever hidden from their view in that eternal mist was the island.

All three men sat facing in that direction, silently regarding the damnable fog. A long holiday had been declared some 40 years ago when a camera was at long last developed that permitted them to see through the mists. It was a small and largely hollow victory—but a victory nonetheless.

Even so, they were unable to see where and how the women actually lived. Old maps existed from the days when men still could go there, and from them they knew that the original settlement lay in a narrow valley beyond a ridge. The far side of the island was known to be mostly barren and inhospitable, whipped by constant winds and occasionally buffeted by tremors.

Jorlan sat staring balefully at that white line, wondering anew at the stupidity of their ancestors who had permitted the women to continue going there after the mist had become lethal for men, but he supposed that it just never occurred to them that the women who shared their beds and bore their sons and did their bidding in all things could turn against them. After all, those women had been taught from birth that men were their natural masters and that their happiness lay in making their men happy.

Why, then, had the system failed? What had gone wrong? It seemed to him to be a perfectly logical system, clearly based upon biological and mental differences between the sexes. Furthermore, it appeared to work on the other worlds they'd encountered. Nowhere had they found a society where females challenged male supremacy.

It was a question without an answer, although Jorlan sensed in some obscure way that it sorely needed an answer.

The trio took out the food packs they had carried with them and began to talk as they sated appetites whetted by the strenuous climb. Jorlan let the conversation go on for some time while he continued to stare moodily at the horizon.

"Is there any news on the latest tests?" he inquired when there was a momentary lull in the conversation.

The other two followed his glance briefly before Solov, the third member of their group, spoke. He had spent the past six months at home recuperating from a battle wound.

"Not yet, but the results should be in soon. A waste of time, in my opinion. Those minds could be put to better use improving the firing range of the tavids."

Zakton nodded with a chuckle. "True

enough, but we seem to find it necessary to keep trying."

Solov grunted his acknowledgment of that fact, then went on in what was for him a surprisingly philosophical tone. "I wonder if anyone has ever seriously considered what would happen if we did somehow manage to get through the mist."

His companions looked from him to the horizon and then back again. Jorlan broke the brief silence with a laugh.

"What is there to consider? If we get through, we bring them back and then blow the damned island to eternity."

"I think," Zakton put in drily, "that Solov was wondering just what it is that we'd be bringing back. Surely they've changed."

There was another brief, almost wary silence—a common occurrence when the men contemplated their women.

"Changed?" Jorlan scoffed at last. "They're still women. We can see that."

Zakton smiled as he contemplated the distant mist. "What if they're all like Amala—the original Amala, I mean?"

Jorlan and Solov exchanged long-suffering looks. Zakton was their very good friend, but his incessant championing of his ancestress could try even their patience.

Jorlan let himself consider that possibility for all of ten seconds. He was willing to admit to a grudging admiration for Amala, but in the final analysis, she'd accomplished her treachery only because she'd had a very busy and overly indulgent husband, not because she was the brilliant "man in a woman's body" that Zakton often portrayed her to be.

The great starship fell slowly through the atmosphere of Bethusa as the planet loomed ever larger beneath them. They were close enough now to see, through wispy clouds, the outlines of continents and large lakes.

Jorlan sat with controlled impatience in the captain's chair, strategically placed to afford him an unobstructed view of the entire control room. Officers' uniformed backs were to him as they watched carefully over their various areas by means of video displays and flashing lights.

His presence now was useless, but tradition dictated that the captain remain on the bridge until the ship had landed and all systems were shut down. With a ship the size and complexity of this giant starship, the process would take well over an hour. The smaller vessels of his fleet would already have landed and been hauled into the gigantic repair complex.

Another battle was over, and with its conclusion had come his greatest victory yet. Furthermore, not one man had been lost from his entire fleet. He'd received reports on the score of wounded and knew that all would live, although one or two of them might never see space duty again.

Jorlan felt a moment's sympathy for them; to

be condemned to a life spent planetside was the worst nightmare for all spacemen. Even death might be preferable. Those who were chosen for the Space Command were unquestionably the elite, as the planetbound military had been before them. The highest ranks were reserved for men from Great Families, but even the lowliest could aspire to space duty—and all of them did.

Unconsciously, he rubbed a hand over his black, curly beard, the trademark of the spaceman as it had been generations before for the military. The tradition had developed from the necessity of battlefield conditions, then continued into space where living conditions were far better though water was precious. There was no actual law that forbade the wearing of beards by the planetbound, but none wore them, although a few affected mustaches.

The ugly Viboldans, their erstwhile foe, had proved to be every bit as tenacious and ferocious as expected. But now, their world, with its surfeit of precious minerals and its highly convenient location, belonged to the men of Volas. Furthermore, there'd been no reason to leave any overlords, since there were no Viboldans left. Every last one of the world's inhabitants had been eradicated at Jorlan's orders.

The ugly, lizard-like creatures had retreated, together with their females and offspring, to their underground cities. Faced with the unwelcome prospect of losing some of his own precious troops to capture those hidden cities,

Jorlan had elected to blast them all. He had no second thoughts about his decision, but the unnecessary destruction of civilians did not sit well with him, either—even if, as in this case, they weren't human. Life was life, even if it were less than human, and he would have much preferred to bend the Viboldans to the acceptance of his race as their masters.

The aftermath of battle, even when victory had been absolute, always left him vaguely irritable and depressed. The pleasures that awaited him on Bethusa, followed by a sojourn at home, eased that feeling somewhat, but it never quite vanished until he once more set forth into battle.

Yet it perhaps would be unfair to say that he was blood-thirsty, as some of the others surely were. Instead, he was a man who lived for challenges, and war offered him the only true challenge he could find. He was temperamentally unsuited to a life spent in the pursuit of scientific knowledge, which was also an acceptable career for a man of his stature, and his membership on the Council gave him as much a taste of politics as he wanted. Besides, there was the matter of tradition. The men of his family had always been warriors, as had the men of his friend Zakton's family.

Far back in the turbulent history of their world, these two greatest of the Great Families had battled each other for supremacy. Then, after several generations and many deaths had produced no clear-cut victory, both families had wisely agreed to put an end to the bloodbath and join forces against outside foes.

Still, the two families had remained wary of each other, and only with the marriage between the first Jorlan and Amala had they been fully united. Following that disaster, each family had retreated once more to a skeptical distance—until the present generation.

To the surprise of all, Jorlan and Zakton had become the best of friends virtually from the day they'd first met at the academy at the age of 12. Since the two men were now the heads of their respective families, the old rivalry appeared finally to be at an end.

As the starship neared touchdown, there was an increase in activity in the control center. Lights flashed, sirens whooped, and there was the occasional verbal confirmation that all was well. The great ship swayed slightly as it drifted down to meet the surface of Bethusa. Jorlan dutifully scanned all systems, knowing full well that his actions were superfluous. Touchdown was computer-controlled, and the officers on deck were skilled.

Then at last came the slight shudder that told them they'd made contact with Bethusa. Through the large porthole in the control center, they could see the barren desert they had chosen long ago as a docking and repair station.

Bethusa was a large world—far larger than Volas—and possessed a richly varied topography and climate. The inhabitants, surprisingly few in number, were a tall, lithe people with bronzed skin and light hair. To the amazement of the would-be conquerors from Volas, the Bethusans had offered no resistance at all. Their primitive religion was filled with stories about gods arriving from the skies, and the newcomers, somewhat to their chagrin, found themselves worshipped.

Disinclined to pass up such an opportunity, the men of Volas had turned Bethusa into a pleasure world. Many of the women were quite beautiful in their way, and to a race of men too long deprived of pleasures of the flesh, they were fair and easy game. No woman was taken against her will, although a case could be made that the childlike, primitive Bethusans were incapable of self-determination.

It was altogether a satisfactory arrangement for both races. The men of Volas satisfied their lust while taking care to ensure that no offspring resulted from these liaisons, and the Bethusans received payment in the form of medicine, buildings and such technologies as the men of Volas deemed they could utilize.

Jorlan got up and began to pace restlessly about the large, circular room, betraying his impatience with the tedious docking maneuvers. He was standing before the large porthole, staring at the endless desert, when a youthful voice sounded from behind him.

"Request permission to discharge the crew, sir."

Jorlan turned to the young officer with a smile. Although he hadn't actually timed it, he suspected that the apprentice spaceman had gotten to the bridge in record time. He recalled for a moment his own eagerness at that age to be off to the pleasure pits. It seemed very long ago. He nodded to the young man.

"Permission granted, and the drinks at Wallee's are on me."

The youth beamed. "Thank you, sir, and enjoy your rest."

Jorlan watched his hurried departure with a slight frown. Rest? Is that what they thought the "Old Man" did here? Then he sighed heavily. This time, they just might be right. The pleasures of Bethusa were becoming stale. If it weren't for the debt owed to his men, he might very well have opted to head for home.

His broad shoulders slumped briefly as he momentarily felt every bit as old as he must seem to the youth. The years were passing far too quickly, and just this morning he'd noticed a few strands of silver in his thick, black hair.

No sooner had he given into this uncharacteristic burst of self-pity than an image of the golden-haired Amala imprinted itself upon his mind. Could she be carrying his son? That all-too-familiar rage coursed through him. If she weren't out of his reach on that infernal island, he would have made damned sure that he'd fathered several sons by now—and would have certainly enjoyed every moment of it, too.

Furthermore, he thought with a spurious satisfaction, she would have enjoyed it, too. He'd have long since tamed that arrogance and found the key to unlock the passion he was sure existed beneath that cool, self-possessed exterior.

Then, in an abrupt shift back to reality, he thought about her bearing his son and then being forced to give him up. Over the years, he'd occasionally thought about the women's attitudes toward their sons. In the old days, they'd always been very proud of their sons, regarding them with far more favor than they had their daughters. Surely they must find it heart-wrenching to give up those sons and never see them again.

And yet, not once in all these years had a mother inquired after her son. Jorlan could recall with a secret shame the times as a youth when he had gone to the observatory, hoping to be able to identify his mother. He could never be sure, but there had been one woman who appeared to be the right age and who bore the traits common to her family. Then, when he was 17, he had learned through the lists that were exchanged that she had died, and he'd never seen that woman on the mountain again. For weeks he'd wondered if she'd regretted dying without seeing him. Surely she had.

No other single aspect of their peculiar society was as troubling to Jorlan as this seeming lack of interest on the part of the women, and the chief reason it was unsettling to him was that it seemed to argue in favor of Zakton's thesis that they might have changed greatly over the years. Although the matter was rarely discussed among them, Jorlan was certain that others also had these thoughts.

It was somehow very important to maintain the belief that the women hadn't changed, just as it was equally important to believe that one day they would find a way through the mist and bring them back. Each new generation believed that implicitly and carried that belief to their graves.

Around him, the control center began to empty out, as the ship's complex systems were shut down and officers made their final reports to him and then took their leave. The crew carriers had arrived from the still-distant repair complex, and the six tugs that would nudge the now powerless starship to the repair bays were drawing alongside.

The officers had filed their final reports into the computer prior to leaving, and Jorlan now reviewed these and added his own instructions to the repair crews, then hesitated with his fingers poised over the keyboard.

The beautiful Asroth awaited him at the beach house he had chosen for this stopover, and he thought briefly about her before tapping out an inquiry about other starships in port at the moment. Starfleet captains were the elite among an already elite group, and they generally preferred to associate only with their peers.

Two other captains were in port at the moment, he saw, but neither one was a particular favorite of his. He knew that both of them would likely choose some of the more exotic pleasures Bethusa offered—sensual pleasures in houses set up for that purpose that he had tried as a young man but had quickly found boring.

So, with something less than enthusiasm, Jorlan contemplated a few days with Asroth. He knew he could always send her packing and find a new woman, but that prospect didn't appeal to him, either.

Most of the men opted for variety in women, but Jorlan found that tedious. He preferred one woman who knew his needs and desires, and about whom he knew all there was to know. He'd been seeing Asroth for several years now, and she suited him as well as any woman ever had. Whether or not she had other men in his absence, he didn't know and didn't care, and if she had decided to mate with a man of her own race, he would have regarded it as nothing more than a minor inconvenience to be forced to select another woman.

Still with a lack of enthusiasm, Jorlan joined his second-in-command in the lift that carried them down to the point of disembarkation. At the bottom, they crossed a wide stretch of nearly empty cargo space, then took a second, outside lift to the planet's surface.

Both men breathed deeply of the hot, dry desert air, grateful for the change from recycled shipboard atmosphere. It had been a stroke of great good fortune to find that the Bethusan atmosphere differed only slightly from that of Volas. When a ship planned to make for that port, the shipboard atmosphere was adjusted gradually by the computers so that by the time they landed, no adjustment at all was required on the part of the crew.

Airsleds awaited both men, and they parted quickly. A moment later, Jorlan was airborne, heading west into the burnished light of the setting sun. He set the controls at a moderate cruising speed and an altitude of 500 meters above the undulating desert floor, then tilted back the pilot's seat and stared out at a landscape whose alien nature had ceased to fascinate him long ago. Far to the west was the mountain range that separated the desert from the lush seacoast where Asroth awaited him.

When he reached over to check the contents of the bag his aide had packed for him, he saw that the man had remembered to include his gift for Asroth. Like all women, she enjoyed the small presents from places she would never see. This time it was a particularly exotic plant with scarlet foliage and tiny, irridescent flowers, sealed into a clear plastic bubble. It would not survive indefinitely in its mini-atmosphere, but she would treasure it nonetheless. Normally, he simply detailed one of his crew to find something appropriate, but this time he'd actually found it himself, growing among the rocks near one of the openings to the Viboldan underground cities.

Then he settled back once more to watch the white and tan desert pass slowly beneath him. He was aware of the sensual delights to come, but those thoughts were not sufficient to propel him to greater speed. Once more he wondered if he should find himself a new woman, and once more he pushed the thought aside. It just wasn't worth the effort.

Deep down inside Jorlan, in a part of him that he rarely acknowledged, he knew that no woman could truly satisfy him—except possibly the one he couldn't have. A vision of Amala hovered tantalizingly before him, framed as always by the screen that reminded him of her inaccessibility.

Part of this feeling, he knew, was the result of the fierce racial pride that was at its most intense among the men of the Great Families. If the men of Volas in general regarded themselves as being vastly superior human beings, those of Great Families exhibited that chauvinism to an even greater degree. No man of a Great Family had ever taken a mate from the lower classes in all their history, and very few had ever even taken a mistress from their inferiors.

Since girls of Great Families had been chosen by their future mates around the age of 12 and to infringe upon another man's property was an unforgivable sin, the men of Great Families had nearly always been faithful to their wives. It was, perhaps, their only virtue as husbands.

When they had discovered Bethusa with its very willing women, there had been considerable hesitation on the part of men from Great Families to become involved with an obviously inferior race, but the lower classes had had no such compunction. When foolproof birth control had been quickly devised, any lingering inhibitions disappeared.

Still, in a few men like Jorlan and Zakton, prouder than most of their heritage, there remained a slight distaste, even a vague wish that their bodies would cease making such demands upon them.

The fact that Asroth and the other women of Bethusa accepted this thinly veiled contempt toward them only increased that feeling among the men. The Bethusans were unfailingly docile and compliant and in the estimation of the men of Volas possessed only slightly more intelligence than the furry Feloths that had been domesticated centuries ago on Volas. Fortunately, however, they were far more attractive.

The airsled issued a warning that the mountains lay dead ahead, then, when Jorlan did nothing about it, it corrected its altitude and ascended over the rounded peaks. Beneath him, the landscape was dramatically transformed. A melange of pleasing blues and brilliant scarlets ringed the edges of the land and provided a perfect border for the silvery sea beyond.

Flicking off the autopilot, Jorlan took the controls and brought the sled down to an altitude just above the frothy treetops. A moment later the distinctive white landing pad appeared, and he dropped the small craft gently onto the square.

Inside the cottage, Asroth raised her head and listened for a moment, then leapt up from her chair, smoothing the wrinkles from her gown as she hurried outside.

He was just alighting from the airsled when she saw him. She smiled with secret pleasure, knowing how the others would be envying her now. Not only was she being favored by the gods, but by one of the greatest of them all. They all knew by now that the gods from the skies had their own hierarchy, and Jorlan was at the very top.

Besides that, he was a great lover. Asroth, who was older than Jorlan believed her to be, had known other men before him—although none since he'd chosen her. She also knew some of the women who had served in the pleasure houses when Jorlan had frequented them, and all agreed that he was indeed blessed with great skills, befitting his status.

At the very least, Jorlan would have been bemused to know this—first of all because he never gave any thought to his "skills" as a lover, and secondly because he had no idea that the women ever discussed such matters.

He was a skilled lover because he was a highly intelligent man, and he had noticed very quickly that his own pleasure was greatly increased when his partner was stimulated, too. Therefore, he had taken care to learn just what women enjoyed and assumed erroneously that other men did, too.

He also assumed that women never discussed such matters simply because most men did—and in considerable detail. It was his firm belief that whatever men did, women did the opposite. That, he was quite sure, was the natural way of things.

He saw Asroth coming toward him and felt desire begin to stir, but then, for one tormenting moment, he saw instead a much smaller woman with golden hair. Desire quickly ebbed, until he shook himself mentally and saw that Asroth had paused a few meters away with a hesitant frown. He belatedly held out his arms to her, and she quickly ran into them.

But that taunting image would not dissipate completely, and after a moment, he disengaged himself from her and gave her the present. She squealed with delight and exclaimed over it in her thickly accented version of his language until he announced his intention of bathing in the pool while she prepared their meal.

He stripped off his uniform and left it in a heap beside the small pool, then stepped into the swirling, heated waters and sank back as she brought him a glass of the potent Bethusan wine he preferred. A few moments later, spicy aromas began to drift out from the small cottage.

When she had brought their dinner to the poolside terrace, Jorlan climbed out of the pool and allowed her to dry him off before sitting down, still naked, to enjoy the meal. She sat across from him, both demure and erotic in her diaphanous gown. There was little conversation between them—what did they have to say to each other? She knew that he had a limited tolerance for her chatter, and he had virtually nothing to say to her.

After they had finished the meal, he wrapped himself in a silken robe and settled down in a lounge chair while she cleared the table. Dusk crept slowly over the colorful landscape, softening it to more peaceful hues. When she returned, he asked her to play and sing for him. She was very talented, although the words, in her own language, were meaningless to him.

She played and sang through the long twilight, then finally set aside her stringed instrument and came over to him. Hesitantly, she reached for the sash of his robe, then loosened it when he nodded. She bent over him, and he let out a long, low groan of pleasure. Yes, she knew exactly how to please him.

Her lips and fingers played his body as skillfully as they made music, and he gave himself up to that brief but powerful release that left him spent and languorous. This time he had been far less attentive to her needs, but that fact didn't really register. Shortly thereafter, he went off to bed alone, leaving her to sleep in the small anteroom of his chamber, where she would awaken if he called to her during the night.

But Jorlan didn't call. Instead, he spent a restless night in a tormented world of mist, where a small golden-haired figure danced just beyond his reach, pausing every so often to stare at him in open challenge.

CHAPTER TWO

AMALA SANK DOWN ONTO A LARGE BOULDER. THE ceremony was ended. Her breasts rose and fell beneath their gauzy covering, betraying the enormous exertion required of the dance. The others had left, and she was alone near the summit of the holy mountain, surrounded by the thin veil of mist that drifted down from the crater.

She lifted her head and stared, frowning, at the volcanic peak. Had Aleala seen fit to make her pregnant this time? Or did the goddess truly see into her heart and know that she was ambivalent on the subject?

Blasphemy, she thought with a wry shake of her golden head. Whether or not she believed in the powers of the goddess, she knew that there was no getting around the fact that she must soon bear a child—two children, actually. The bloodlines must be maintained at their present strength. Her mother and aunt had been reminding her—and with decreasing subtlety—that it was past time. Most women bore their first child in their late teens or early twenties and had already had their second by the time they reached her age.

But Amala was the acknowledged ringleader of a group that had begun to question the old dictum that each of them must bear two children and a few who chose to do so could bear three.

"Why even two?" she had questioned some years ago. "Why not a single child to preserve the bloodlines? Why should we provide them with more fodder for their cannons? If we allow the population to decrease, they might be forced to stop making war."

The other women had no answer to that. They all knew that the men must still be making war because the death lists that were sent across showed the pattern very clearly—clusters of deaths of mostly young men, followed by periods of few to none at all, during which time they were presumably gearing themselves for yet another war. Thus it had been ever since they had come here, and thus, they all knew, it would always be. Men lived for two things—to make war and to father sons to carry on their bellicosity into the next generation.

There were fewer deaths in recent years,

however, which some women argued indicated that they might indeed be less warlike, but Amala and her friends believed that the decrease meant only that they had become more proficient. Besides, they argued, if it was true that they were less warlike, they would be forced to become even less so if the population decreased.

Amala had no misplaced love, as a few others did, for the male infants who were sent across as quickly as possible, but she did often look at them and wonder what happened to change them from happy, gurgling little creatures like the girls into vicious, death-wielding machines.

They had all speculated endlessly about this and had reached the sad conclusion that male children must be born with some defective gene that would transform them at a certain age into something less than human.

She stared off through the mists toward the land her forebears had left behind—the land where the dreaded men still lived, and where they had once held women in terrible bondage. Years ago, she and her best friend Felis had stolen one of the little fishing boats and made their way through the mist to the very edge, where they had drifted for a long time, staring off across the wide expanse of water to the dark blur of land at the horizon. They had stared and speculated about the other half of their race. Such speculation, Amala's mother had once remarked, was the peculiar province of the young.

She passed a hand across her flat abdomen, wondering once more if she were carrying a child—Jorlan's child.

Each of them was permitted, at the age of 12, to choose the future father of their children—aided, of course, by those who kept track of bloodlines. Not all of them chose; in fact, most left the decision to the keepers of the charts. After all, except for the bloodlines, it mattered little who their future "mates" were. But in the terrible old days, particularly among Great Families, brides had been chosen by their future husbands at around the age of 12. The tradition had therefore been continued by the women but with a decidedly new twist.

Amala's choice had been the cause of many raised eyebrows and quite a few voices of disapproval. Not since their arrival here had there been a union between the two greatest of the Great Families—and an Amala and Jorlan at that!

Amala's elderly aunt had been very disturbed and had begged her to change her decision. Verta had a reputation as a seeress, and she had forecast vague but dire consequences to such a decision. But 12-year-old Amala had stood firm, demanding her right to choose her mate. Even at that tender age, she'd had a fine sense of irony. The only dire consequences she could see were that the present bearer of that hated name would be forced to accept her choice—and not the other way around.

Amala felt quite strongly that she was, by her

choice, avenging her own famous ancestress, who must surely have hated that most terrible of warriors who had chosen her.

Furthermore, she had told her distraught family, if Aleala believed her choice to be wrong, she could always prevent her from conceiving.

And perhaps her half-jesting words had been accurate, after all, for she'd now been impregnated twice without success.

Had Jorlan guessed by now that she had chosen him? He must surely have noticed her name on the birth lists. Did he eagerly seek out those lists now to see if he'd finally fathered the son he must want so badly? He was the last male of his particular branch of his family, the final direct descendant of the original Jorlan. Amala hoped fervently that if she did conceive, the child would be female.

She rather wished that she believed more strongly in the powers of Aleala so that she could pray for just such an occurrence, but like most of her generation, her faith was tempered by rational thought. It was obvious that something kept the men away, but they were no longer so sure that it was the goddess' powers.

Felis, Amala's scientifically minded friend, thought that it might be some sort of chemical that was lethal to males but not to females. They knew from their history studies that the men had created deadly gasses for use in warfare, so it did not seem beyond the realm of possibility that some sort of natural chemical reaction within the volcano had created the same thing —but with devastating effects for males only.

"Nature playing a game of one-upmanship," Felis had suggested with a grin.

Amala really hadn't sorted all this out in her own mind. A part of her still believed, or wanted to believe, in the powers of Aleala. She had remarked to Felis once that if they weren't here by divine intervention, then there was always the possibility that the men would one day find a way to neutralize the chemical. But more recently, she had been leaning toward Felis' explanation, regardless of the fear that inevitably called forth.

She got up slowly, and after one last defiant look toward the land where the hated men lived, she started down the path into the valley.

On the gently rolling valley floor, she passed a group of women who were busy tending crops and offered a silent prayer of thanks that her turn at this odious chore wouldn't come again before winter set in. Democracy, she had drily remarked to her mother, did have its drawbacks. In the old days, no daughter of a Great Family would ever have gone into the fields or done any other type of physical labor, for that matter.

But despite her dislike of some of the tasks, Amala was an ardent supporter of the system begun by her ancestress. That Amala had decreed that all must tend the crops if they intended to survive their first winter on the island. That the men had not expected them to become self-sufficient had been amply demonstrated by the food-laden barges sent across as winter set in. The date those barges arrived—and were sent back—was still celebrated as a revered holiday among them.

As that first year on the island progressed, a great change had taken place among the women. The hard labors of all able-bodied women were needed to erect the additional shelter required, plant and harvest crops and do the many other chores that turned a temporary haven into a permanent home.

In the midst of all this, it quickly became apparent that the women of the lower classes, who had never been as pampered and cosseted as the Great Family women, were far better equipped to endure such hardships. They were content with less, they knew how to build houses, and they were already expert in the matter of agriculture. Amala, their leader, was among the first to take note of this and then to act upon it.

All women over the age of 25 were invited to apply for Council positions, and all were permitted to vote in the elections. The result was a Council nearly equally divided between women of the Great Families and those of the lower classes.

To be sure, some class distinctions remained for several more generations, but those too had gradually died out, to be retained now by only a few older women among the present population.

Only in the matter of breeding were the old ways continued, and Amala, among others, had been agitating for a change there, too. But the proponents of the status quo maintained that breeding across class lines would result in dire consequences for male babies. They would undoubtedly be put to death as soon as they arrived. There were historical records of such murders.

Amala doubted that thesis, although she could not disprove it. In her opinion, the men would be very reluctant to murder any male babies, when they were so sorely needed for war. In the old days, when women were expected to bear as many children as possible, life had been considerably less precious.

Still, it was an unshakable tenet that men simply did not change. That fact was drilled into every girl from an early age and was therefore accepted by them all.

Amala walked on through the ripening fields and finally came to the outskirts of the village, where she left the path to seek out her friend Felis. The small cluster of crudely built buildings here housed the few workshops the women had. The grains that constituted the mainstay of their diets were processed here, the herbs that were used for cooking and for medicinal purposes were dried and prepared, and simple utensils were made or repaired.

She headed for the smallest of the buildings, certain she would find Felis there. Her friend was a highly valued member of the community, because she alone seemed able to coax additional life out of their two remaining jepsas—the only form of transportation on the island except for crude, human-drawn wagons.

It hadn't been possible to bring jepsas to the island at the time of their departure from the mainland, but fortunately four of the sturdy, little, solar-powered vehicles had already been here for the use of older or handicapped women. It was a major miracle that two of them remained after all these years—a tribute, Felis had acknowledged begrudgingly, to the craftsmanship of their male makers.

In Amala's opinion, it was even more a tribute to those like Felis who had learned how they operated and then had fashioned replacement parts from what little they had on the island.

Amala entered the garage and saw a pair of sandals protruding from beneath one of the jepsas. After smiling at the muffled curses coming from beneath the vehicle, she squatted down to gain her friend's attention just as Felis' dark, curly head emerged.

"Will you be able to get it running again?" Amala asked with some concern. She had to make a trip soon to visit the Others, and she didn't relish the prospect of a 30-kilometer walk over rough, lonely terrain. One jepsa was always kept in the village for emergencies, so it was this one or nothing.

"Don't I always?" Felis grinned, her black eyes sparkling.

"Hmmmpphh! Last time, you got it running just long enough to strand me in the middle of nowhere."

"It was your reckless driving, not my fixing, that got you stranded," Felis protested smugly. "And anyway, what's your hurry? I still can't understand why you're always so eager to visit them."

Amala shrugged. Felis, like most of the women, found the Others a subject to be avoided as much as possible.

"They're very interesting. Why don't you come along and see for yourself?"

Felis wrinkled her upturned nose. "No thanks, I don't need to visit them to know that they're weird."

Amala stared thoughtfully into space. "Oh, I don't know about that. Sometimes I think they're just the next step on the evolutionary ladder."

Felis' mouth dropped open in dismay. "You can't be serious! How could that be? It would mean extinction."

"Not necessarily. They have no real strictures against having children; they've just chosen not to have them. If we all became like the Others, at least some of us would have to have children."

Felis just shook her curly head at Amala's outlandish ideas. She'd once remarked to a mutual friend, only half in jest, that Amala thought too much. More than any of them, Amala seemed to chafe at their life here and talk about change. Hers was a restless spirit, and Felis was of the opinion that if their life were any less protected, Amala would get herself into serious trouble. Fortunately, there wasn't much trouble to be gotten into on the island.

When Amala seemed about to pursue the topic of the Others, Felis quickly decided to change subjects.

"Do you know yet if you're pregnant?"

"No."

Felis snorted. "If it's true that Aleala can see into your heart, you won't be, either. She'd know that you don't really want a child."

"That's not really true," Amala protested mildly. "Of course, it *is* true that the idea doesn't excite me much, either."

Felis shook her head in an expression of mock sympathy. "Poor Jorlan. I can just picture him, running to see the birth lists each time, hoping in vain."

Amala smiled. "He doesn't deserve to have children, and I'm not sure I want them. That makes us a perfect match."

"I wonder what he's like," Felis went on, warming to a favorite topic between them. "I wonder if he's as much like the original Jorlan as you are like the first Amala."

"Thank Aleala I'll never know the answer to that question," Amala said with a slight shiver.

"But they *could* have changed. I don't understand why you won't at least consider that possibility when you know that we have."

"Because, as I've said before, it's perfectly

obvious that they haven't changed. They're still making war."

"Well, we assume they are, but we can't know for certain."

"*I* know for certain. They're men and that's what men do."

"I still think there could be other explanations for the clusters of deaths. They could be dying of some plague or even dying in attempts to get through the mist."

Both women shuddered at that thought, rarely expressed openly among them. They all preferred to believe that the men had given up long ago.

There was a nightmare shared by every child on the island—great hairy monsters coming suddenly through the mist to carry them off. There were no pictures of men and no written descriptions, either, but the myths persisted from one generation to the next of huge, hairy creatures with bulging, misshapen bodies and loud, booming voices.

"It's strange, isn't it," Amala mused aloud, "that we still persist in believing those old tales, even when we can see that they look almost like us."

"Almost," Felis agreed. "But there's still something grotesque about them."

"Well, I daresay they don't think so," Amala responded with a grin. "But that thing certainly looks uncomfortable to me, especially if it grows along with the rest of them. Imagine having to go through life with something like that dangling between your legs."

Then she sighed. "I really would like to see one of them—even a picture. I'll never understand why the first women didn't keep some pictures or at least write some descriptions."

"After what they'd suffered at the hands of men, why should they? They came here to escape from men, not to be reminded of them."

"Corla says that myths generally have some basis in fact, or they wouldn't have gotten started in the first place."

"Oh, I agree with her," Felis said, "but she also said that exaggerations occur as they pass through generations."

"Mmmm . . . still, if it had been up to me, I would have kept some pictures around, just to remind future generations about how awful they are."

"I don't need to be reminded," Felis stated firmly, "and neither do you. We know what they are, even if we can't be sure what they look like."

Amala peered thoughtfully into the tiny cradle. Her cousin's son lay there sleeping peacefully, less than two hours old and totally naked on the soft blanket. Behind her, her mother and the other women were talking softly. There would be no celebrating here tonight. Amala felt very sorry for her cousin, since this was her second son. She was truly fond of children and very good with them, so she would probably petition to have a third, in the desperate hope that it would be a girl.

Amala continued to stare at the sleeping baby. They definitely were strange-looking little things, with that ugly, rubbery appendage. If indeed it *did* grow in proportion to the rest of the body, it would surely be enormous by adulthood, and that could certainly explain all the stories that persisted about the pain of conceiving in the old way.

Amala grimaced and thanked Aleala for having spared them such a horror all these years. The thought of even being touched by the creature this baby might one day become—let alone actually mating with it—was enough to cause nightmares for a week.

The infant stirred slightly, then settled down once more into untroubled sleep. Surely, she thought, the grownup version of this baby couldn't be as bad as the myths suggested. There was no hair at all on its body, save for its dark, downy head, and no hint at all of the misshapen body of the stories. Furthermore, the boy babies were no larger than the girls.

She turned away, spoke a few words of consolation to her cousin, then let herself out into the pleasantly cool night. Her thoughts drifted for a moment, then centered on another boy baby—her only nephew. His father was her brother, Zakton. He'd been named Levyan, an old family name, and he would be nearly five years-old by now.

Could he already be turning into some kind of monster, or did that happen later? Girls' bodies began to change shape at about the age of 12, when the monthly flow signaled approaching womanhood. Perhaps that was when it happened to boys, too, but if the changes were as dramatic as the stories indicated, it might begin earlier. Amala was irritated at her lack of knowledge, although no one else, not even Felis, seemed much interested.

Unconsciously, she passed a hand over her flat stomach. Still no child in there. Soon there would be pressure exerted upon her by the keepers of the lists to relinquish her claim to Jorlan.

She knew she should give up. Perhaps she was incapable of conceiving—it happened—or perhaps the fault was his. That happened sometimes, too. The only way to know was for her to give up her claim to him, choose another mate, and allow him to be chosen by someone else. But in some strange, unfathomable and perhaps unholy way, Jorlan belonged to her. If she had to bear children, she wanted them to be his, and she wanted them to be female.

A few weeks ago when an exchange had been made, she'd hurried to look at the death lists, just as she always did. Jorlan's name had not appeared, although a rather large number of young men had indeed died. She'd been perversely happy about that, just as she always was. Not that she much cared whether he lived or died, but if he were dead he could hardly be seething with frustration over his failure to have produced a son.

Amala was uneasily aware of what amounted to an obsession with Jorlan. It had to be wrong—or at the very least, unhealthy—to hate someone you've never met and never will meet. But hatred didn't really describe the complex set of emotions she felt when she thought about him.

Sometimes, he seemed frighteningly real to her—a shadowy, hulking figure at the edge of her mind's eye; a dark monster, waiting and watching. There'd been a few occasions up on the mountain when she'd actually felt the force of his gaze upon her. She'd spoken of this to Felis, who had stunned her by suggesting that the men actually might be watching them up there. They all knew that such things as telescopes and cameras existed since there'd been some on the island years ago.

Felis had pointed out that if they'd had such technology way back then, they might well have found a way to see through the mist by now, and the mountain was the only spot that would be visible to them from the mainland.

Amala had immediately wanted to deny that horrifying possibility, but she couldn't. What Felis had said made a terrible sort of sense.

In the end, she'd insisted that such talk go no further than the two of them, since the other women would be aghast at the possibility that the men were spying on them in their sacred place.

But she wondered what it would be like for them, watching former slaves enjoying their freedom. If one were male and therefore determined to dominate, it must be frustrating indeed.

She had reached the doorway of the cottage she shared with her mother, and she paused for a moment to stare up into the heavens. The nearer of the two moons was full this night, and that strange spot on its surface was outlined starkly. According to the older women, that spot had appeared suddenly many years ago.

Felis and some others believed it could be a base of some sort, that the men had found a way to travel into space. It made sense, Amala thought, since they would have long since conquered this world—with one all-important exception. Now they were probably carrying their wars to other worlds.

That aching, bitter sadness overtook her once more, and she lowered her head quickly. Had they really accomplished so much by coming here and staying? The men had surely moved on, discovered new worlds and invented fabulous new technologies—even if they were putting them to bad use.

She understood and accepted the reasons for coming here, but was it really necessary to remain in this self-imposed prison? Despite her fear of the men, Amala chafed at their life here. Nothing changed; nothing happened. There were times when she would have willingly faced those monstrous men at their worst just to find some purpose to her life.

Although no one else had ever given voice to

it, Amala sensed that she was not alone among her generation in feeling this way. In order to gain their freedom, they had given up so very much. She knew about computers, the magical machines that had enabled her namesake to gain the information she needed, and she had listened and watched as Felis explained the workings of the jepsas to her. She knew about other machines that could fly through the air and probably even into space.

What must they have now, more than 100 years later? The world beyond the mist must be a fabulous place, filled with wonders beyond imagining. But here they were, locked forever away from all that.

All their teachings told her that men were evil and that men couldn't change, but sometimes Amala wondered if those teachings might be nothing more than the rantings of old women who had to justify their remaining on this island prison.

"Please remember to treat it gently," Felis implored in the long-suffering tone of one who knows she'll be ignored. Amala had a distressing tendency toward recklessness, a trait Felis was sure she must have inherited from her ancestress. And since that unfortunate tendency could find no other outlet, it surfaced in her driving.

"If you're so worried about the jepsa, you could always come along and do the driving yourself," Amala challenged as she climbed into the driver's seat.

For a fraction of a second Felis seemed to hesitate, and Amala hoped that she might actually come along this trip. The invitation had been extended many times before without acceptance. But then Felis shook her dark curls and backed away. With a wave and a goodbye, Amala drove off, tormenting her friend a bit by accelerating quickly and scattering pebbles and dust in her wake.

Felis stood there watching until the sturdy little vehicle had crested a low hill and disappeared from view. A fleeting pang of envy came and went quickly. Amala, so totally secure in her place in the world, could easily afford to be reckless and take unpopular positions. As a member of the lowest class in this outwardly classless society, Felis felt she could take no such liberties.

For all her life—and despite her close friendship with a member of a Great Family—Felis had always been aware of the tenuous nature of her position. Here on the island, her position in society was reasonably secure, but if they should ever be forced to leave . . .

She shook her head, denying the possibility. It was only that generations of enforced inferiority could not be undone in a few years. The feelings went too deep.

And yet, she too occasionally felt that restlessness and dissatisfaction that so often afflicted Amala. Life was at a dead end here. There simply was no possibility of true progress. They lacked both the raw materials and the technical skills to improve their lives. This was particularly frustrating for someone like Felis, who knew that she had the ability to learn those skills. Yet all that was available to her were old science books in the library that she knew were terribly outdated and a few precious remnants of that male technology like the jepsas.

Felis knew, deep down inside, that Amala was right—the island *was* a prison—but she also knew that only in this prison could someone like her be truly free. She understood that Amala's campaign for inter-class breeding was the result of her desire to end those fears for Felis and others of her class.

Amala was an idealist, a philosophy that dwells easily in one who has all the advantages of life, but Felis did not have that luxury; she remained firmly rooted in reality. And that reality told her that she could never leave this place.

Felis cast one final look at the spot where Amala had vanished, then returned to her workshop, where she was presently engaged in trying to fashion a particularly intricate replacement part for the other jepsa from the broken remnant of a third machine now long out of use.

In the meantime, Amala bumped along the well-worn path, curbing her desire to push the jepsa hard. As she drove along, her thoughts flew ahead to the Others.

The Others was the name given to them by the main colony, but Amala always referred to them by the name they preferred—Semlians. She had a deeply ingrained sense of fairness and recognized the pejorative nature of that term.

In a world that offered true career choices, Amala would certainly have been a lawyer or judge, but here in their restricted society, such choices weren't possible. Since the women were a very law-abiding group and their society hadn't really changed in all their years on the island, the pursuit of law was more academic than practical. She had read all the legal tomes in their library and was unquestionably the leading expert among them on the ancient laws that had governed their people for centuries.

She was the youngest member ever of their governing Council, but even that singular honor was not enough to keep her very good mind fully occupied. So she pursued several other interests.

The first of these interests was undertaken in secrecy, and only Felis now knew about it. Amala was working on nothing less than a complete restructuring of their society—a re-write of the body of law that formed its basis. Felis had been shocked to learn that the project included the hated men, but Amala had pointed out that it was nothing more than a mental exercise.

Her other interest was the post of Ambassador to the Semlian colony. She had always found them very interesting.

Nearly two generations ago, the Semlians had separated themselves from the main colony and moved to the far side of the island to live in far harsher conditions. Long ago, when men could still come to the island, they had forbidden the women to venture into that land, and even after they themselves had been banished from the island by the mist, most women had chosen not to go there. But for this very reason, the Semlians decided to settle there.

The group's founder was a woman named Semle. By all accounts, she had been a commanding figure, perhaps the most powerful among them since the first Amala. She had severely criticized the women for what she viewed as complacency—their total trust in the powers of Aleala to protect them from the men.

Semle had been the first to openly voice disbelief in the old goddess and to suggest that the women might one day be forced to live again with men. In anticipation of this day, she espoused a strenuous regimen of body-building and rigorous training in mental discipline, not unlike the warrior training of the men. It was her firm belief that only through attaining the strength of men could women hope to live as equals in a reunited society.

Furthermore, she refused to bear children, stating that child-bearing and rearing weakened women and made them dependent upon men.

So vehement was she in her views that she was finally called before the Council and given a choice—either tone down her talk or leave the colony. She chose to leave, and her followers went with her. The Council was stunned but refused to back down.

Two generations later, the small renegade colony still existed, their numbers having grown slightly from the original group. With each new generation, there were a few who chose to join them, to the dismay of their families.

Amala herself had once secretly considered joining them, but she gave up on the idea chiefly because of the shame she would bring to her mother.

The Semlians refused to set foot in the main colony, and its residents would not make the long, difficult journey to the far side of the island. Therefore an emissary became necessary. Trade between the two groups was desired by all, and despite their differences, each group was always hungry for news from the other side.

The Ambassador was selected by the Council but also had to meet with the approval of the Semlian Council. When Amala had proposed herself for the post, she'd never doubted that she would be acceptable to the Semlians—and perhaps for that very reason, she was. She had now been making the arduous journey monthly for nearly a year.

The road she was following had by now deteriorated into an unending series of bumps and dips, and Amala had no difficulty in keeping her speed down to a level even Felis would have approved. Although she was less than seven kilometers from home, the lush green was already giving way to stunted shrubs, and she knew that beyond the next hill, even that would be gone.

The men had once enjoyed exploring this wild land, and there wasn't a child on the island who hadn't heard stories about their ghosts lingering here. Amala was no believer in ghosts, but after her first trip out here, she'd decided that if they did exist, this would surely be the place for them.

She crested the hill and stopped as she always did to survey the otherworldly scene below her. Nothing grew here, not even the hardy shrubs and stunted trees that clung to a precarious life further on where the Semlians lived. The land was utterly barren, pockmarked by craters and strewn with boulders, and over it all hung a yellowish haze that escaped from deep fissures in the earth.

Amala always found it necessary to remind herself that she was free to travel through land that had once been forbidden to women. It did nothing to improve the scenery, but it did lessen her uneasiness. She accelerated again, eager to be through this desolate land. She had a recurring nightmare (and a perfectly understandable one, given the condition of the jepsas) that she would be marooned here one day.

She steered carefully through the rocky land, trying to avoid the worst of the foul-smelling haze. Before her was a long, rocky slope and beyond that, yet another lifeless hill—and then the small Semlian colony on the seacoast.

When at last she had reached that far hill, she brought the jepsa to a halt and got out to stare back at the land she'd just crossed. It seemed to her that the haze was thicker than it had been at the time of her last journey only a month ago, and although the ochre vapors partially obscured the landscape, she also thought that there had been a few more fissures.

She lifted her gaze to the holy mountain in the distance, its peak enshrouded as always in the mist. Only once in history had the mountain erupted, and that had been just before the mist had turned lethal to men. None of them ever spoke openly about the possibility that the mountain might erupt again, but many of them, including Amala, thought about it.

If it erupts, she thought, we could be forced to make a terrible choice—perish in this prison we have chosen for ourselves or return to a prison the men would recreate for us. It was a choice no sane woman could contemplate for long.

She turned quickly and got back into the jepsa, but just as she reached for the ignition switch, the little vehicle convulsed violently. Amala gripped the seat and door and held on tightly. It was nothing more than one of the tremors that regularly shook this part of the island, but coming just after her thoughts of an eruption, it left a metallic taste of fear in her mouth and a prickly sensation along her spine.

When the tremors subsided after a few moments, she began to weave her way slowly down the slope. After a year of making these monthly journeys she knew her way well. She'd remarked to Felis that she believed she could find her way blindfolded, and her friend had responded drily that she suspected Amala did just that, given the condition of the jepsa when she returned.

But now she suddenly stopped in confusion. Had she let her mind wander and lost her way? Directly ahead of her and stretching for about 15 meters on either side was a fissure at least two meters wide. Trails of sulphurous vapors rose from its unseen depths.

She looked around her and became very certain that this fissure hadn't been here at the time of her last visit. She hadn't lost her way; the land itself had changed. She'd occasionally seen other new fissures but never anything quite like this.

Filled with an uneasiness that she couldn't will away this time, Amala carefully drove around this new obstacle, then pushed the jepsa to its limits, eager to gain the familiarity of the Semlian colony.

The Semlians had claimed for themselves a strip of land along the coast that, while lush by comparison with its surroundings, was still far from hospitable. Some plants, however, did thrive here, despite the almost constant winds and regular storms that swept in from the sea. Chief among these plants in importance to the women was the datera. When it was ready to be harvested, datera stood nearly two meters high on tough stalks, its leaves a mottled brown and tan. Datera grew wild on other parts of the island, but only here had the women been able to cultivate it.

The datera produced a very durable fiber that had for centuries been woven into rugs, wall-hangings and sturdy sandals. By the time of the exodus, synthetics had long since replaced it, and even the art of weaving the tough fibers was all but forgotten. But when the shoes and rugs the women had brought with them had worn out, the ancient art was revived out of sheer necessity.

The fibers shaded from the palest of golds to the darkest browns, and a skillful weaver could create something that was both highly practical and esthetically pleasing. The production of these items was the chief occupation of the Semlians, who had become highly skilled crafts-women.

Prior to Amala's assumption of her post, the Semlians had refused to trade the raw datera, but she had persuaded them that her people had no desire to compete in the production of mats and sandals but rather wished only to indulge their own creative talents. Now, small quantities were traded regularly.

It was with considerable relief that Amala now approached the outer edges of the settlement, where fields of nearly mature datera rustled distinctively in the breeze. Datera grew rapidly, and several crops were harvested each year.

Here and there she saw women in the fields,

checking the ripeness of the crops that were already taller than their heads. Those who saw her paused in their labors to wave at her, and she slowed down briefly to return their greeting. As she looked at this harsh and primitive tableau, she thought of the men undoubtedly out challenging the frontiers of space. But before the sadness and bitterness could overwhelm her, she accelerated once more and drove on into the village.

Her entrance into the settlement was always an occasion for stopping all work and gathering to see what she had brought and to hear the news from the main colony. Despite their decision to remain separate, the Semlians were always interested in news of relatives and eager to have the goods she brought to trade. Amala's friendly manner and the respect she showed for the Semlian ways had made her far more popular among them than her predecessors had ever been.

By the time she came to a halt in the small square that formed the center of the village, a veritable parade was following along behind her. But her eyes were already searching for Glea, the current Semlian leader.

Finally she saw the familiar tall figure emerge from one of the small houses and start toward her. Glea was easily the tallest woman on the island, with a lean, angular body that was the opposite of Amala's petite, rounded figure.

Glea and Amala had approached each other warily at the beginning, although Glea had readily assented to Amala's holding the ambassadorial post. She was the ranking member of the only other Great Family that was the equal of Amala's own family—the family to which Jorlan belonged. They were first cousins, although Glea was some years Jorlan's senior.

Glea knew that Amala had chosen Jorlan and found that choice highly amusing. If anyone might have given Amala trouble over her failure to produce a child and her refusal to give up her claim to Jorlan, it would have been Glea, as head of the family. But Amala knew Glea was unlikely to do so, and in fact, might be displeased if Amala *did* become pregnant. She had once remarked to Amala that the end of that particular branch of her family would cause her no grief at all.

Amala brought the jepsa to a halt and got out to exchange greetings with Glea. The greetings were the ritual greetings exchanged between Great Families for centuries. Despite the democratization of their society, such greetings were still used on formal occasions.

"Was your journey pleasant—or as pleasant as possible?" Glea inquired with a trace of a smile as they walked across the square.

"I had no real problems, thank Aleala, but I am eager to discuss some observations."

"Come in out of the wind then," Glea suggested, taking Amala's arm and leading her toward her cottage. The other members of the Semlian Council assembled behind the pair, while still other women began to unload the contents of the jepsa.

A tasty meal of nuts and berries was laid out for them, together with a chilled jug of the excellent wine that was the second most important export of the Semlian colony. It was made from the berries of a vine that grew in the shelter of the datera plant, and the secrets of its recipe were closely held by the Semlians.

To this excellent repast, Amala contributed several delicious melons harvested that morning, and the Semlians were quick to exclaim over this delicacy. The conversation during the meal was casual, but as soon as the food had been consumed and the wine glasses refilled, Glea settled back into her chair and regarded Amala solemnly.

"Tell us about your observations."

So Amala described her impression that there were more geysers in the blasted land and then told them about the large new fissure. As she spoke, the women nodded gravely.

"We've not seen the fissure you described, but it probably opened up two days ago. There was a violent tremor here, bad enough to damage a few foundations. And yes, we too believe there are more geysers and that the ground even appears to be warmer in some places."

"What do you think it means?" Amala asked. Because it was in their self-interest, the Semlians kept a close eye on the land surrounding their colony.

Glea shrugged, but Amala thought it was a strangely tense gesture. "Perhaps nothing.

There are always tremors, and fissures have opened up before, too."

Amala waited for her to say more, then belatedly realized that Glea was probably waiting for her to make the terrible suggestion herself. Glea knew that Amala wasn't strong in her worship of the old goddess, but she obviously didn't want to risk offending her.

"Do you think it's possible that the mountain might erupt again?" Amala's words were carefully neutral in their failure to refer to Aleala.

There was a heavy silence in the room, and Amala was more than ever aware of the Semlian belief that they would all be forced to leave the island one day. Finally, it was Glea who broke the silence.

"The mountain is a volcano," she stated firmly, "and we know that when sufficient force builds up, a volcano erupts. It hasn't erupted for nearly two hundred years now. Is there any change on the mountain itself, Amala?"

"Nothing that I've noticed, and no one else has remarked about it."

"Has Verta said anything?" An older woman asked in a tense, eager voice. The psychic talents of Amala's aunt were well-known to all.

Amala shook her head. "She hasn't been well of late. In fact, she rarely leaves her home now, and she hasn't been to the mountain for more than a month."

The women took this news with varying degrees of uneasiness. There was no one else who possessed Verta's talents. The common belief among the women of the main colony was that her talents resulted from an especially close relationship with Aleala. Although the Semlians didn't believe in Aleala, they did respect Verta's powers.

The conversation shifted quickly to other matters, and Amala thought that in this respect at least, the Semlians were no different from the women of her colony. When the subject became difficult or frightening, they changed the topic. The Semlians might believe that they would all have to leave one day, but Amala now suspected that they were in no hurry to be proved right.

After a while, the other women took their leave. Amala always stayed with Glea during her visits here, and so the two of them were left standing in the open doorway as dusk began to settle over the land.

"Shall we walk along the beach for a while?" Glea asked. "The wind has died down a bit."

Amala quickly assented. She needed to stretch her legs after a day's confinement, and she enjoyed the rugged, wild coastline on this side of the island.

They walked in a companionable silence along the path that led to the shore. Then they emerged on a low bluff from which a steep path led down to the rock-strewn water's edge. They paused for a moment, staring down at the water hurling itself in perpetual anger against rock jettys before retreating to leave a path of foam that glowed beneath the light of the two moons.

They climbed carefully down the path, then

began to walk slowly along the narrow strip of beach, just beyond the reach of the cold, angry sea. Amala turned her face up to the heavens and stared at the dark patch that was now so obvious on the full face of the closer moon that was called Ethera after some long-forgotten god.

"My friend Felis and some others believe that dark patch may be a base of some sort. They believe the men have found a way to travel into space."

Glea followed her glance, then nodded. "I'm sure they have. There was already talk of going into space even before we came here, and since the wars continue, they must have found new enemies out there."

Amala cast a quick glance at Glea. "Have you ever thought about how much they must have advanced while we've been . . . here?" She had almost said "imprisoned here" but wasn't quite willing to voice such a thought to Glea.

"Imprisoned here, you mean," Glea said drily, causing Amala to turn sharply to her. "Don't look so shocked. I know you've thought the same thing yourself. Any intelligent woman would think about that."

Amala nodded slowly. "Back home, it's considered a traitorous thought . . . but yes, I *have* thought about it."

"It isn't traitorous at all," Glea scoffed. "We haven't advanced here at all. In fact, we've backslid into an existence that was primitive even a hundred years ago when we came here."

"Well, we can't be blamed for that. We have

no raw materials on the island and no way to gain the knowledge we need."

"I know that," Glea acknowledged. "I'm not blaming us for it; I'm merely stating a fact. They've moved ahead, and we've moved back."

"But we *have* become stronger, Glea—and we're free."

"True, but are we really free and have we become strong enough to face them again?"

Amala stopped and stared at her. "You believe that we're going to have to leave the island soon, don't you?"

Glea sidestepped the issue temporarily. "How would you feel if you knew that it could happen soon within your lifetime?"

"Scared—terrified, in fact," Amala replied honestly, then added in a quieter tone, "but excited, too, I think. It's the challenge. There's so little to challenge us here."

"That's exactly how I feel, too," Glea admitted. "And I *do* believe that it will happen soon."

"Do you really?" Amala asked, stunned by the certainty in Glea's voice. "Why?"

"The changes out there." Glea gestured behind them, to the hideous land Amala had crossed earlier. "I go out there often. And I've been having some dreams, too." Then she shrugged.

"Mostly, though, it's just a feeling I have, a feeling that something is coming to an end."

Amala said nothing as icy fingers seemed to play along her spine. She knew the feeling, although she'd never voiced it to anyone, not even Felis. It couldn't be described. It was almost like the subtle, invisible signs of a change in the seasons—something felt, rather than seen or heard.

"Yes," she said finally, not trusting herself to say more at the moment.

"Are you pregnant yet with Jorlan's child?" Glea asked suddenly.

"No. I suppose I'll try once more, and if nothing happens then I'll release him and find someone else."

Glea put out a hand to touch Amala's arm in a beseeching gesture. "Don't try again—not with Jorlan or even with anyone else. If we're forced to go back, you can't be pregnant. It would give Jorlan or some other man a hold over you, and we're going to need you, Amala. You and I—especially you—are our only hope."

Amala was shocked into temporary speechlessness. She knew that Glea was echoing the Semlian belief that bearing children could put a woman into thrall to a man, but why should she think that only the two of them could save the women?

"But what about the other Semlians?" she asked finally. "Surely they . . ."

"Most of them are not as strong as they think they are," Glea said sadly. "To them, it's almost a game. They pretend to be men, yet they've never seen one. And imitations are never as good as the original."

"Then why do you think that *we* can do anything?"

"Because we *are* strong, and so are a few others here and presumably among your people, too. They'll follow our lead, and that's the only hope we have. Do you honestly believe that we would ever have made it here if it hadn't been for a few strong women like your ancestor?"

"But we did come here. We've proved we don't need the men."

"We don't need them because we don't have them. Don't assume that will continue if we have to go back."

Amala didn't reply, and they both turned to return to the village. She just couldn't accept all that Glea had said. Why should women who had been self-sufficient all this time suddenly revert to dependence just because men were around? That made no sense whatsoever to her.

The silence between them continued all the way back to Glea's house, where they both quickly went off to bed. But Amala lay awake far into the night, replaying their discussion and thinking. Now that they'd spoken openly about the possibility of leaving the island, that possibility began to take on a terrible reality.

Chapter Three

Jorlan felt the tension in the Council chamber from the moment he strode through the door. He'd known that something important was afoot, since he'd been summoned here the moment his starship had docked at the Ethera base, but discreet inquiries of other passengers on the shuttle had produced no information. Whatever the nature of the emergency, it was obviously being kept from the general public for the moment.

As he took his seat, the only one vacant, the expressions on the faces of his fellow Council members told him that whatever the problem was, it must be serious. All looked grave, and many actually looked fearful. Then, just as the Chairman called the meeting to order, he saw that, alone among the group, Zakton appeared no more than bemused.

After congratulating Jorlan on his latest expedition, the Chairman hesitated for a moment. Watching that utterly uncharacteristic gesture on the part of this very self-assured man, Jorlan felt the first real stirrings of true alarm. Then the Chairman spoke, addressing himself once again to Jorlan.

"The others have already been told, so let me bring you up to date. The mist is receding and at a remarkable rate. Over a period of ten days, it has receded by nearly one hundred meters."

He paused to let Jorlan absorb that news, a respite Jorlan sorely needed. Of all the possibilities he'd considered, this was one that had never entered his mind. In all the centuries since they'd discovered a means by which to measure it, the mist had held perfectly steady, neither retreating nor expanding. That fact alone had always unnerved those who sought a scientific explanation.

"In the past two months while you've been away, Jorlan, there have also been notable increases in the number and intensity of the tremors on the island. We have every reason to believe that an eruption is imminent, but no one has yet been able to see a link between these two events."

Now, finally, the full import of this information began to hit Jorlan—in the form of a golden-haired woman dancing at the very edge of the awakening volcano. The result was a volatile mixture of fear and rage—fear for her life and a rage that she might be taken from him before he could make her his.

At that moment, Jorlan was as close to irrationality as he had ever been in his well-disciplined, highly logical life. Mercifully, the moment passed quickly as others began to speak.

Before long, however, the Minister of Science began to address them in his dry, pedantic tones, and the others gave him their undivided attention. Normally, when he began one of his lectures, they drifted off into thoughts of lunch or hunting expeditions or the conquest of new worlds. This time every eye was on him, focussed and intent.

"Three tremors in the past two days have been strong enough to have caused damage, although we believe that such damage would have been largely confined to the far side of the island, which we assume to be uninhabited. It is the opinion of our top scientists that the volcano is building a large dome of magma, and an eruption is quite likely within the next few months—or sooner."

"How accurate can you be with your predictions?" one member asked.

"Not very, I'm afraid," the Minister admitted. "We would, of course, be able to predict with greater accuracy if we could get to it ourselves. Nevertheless, our projections show nearly a one hundred percent certainty that a major eruption will take place. But the last eruption did very little actual damage . . . to the island, that is," the man hastened to add, since that eruption had driven them from the island and set into motion the chain of events that had culminated in the women's flight.

"It is our opinion that this time the island is likely to suffer extensive damage. The readings suggest that there are now huge underground rivers of magma throughout the island, which we believe could not have been the case last time."

"How are the women taking this?" Jorlan asked, his mind still tormented by the image of Amala dancing blithely at the very edge of a holocaust.

"We haven't seen any evidence that they're paying it any attention," the Chairman stated. "There is no increase or decrease in the dancing."

"It seems to me," rumbled one senior member, "that they'd be up there all the time now, trying to placate their damned goddess."

"They're probably too silly to understand the danger they're in, or else they have total faith in her ability to protect them," another man said disgustedly.

"One could excuse them for that," Zakton put in drily. "After all, she hasn't failed them yet."

Jorlan stared at his friend. Now he understood that expression he'd seen on Zakton's face. Perhaps alone among them, he would welcome back the women unreservedly.

The irony of the situation was not lost upon Jorlan. Here they were, faced with the prospect of victory in the one battle they hadn't been able to win, and no one appeared to be in a mood for celebration. But if the mist didn't recede quickly enough to get the women off the island before the eruption . . .

"It seems to me," the Chairman mused, "that we're in a deadly race here. If the mist doesn't disappear in time to get them off the island . . ."

"They have boats," someone cut in. "They could get away themselves."

There were dismissive grunts around the big table. None of them believed the women would have enough sense to leave voluntarily. They would cling to their faith in Aleala even as the lava obliterated them, or maybe they would even choose to remain on the island and die. They'd made such an irrational choice once before; such was the nature of women.

The Chairman spoke again. "Our best computer projections show the mist disappearing entirely within a month."

Throughout the room, men shifted in their seats, glanced at one another and then away again. Many of the older members suddenly looked even older, and even the younger men seemed wary rather than eager. Jorlan's expression was closed, betraying nothing of his own inner turmoil.

"We must make some plans now," the Chairman stated, although his tone indicated that this was something he would far rather contemplate at his leisure. The others nodded with a notable lack of enthusiasm.

Zakton, despite his fear for the women's safety, was amused at his fellow members' reactions. Most of them appeared to be in a state of shock. He glanced at Jorlan and saw his friend's neutral expression. He might have been contemplating nothing more than a request for funds. But that was Jor; he never gave anything away—or almost never, Zakton amended as he thought about Jorlan's expression when he watched Amala on the screen.

Was it, he wondered, mere coincidence that this was happening just at the time when there was once more a Jorlan and Amala among them? It had to be, and yet . . . He turned his attention back to the Chairman.

"First of all, if the mist disappears, or if there's an eruption, we'll have to mount a rescue mission quickly."

"We can't mount any rescue mission unless the mist disappears," someone interrupted. "All we can do is wait outside and hope they'll have enough sense to get into their boats."

"Perhaps not," the Science Minister stated, once again drawing the attention of all present. "As you all know, we've been working for some time on protective clothing, and it's possible that we might have come up with something this time. It hasn't been tested yet, but that could be scheduled soon."

"Then send out some prisoners," someone suggested. "And the sooner the better."

For many years, the men had been working to develop a fabric that could protect them from the mist. The breathing apparatus had long since been perfected and was used in space, but thus far the infernal mist had managed to penetrate the best fabric they could invent—and very quickly, too.

Taking note of the nods that followed this suggestion, the Chairman directed the Science Minister to proceed forthwith. Then he returned to the issue at hand.

"There are preparations to consider, in the event that we can get through or that they leave the island on their own."

"What preparations?" a graying veteran inquired testily. "We bring them back where they belong, and this time we make damned sure it doesn't happen again. If the volcano doesn't destroy the island, we blast it out of existence."

There were general murmurs of agreement around the table, but the Chairman spoke with a trace of impatience.

"And just where do they belong, Herva? What do you suggest we do with them while we sort things out?"

There was a very uneasy silence in the room while they all considered that. Every man present had certainly thought about the return of the women, but it now became apparent that few of them had ever gone beyond those initial speculations. Furthermore, to judge from most of their expressions, they weren't ready to consider it now, either.

But Jorlan smiled with satisfaction. He knew exactly what was to be done with one of them, in any event. He knew he should be considering the problem in its entirety, but he permitted himself a moment to savor the prospect of claiming Amala. Then he looked up to see Zakton watching him with amusement.

Jorlan's smile drained away. As Amala's brother and the head of her family, Zakton could deny that claim. It wasn't likely, but Zak did have some damned strange ideas sometimes. He might even think that his sister should be permitted to choose her own mate.

Suddenly, Zakton spoke up. "I suggest that we house them temporarily in the old fortress at Savleen."

The Chairman looked interested, as did many of the others. Savleen was a mountain stronghold of their last enemy in this world and had fallen to the first Jorlan's army not long after the women's departure.

"An interesting idea," the Chairman said. "Does anyone know what condition it's in? I haven't been up there in years."

"I've been up there quite recently, as a matter of fact," Zakton replied. "The buildings are structurally intact. Only the outer wall is in ruins, and that won't matter."

"Well, unless someone has a better idea, I suggest that Zakton put a regiment together and get the place ready."

No one offered an alternative, and Zakton

said he would see to it immediately.

"Good." The Chairman nodded. "Now we need someone to plan the rescue and have it operational as quickly as possible."

Jorlan was lost in his own thoughts and so was slow to notice that all eyes had turned upon him. He was considered by them all to be their greatest tactician. He nodded quickly, and his eyes met those of Zakton in a mutual appreciation of the irony.

Then Zakton spoke up again. "I suggest that we send them a message, asking for damage reports and stating our concern for their safety. The exchange is due in a few days, and we can send it then."

"They'll ignore it," someone grumbled.

"Perhaps," Zakton agreed. "But I'm inclined to think that they do know the danger they're in, and a message from us just might tip the balance in our favor."

The others contemplated this in silence. No one had ever attempted to communicate with the women; to have done so would have been too great a blow to masculine pride.

"I agree with Zak," Jorlan said after a few moments. "It's worth a try."

The others then nodded their agreement. Zakton was pleased by Jorlan's support. He knew that he himself was regarded by most of them as being something of a renegade, but Jorlan commanded the greatest respect among them. It was widely accepted that he would one day become Chairman himself.

Then a new and somewhat hesitant voice drew their attention. Most of them regarded the speaker with quizzical expressions, as though they weren't quite sure who he was and what he was doing there. But when they remembered just who and what he was, at least some of them looked at him with sudden interest. Feza was a psychologist, a profession not held in very high regard among the men. His presence on the Council was owed to the fact that he was the last male member of his particular Great Family, his heroic older brothers having died in the galactic wars.

"We need to be mindful of the shock to them if Aleala fails to protect them," he said in a voice that grew noticeably firmer when he realized that he had their attention. "All of them have grown up accepting the security she has provided for them."

The men nodded. They understood the frailties of women.

"No one is suggesting that we treat them with anything other than gentleness," the Chairman stated, looking around the table as though he half-expected some dissent.

After that, they returned to matters they understood better—gearing up the medical facilities in anticipation of casualties if the volcano erupted, putting factories into high gear to churn out the goods that would be required for double the present population.

Most of them began to show some enthusiasm. Here at least were recognizable and solvable problems.

When the meeting was adjourned, Jorlan and Zakton left the Council building together, then paused in the plaza. Jorlan gave his friend a wry grin.

"I wonder how many of them really want to see the women return."

Zakton chuckled. "Damned few, I suspect. And that probably includes you, too."

Jorlan shot him a baleful look. "I suppose you're looking forward to it."

"As a matter of fact, I am."

In the face of his friend's sincerity, Jorlan remained silent for a moment. Was he looking forward to it? At the back of his mind was a nagging thought that watching Amala on the screen might be preferable to dealing with her in person. In his experience, women tended to be that way—pleasant to look at, but very tedious to deal with. He was beginning to realize that his fantasies of Amala had always consisted of having a bed partner when he chose, and nothing more. After all, his total knowledge of women came from the pretty but dim-witted Bethusans.

"Feza was right, you know," Zakton went on, as they both stared down at the city spread beneath them.

"And it won't just be the shock of having Aleala fail them. There's also the matter of exchanging a primitive existence for all this."

Jorlan, who was becoming irritated with his

own confusion, snorted derisively. "They'll get used to it easily enough. When has a woman ever disliked luxuries?"

"Those luxuries might not mean space dust to them if they have to go back to the old ways," Zakton replied.

"Listen, Zak, we have enough problems without you conjuring up more. They're women—nothing more. Try to keep that in mind."

"Even Amala?" Zakton queried with a smile.

"Even Amala," Jorlan stated firmly. "She probably hasn't any more brains than Asroth."

"Since she's my sister, I could take umbrage at that," Zakton said, still smiling. "But what if you're wrong?"

"I'll deal with that if necessary."

"Am I to assume that you intend to claim her then?" Zakton asked with feigned innocence.

Jorlan stared at him fixedly. "Naturally. And I don't expect any trouble from her brother, either."

"The trouble might well come from the lady herself—without any help from me." Then he shot Jorlan a quick look.

"She could be pregnant, by the way. She's been at the dances every day lately."

In spite of his effort to remain impassive, Jorlan felt his pulse quickening. "She's done that before occasionally."

"But what if she *is* pregnant this time?"

"If she is, it's mine," Jorlan stated. "Then she can't refuse me."

Zakton was staring off into the distance thoughtfully. "Jor, we can't go back to the old ways. I'm convinced of that. If we're going to get a second chance, we have to do better this time."

"Beginning with Hoshe's suggestion that we blast that damned island out of existence, if the volcano doesn't do it for us."

Both men were silent for a moment, contemplating the fragility of the situation. Neither wanted to talk about what would happen if the volcano erupted before the mist disappeared and the women didn't escape on their own. To think about such a thing was to tempt madness.

"Try putting yourself in their places," Zakton said softly. "If you had to choose between slavery and death, what would you choose?"

"Dammit, Zak, they weren't slaves. All right, maybe they should have been given the right to own property and to choose their own husbands."

"That's a start." Zakton nodded, surprised to hear even that concession from Jorlan, but he suspected that Jor hadn't considered the personal ramifications of women choosing their own mates.

"But I have a feeling that they're not going to settle for just those concessions," he went on. "After all, they've been running their own lives for generations now."

Jorlan threw him an amused look. "I suppose you think they should be allowed to vote or maybe even sit on the Council?"

"Maybe I am. They must have their own Council."

"Then let them keep it if it makes them happy. They can decide what to plant in the public gardens and which artists to encourage. That should keep them occupied."

"What about children?"

"What about them?"

"They might decide to keep things as they are now."

Jorlan laughed. "If they think they're going to continue to keep the population in check, they're in for a rude awakening. The only thing that restricts us now in space is a lack of manpower. Besides, there's no way they could have developed any means of birth control."

Zakton acknowledged the truth of that. "But I wasn't referring just to population control. I also meant that they might want to continue the present method of conception."

When Jorlan looked at him, dumbfounded, Zakton shrugged. "Remember that reference in Amala's diary about intending to expunge forever the need for men? I've always thought she meant more than just artificial insemination, since they still need us for that. They've never even seen a man, let alone gotten to know one. Who knows what they may believe?"

Jorlan frowned thoughtfully. He too had read Amala's diary. She'd made very certain that it would be read, by leaving a copy of it in the computer. No doubt she'd feared that it might be suppressed by his ancestor.

The diary was a long litany of complaints against men and their society. It was also a step-by-step description of her treachery, written in a vivid style that had even Jorlan admiring her by the time he'd finished it.

What Zakton had said was indeed possible. The women had undoubtedly been fed a pack of lies about men for generations now without reason to doubt them.

"They'll learn to want us again," he said finally, in a gentle tone that surprised Zakton. "It will take some patience, that's all."

Zakton refrained from pointing out Jorlan's notable lack of that particular quality.

The old fortress at Savleen had always interested Zakton. He'd been coming up here occasionally ever since he was old enough to pilot an airsled. Jorlan had accompanied him a few times back then, but once they'd replayed the ancient battle, he'd lost interest in the place.

He stood now on an intact portion of the outer wall, staring off into the narrow valley below where so many of their people had lost their lives.

Their old enemy had chosen their final position well, taking advantage of the most forbidding terrain on their planet. A narrow, rocky valley lay before the fortress, and still higher peaks surrounded it on the other three sides.

That location had made invasion by air or by land a near impossibility. Furthermore, the enemy had a source of fresh water within the walls and a huge supply of food and ammunition.

Many of the military men of the time had counseled patience, knowing that sooner or later the enemy would run out of supplies, but the great Jorlan had been far too impatient to wait. Instead, he'd formulated a plan that he then rammed through Council.

Troops had been airlifted to the far side of the closest peak under cover of darkness, while at the same time the troops in the valley had made a great show of preparing to attack. The ruse had worked, but not without a terrible loss of life.

Most historians considered Savleen to have been Jorlan's greatest victory, but Zakton had always privately disagreed. Any victory that had cost so many lives seemed to him to be a hollow one, especially since by that time the women were keeping the population in check.

Zakton was inclined to believe that Jorlan had been a driven, half-madman. Thwarted by Amala's treachery, he'd sought a victory at any cost. They'd lost nearly a quarter of the adult male population.

In a sense, Savleen had really been Amala's victory, since years had passed before they'd dared to risk war again—in space. And always after that, the fruits of victory had been carefully weighed against the cost in lives.

The great Jorlan had never fought another battle, although he survived for many more years to see the dawning of the space age.

Zakton supposed that the real reason he was fascinated by this place was that it was here that he could feel most strongly the presence of that most famous of couples.

A careful reading of Amala's diary showed not just her brilliant scheme—but an anguish as well. And Jorlan's own writings in the period after the women's departure were so singularly devoid of any references to her that Zakton was convinced of his own anguish. There was even an old story that he had died begging her to forgive him and take him back, although his family refused to credit it.

To Zakton's way of thinking, the two of them had loved and hated each other in equal measure, unable to live together and unable to be happy apart.

Zakton felt a secret longing to know that kind of passion. Certainly, he'd never known anything more than a brief physical pleasure with the women on Bethusa.

He continued to stare out over the valley, thinking about their future. By now, the entire population knew of the conditions on the island and the receding mist. The talk among men was of nothing else. Zakton kept silent for the most part, listening to others talk, and what he heard was not reassuring.

The majority of the men seemed to believe that the return of the women would signal a resumption of the old ways. Men who had fathered children were grumbling openly about being forced to live with women they hadn't chosen. Younger men of the Great Families were studying the charts with an eye toward selecting the best possible mates. And a few crusty old spacemen were even talking about creating a female-free zone where they could live in peace.

They won't accept that, he thought. They will demand changes. Then he wondered if perhaps he was basing this assumption on the rather dubious belief that the present Amala was a reincarnation of her infamous ancestress. He didn't for one minute believe that she was brainless, as Jorlan had suggested, but that didn't mean that she was the extraordinary woman her namesake had been.

Ah, but if she were . . . He smiled at the prospect of Jorlan facing a woman like that. It could well be the greatest battle his friend would ever fight—and the only one he might not win.

Zakton was still contemplating the fireworks such a meeting would produce when one of his officers came up to report that their examination of the buildings had confirmed his belief; they were all structurally sound. Certainly they would be adequate housing for women who were presently living in such primitive conditions.

After some repairs and considerable cleaning, they would begin to bring in furniture and other provisions. A whole fleet of airfreighters would be required to get everything up to this isolated spot. Zakton had already issued the orders and the supply officers had raised their brows at the lengthy list, but he wanted the women to be comfortable. He'd even ordered solar generators, although he wasn't certain they'd have the time required to electrify the place.

He climbed down from the wall and walked into the great courtyard, where some of the men were beginning to clean up the rubble from that ancient battle. His chief supply officer followed after him.

"Add to the list some tubs of flowers and shrubs, Jeska. That should improve the looks of the place. And some comfortable benches as well."

The man wrote it down, but Zakton could see that he thought it was all crazy, since everyone assumed the women would be here only a very short time.

"How many heaters are available?" he asked.

When Jeska told him, Zakton nodded. That should be sufficient, if they also used the fireplaces. Already the nights were cold up here. If they were still here when winter set in, more would have to be done. The climate on the island was far gentler than up here in these mountains.

And Zakton had a feeling that they *would* still

be here when the snows arrived. He hoped that Amala could be persuaded to come live with him in their compound, but she might well choose to stay here with the other women.

He walked about, observing the work and reassuring himself that it would not be fruitless. The mist was still receding at the same rate, and there'd been no more tremors on the island. But there'd also been no reply to his message. Every day now they'd sent out a boat to await a response.

At the request of the Chairman, Zakton himself had written the letter. He'd labored hard to strike just the right conciliatory note, without actually promising any changes. He'd even gone out himself on exchange day, when it was sent across with the death lists.

The exchanges were a humiliating experience, and no man ever volunteered to go after one trip out of curiosity. They were made on a monthly basis, according to a lunar schedule devised by Amala at the beginning. The time was always the hour of dawn, which added to the unreality of the scene.

The men were required to remain a kilometer away from the mist while the women set the babies and birth lists adrift in small boats. As soon as the tiny boats had been lowered into the water, the women retreated back into the mist in their weather-beaten, old Great Family boat. The men then advanced to gather in the babies and set the boats adrift once more with the death lists—and this time with Zakton's message. Sometimes, too, the precious seed of life was sent across, stored in labeled cylinders. And that was surely the most humiliating aspect of the whole unpleasant business.

Naturally, the men carried with them high-powered glasses to see what they could of the women, but the few women aboard always wore heavy, hooded cloaks and from their movements appeared to be elderly. Zakton had watched them, wondering if they still carried the poison pellets Amala had written about.

Zakton had returned feeling angry and frustrated, knowing that his feelings were shared by the others on board. Only the furry Feloths who provided for the infants were happy, making their soft, warbly sounds as they examined the babies.

He stood now at Savleen, worrying that that frustration would spill over into violence against the women when they returned. He wasn't worried about the women of his own family nor those of the other Great Families, but he did worry about the lower classes, whose history of abuse toward women was well-known, despite the old laws that had been written to protect them.

But they would be safe here, at least. He had personally selected the men who would remain here to assist the women, and regardless of how they might feel personally, they could be trusted to follow his orders.

Zakton was about to depart for the city when another airsled glided down to land in the courtyard of the fortress, and to his surprise Jorlan got out.

After the two men greeted each other, Zakton told him about the progress they'd made.

"I'm surprised you found the time to come up here," he observed, knowing that Jorlan was busy with his rescue plans.

"I just wanted to see the place again," Jorlan replied in a somewhat distracted tone. Then he shot a quick glance at Zakton.

"I went over to the observatory, too, and she wasn't there today."

"Maybe she's busy with plans of her own," Zakton suggested, now understanding the reason for his friend's behavior.

When Jorlan said nothing, Zakton went on. "Maybe it would be a blessing if she isn't pregnant just now."

Jorlan just nodded, lost in his own thoughts. He didn't want her to come here; he'd never liked this place. He was always uncomfortable here, despite its having been the scene of his ancestor's greatest victory. Something of her—the original Amala—lingered here, despite the fact that he knew she'd never set foot in the fortress.

Jorlan had spent the past few days burying himself in his plans and trying not to think about the future, but here, amidst all these preparations, the future was proclaiming itself.

"I think they may be here quite a while," Zakton said musingly. "I'm going to have to see to it that there's adequate heat."

Rather to his surprise, Jorlan nodded. "But we can't let them exchange one prison for another," he stated firmly.

Zakton thought that just might be what they would choose to do.

"They voted unanimously to ignore the message."

"Unanimously?" Felis frowned at Amala. "What about you?"

Amala looked uncharacteristically sheepish. "I abstained."

"You did?" Felis gaped at her. "But you said it sounded like a peace offering."

Amala sighed heavily. "It was a very conciliatory letter. Someone obviously labored long and hard over it. When I first read it, I was ready to throw away everything we've always believed about men, but then I read it again and decided that there was too much that wasn't said."

"Like what?"

"No apologies for past injustices—and no guarantees that things will change."

Felis nodded. "I saw that right away."

"You did? I didn't."

"That's because you're an optimist and I'm a pessimist."

"Nonsense. We're both realists, and realistically speaking, we have no choice but to go back. I just think it would be better to go back on our own than to be dragged back or rescued."

"The mist could stop receding?" Felis suggested with a desperate fervor.

"Now you're *not* being realistic. It won't stop, Felis, and even if it does, the mountain could still erupt. Our time here is ending. I know it."

"Most of the women believe that Aleala would never betray us," Felis stated.

"They could still be believing that when the lava buries us all," Amala replied disgustedly.

"You really don't believe in her anymore, do you?" Felis asked.

Amala shrugged. "I don't know. I believed when I was little. But Felis, if she does exist, she might well have decided that it's time for us to go back again. Maybe it will work this time."

"Hmmmpphh! Do you really believe that they could have changed?"

"How could I possibly know, when we know nothing about them? We don't even know what they look like, unless you want to believe those old stories."

"You really want to go back, don't you?" Felis asked.

Amala gestured around them. "This place is a waste of our lives. We can't progress here. Think of the things you could learn if we go back."

"*You* may be able to learn things. You're Great Family."

"That's what you're really worried about,

isn't it?" Amala asked quietly.

"I won't go back to a world where men rule us and your fate is determined by your family's class. I'd rather die here."

"That won't happen, Felis. I promise you."

"You promise me? What makes you think even you can change the system? You may be a member of the greatest Family, but you're still a woman. Your brother, what's-his-name, has all the power."

"I've been thinking a lot about Zakton lately. I refuse to believe that my brother is a monster."

"But even if he isn't, and he listens to you, he's still just one vote on the Council. And if Jorlan is anything like the first Jorlan . . ." She lapsed into an ominous silence.

Amala remained silent. Jorlan was one subject she refused to think about just now, although she was aware of the fact that she would certainly have to do so—and soon.

"We need to find some way to deal with them from a position of strength. It's our only hope."

"I agree. But just where do we find that strength?"

"The one real hold we have over them now is control of the population."

"But we won't have that when we go back," Felis said with a shudder. All of them were having nightmares now, dreams filled with the unimaginable horror of being touched by men, being forced to mate with them.

"Maybe, just maybe, we can. I've spent most of the afternoon at the library, looking for something I remembered from a history text. I finally found it just when I was about to give up, and it could be the answer."

"What are you talking about?" Felis demanded impatiently.

"Birth control."

"I still don't know what you're talking about."

"I remembered reading once about some herbs that grew wild here on the island many years ago, back when men could still come here. The women discovered somehow that they could prevent conception, and they secretly gathered and used them. Then the men found out about them and supposedly destroyed them."

"So how could that help us, if they no longer exist?"

"Don't you see? They might not have destroyed all of them. If they were growing wild, that would have been virtually impossible. They could still be here."

"Did the book say where they grew?"

Amala shook her head. "Only that it was on the part of the island that was forbidden to women."

"But that's a huge area, and we don't even know what they look like."

"True, but it's not as big an area as you think. Most of the part that was forbidden is completely barren. The only part where anything at all grows is the area where the Semlians live."

"Do you think they could know anything about them?"

"It's possible. Semle's journal had all sorts of information in it that isn't in history books. She must have spent her whole childhood hiding around corners eavesdropping or prodding old women for their stories, at least if Glea is to be believed."

"But why wouldn't Glea have told you about them?"

"Why should she? Up until now, it wasn't important. I'm going to see them tomorrow."

"Amala, the trip is so dangerous now. We know there must have been some damage out there, because we even felt the quakes here."

"All the more reason I must go. I have to persuade them to come back here. The Council is drafting a letter for me to take to them. I just hope they'll pay more attention to it than we have to the letter from the men."

"I'm going with you."

"You are?" Amala smiled. "I wanted to ask you, but it's so dangerous."

"I know, but you'll need all the help you can get locating those herbs."

"Is it worse than before? I've never been out this far." Felis brought the jepsa to a halt at the top of a hill and stared in disbelief at the scene before them.

As far as they could see, ugly, ochre vapors covered the land, so thickly that in places the landscape itself was completely invisible. What land they could see was raw and cracked like ugly, open wounds.

Amala didn't know whether or not to tell Felis the truth, but she suspected that her expression and her silence had already said it for her. "It's much worse. I'm really afraid that we'll get sick from the fumes before we can get across it."

"Do you want to turn back?"

Amala shook her head firmly. "I must go on, Felis, but I could take you back first. This isn't your responsibility."

"No, but it's my choice," Felis replied and urged the little jepsa forward once more.

Amala was secretly relieved not to have to make this hellish journey alone, and she was pleased that Felis seemed more alive and interested than she had for days. Ever since they discovered that the mist was receding and then felt the tremors growing worse, Felis had been sinking ever more deeply into herself.

They were all frightened, of course, save for those mostly older women whose faith in Aleala was unshakable. But Amala had noticed that the fear was greatly increased among the women of lower class origin, like Felis.

I will not allow the men to undo what we have done here, she thought. *We have found freedom on this island, if we found nothing else, and we* will carry that back with us.

From the moment the pilots had discovered that the protective mist was receding, Amala had faced up squarely to all that implied. While others sought desperately for an explanation that would continue to keep them safe on their island, she had set the past aside and looked toward the very much changed future.

As they bumped along across the scarred land, Amala recalled the moment when she'd heard the news and the trip to her aunt's home that had immediately followed. Verta, the seeress, had years ago retreated to a small cottage on the edge of the settlement because psychic emanations from within the colony disturbed her as she grew older. Now she had become very frail, and Amala's mother had gone to stay with her.

Nevertheless, when Amala had appeared, the old woman had sat up in her bed, and before Amala could even deliver her news, Verta had nodded and said, "It is ending."

Amala had made another visit to her aunt last night and found the woman's health even more fragile. Her mother said that Verta was drifting in and out of reality, never remaining for long in either state. When her mother had gone off to prepare some broth for Verta, Amala had sat quietly by the bedside, wishing that they could have the benefit of the old woman's knowledge. How very much they all needed to see into the future now!

Then suddenly, Verta had stirred and opened

her still-bright blue eyes. To Amala's surprise, she'd spoken her name and reached for her hand.

"You are the leader now. You have the power."

Amala could still hear those words, as clearly as though Verta sat beside her now. She'd asked what her aunt meant, but Verta had slipped away again.

What had Verta meant? What power did she possess? Was it possible that the old woman was confusing her with her ancestress?

Amala had gone home without telling her mother or anyone else of Verta's words. Then she'd stared long and hard at the only surviving portrait of her famous ancestress. The resemblance was truly remarkable—the same pale gold hair and piercing blue eyes, the same slightly squared face that added to the look of steely determination. It might well have been a portrait of herself in a few years.

She began to wonder now if any portrait of Amala had survived over there in their former home. Perhaps Jorlan had destroyed it. She hoped that was the case, since it now occurred to her that her resemblance to her ancestress could well prove disastrous in her dealings with the men, among whom she would certainly be reviled.

Beside her, Felis began to cough and choke, then turned to Amala with streaming eyes. "This is awful. I feel as though I can't breathe."

Amala, who had been pressing a damp cloth

to her own nose and mouth as she drifted in her thoughts, was overcome with guilt. Felis wasn't accustomed to this, and she should never have let her come along.

"Let me drive the rest of the way so you can cover your face. I think we're more than halfway through the bad part now."

So Felis brought the jepsa to a halt and they switched seats. Amala began to pick her way carefully along the perimeter of the malodorous geysers, then circled around yet another new, gaping crack in the tortured earth. Twice during the slow, tedious journey the little vehicle shook from small tremors. Both times Felis stiffened in fear, and Amala reassured her that this was a common occurrence out here. But she had only to look at the changed landscape to know that far worse tremors had occurred since her last journey.

Then at last they were through the inferno and moving toward the partially harvested fields of datera. Not one woman could be seen, at a time when Amala would have expected virtually the entire colony to be out in the fields, gathering in their precious crop. She said nothing to Felis, but fear for the Semlians slithered through her.

They climbed the last hill that separated them from the colony, and Amala brought the jepsa to a halt as relief swept away her increasing fear. There were raw, jagged cracks in the road just ahead, and beyond that she could see the rubble that had once been the outermost buildings of the settlement. But she could also see a group of Semlians, some of whom were searching through the rubble, while others were busy repairing less damaged structures.

This was not a scheduled visit, but even so, there was no real surprise on the faces of the first women they approached.

"Glea said you would come," one woman said as they greeted her and peered with interest at Felis. "But many of us thought it would be impossible for you to get here."

"How bad was it?" Amala asked, gesturing at the ruins around them.

"Two women died and five were injured," she was told. Amala knew one of the dead women, a highly respected artisan, and one of the injured was a Council member.

"The worst of the damage was here," another woman said, "but even in the square, some of the foundations were cracked."

Then they inquired about the main colony, and Amala said that while they had certainly felt the tremors more strongly than ever before, no real damage had been done, save for items that had toppled from shelves and walls. After that she excused herself to move along to the center of the village, where she was told she would find Glea.

Glea came forward from a small group as they drove into the square. Beside her, Felis made a sound of surprise at Glea's height and her commanding presence. Amala thought she saw a few more silver hairs among Glea's black curls.

They greeted each other, and Amala expressed her condolences over the loss of life before introducing Felis.

"Welcome, Felis," Glea said in that remarkably deep voice that never failed to remind Amala of all the old stories about the men.

"Amala has told us that you are the one who keeps the precious jepsas running. Such skills are to be envied."

Amala noted with a smile that, consciously or unconsciously, Glea had chosen the perfect words to put Felis at ease. Felis was very proud of her mechanical skills—and rightly so, in Amala's estimation.

Then Glea turned her attention back to Amala. "I will gather the Council. Go to my house and refresh yourselves. I will have someone bring you both a change of clothes so you can rid yourselves of the stench."

Amala and Felis exchanged embarrassed glances. They'd apparently grown so accustomed to the strong sulphur smell that they'd failed to notice they'd brought it with them from that hellish land.

A short time later, Amala sat watching the faces of the Semlian Council members as they absorbed her news. She'd brought with her the message sent by the men, and the letter from her Council inviting them to return to the main colony. Both letters were now being circulated.

"What has Verta to say?" an older woman asked.

"My aunt is in a deep coma," Amala replied sadly. "We fear she is about to die." She resorted to that half-truth because she and her mother had agreed to keep Verta's statement about an ending to themselves for fear of panicking the others. Amala had also decided to keep secret the words Verta had spoken only to her, just before she lapsed into the coma. Why speak of power when she didn't have the faintest idea what Verta had meant?

The questioner nodded sadly. "Yes. Treza also died at such a time—just before the exodus."

Amala stared at her in shock, as did many others. She'd quite forgotten about that, but it was true. Treza had been a seeress like Verta. She had died two days before the women's departure for the island, but not before assuring them that all would be well.

Had Verta given her the same assurance? If so, it was certainly a very obscure sort of assurance.

Then Amala told them about the precious herbs and how she viewed them as being essential to guarantee their future. To her surprise, the women began to nod, and a few even smiled. When Amala had finished, Glea looked quickly at the other members, then spoke.

"We do know about them, Amala—and yes, they still exist. The knowledge of where to find them and how to prepare them was passed on to Semle when she was quite young by the only woman who knew about them, and Semle committed the information to her journal.

"They grow now in one small area about two kilometers from here—a small, sheltered valley near the coast. I think you are right. The real reason the men forbade the women to come to this side of the island is that they knew they might not have destroyed them all.

"Their preparation is the key to their success, and Semle left very clear instructions about that. Tomorrow we will begin to gather them. If you can remain here long enough, we could use the jepsa and get there much more quickly."

"Of course we'll stay. I told the Council we might be gone for a few days. I'm so glad that Semle had so much foresight. I wish I could have known her."

Her sincere words, spoken about a woman whose name was virtually anathema among Amala's people, was received with great pleasure and pride.

After that, Amala and Felis excused themselves so that the Semlian Council could debate the offer Amala had brought them. Amala suggested that they walk along the beach, since she wanted Felis to see the picturesque coastline. As they walked along, Amala thought she could sense a definite lightening of her friend's mood. She was about to comment on it when Felis broke the silence herself.

"I was afraid they might not help us, but now I'm beginning to think we might have a chance."

Amala nodded. "The only enemy we have now is time—time to gather the herbs and prepare them, and time to persuade the Council that we should leave the island voluntarily."

"I like them," Felis went on, "especially Glea. She's very level-headed and strong. If she hadn't joined the Semlians, she would have given you some competition."

"Competition?" Amala asked, casting a sidelong glance at her friend.

"As leader," Felis explained.

Amala frowned. "Do you really think of me as a leader, Felis? I may be on the Council, but I'm only one of fifteen—and I'm not the Chairwoman."

"Everyone thinks of you as the leader, especially now, I think."

Amala thought about that. Verta had said she was the leader, but it was that statement that had made Amala think she had confused her with her ancestress, who had clearly been the leader then. She didn't really think of herself as being the leader, since she was young and had been raised in a culture that values the wisdom of age.

"Actually, I think of myself more as a rebel than a leader. I'm afraid that's how most of the Council sees me, too. I'm not sure I want to be thought of as a leader."

"Well, whether you want it or not, you are."

Amala sighed. "I hope that the Semlians will agree to return to the main colony. They'll be so much safer there, and then we'd be facing the future as a united front."

"They'll be in so much more danger from the men than we will be," Felis said quietly. "It could be far worse for them because of their views."

"Yes, and I'm sure they know that. But with Glea as their leader, at least they have some power on their side. After all, she's a Tabor." Tabor was Glea's family name.

"But so is Jorlan, and if he's at all like the other Jorlan . . ." Felis let the sentence trail off ominously.

"Even if he is, somehow I think Glea could be a match for him." Amala smiled.

The two women walked on in silence along the water's edge, then climbed the rocks at the end of the beach. The day was cool and overcast, and even heavily cloaked as they were, they both shivered in the cutting wind from the sea. Both turned their backs on the restless sea and stared instead at the distant, mist-enshrouded peak just barely visible beyond the far hills. There was scarcely a place on the island where the holy mountain could not be seen. But what had once seemed to be a benevolent sentinel had now become an object of menace for them both.

"It is ending. You are the leader. You have the power."

Once again, Verta's words came to her with

such clarity that Amala could actually feel her aunt's presence. She shivered with a sudden premonition of what she would find when she returned home.

If only Verta had been able to tell her what that power was.

CHAPTER FOUR

BY THE TIME AMALA AND FELIS RETURNED TO Glea's cottage, the rest of the Semlian Council had gone. Amala's heart sank. She was certain they must have decided not to return to the main colony, since a decision to accept the invitation would surely have been reached only after a lengthy debate. Her fear must have been very evident because Glea smiled at her and nodded.

"Our answer is yes. We will accept the invitation to return, but only after we gather and prepare the herbs. We think this will be an appropriate peace offering."

Amala relaxed visibly. "I'd expected a lengthy debate."

"You may find some of our beliefs strange, Amala, but we are not fools. The danger here has become too great. Furthermore, we agree with you that we must present a united front to the men."

She paused and smiled again. "I think your year as Ambassador has helped a great deal to dispel any lingering animosity toward your Council. All of us have great respect for you."

"Thank you," Amala replied sincerely, "but I must warn you that not all of the Council—or the rest of the women, for that matter—share my beliefs. Some of them, particularly the older ones, still cling to their belief in Aleala, and your rejection of the goddess doesn't sit well with them."

"We understand that, and I assure you that we respect their beliefs, even if we don't share them. Besides," she sighed, "if the volcano erupts, their beliefs will disappear in the smoke and lava, and they will need the support and understanding of all."

Amala nodded her agreement. "I really worry that some of them may choose to perish here, rather than give up their beliefs."

"Do we have the right to force them to leave?" Felis asked quietly, drawing both women's attention.

"I don't know," Amala replied solemnly, wondering if Felis herself might make that choice. "Our laws provide for holding someone against their will to prevent them from harming themselves, but it's always been a very difficult issue."

"Then let's hope that we don't have to face

it," Glea stated.

The women settled down with mugs of herbal tea as Glea lit a fire. Then she sat down on the rug before the hearth and fixed her dark eyes on Amala.

"Our Council has also voted unanimously to recommend that you be the chief negotiator with the men."

Amala stared at her. "But you and Thurzia are the heads of the two Councils."

"Yes, but you are the most knowledgable among us of the laws. Furthermore," she added with a wry smile, "there's a fitting irony to choosing you. When the men see who they're dealing with . . ." She let the sentence trail off with a low chuckle.

"That may be the very reason I'm *not* the most suitable," Amala said even though her mind was harking back once more to Verta's words.

Thurzia, although a highly intelligent woman, was not from one of the Great Families, which would certainly put her at a disadvantage with the men. And Glea, although she was Great Family, held views that were too extreme to make her suitable as a negotiator.

Was this, then, what Verta had meant when she'd said that Amala had the power?

"The fact that they are dealing with the namesake and virtual reincarnation of the woman who defeated them will be a great advantage," Glea stated firmly. "And don't forget that they want us back, so we have the advantage there as well. What we must do is to be sure that we, not they, dictate the terms. I hope to persuade the Council that you are right—we should leave here voluntarily. That should give us both the advantage of surprise and the appearance of strength."

They began to discuss the laws of their society, and Amala told them about her secret project—the rewriting of those laws. Glea listened carefully as Amala described her vision for their future.

"I agree with all you've said," Glea said when Amala had finished, "but the realist in me tells me that we can't hope to accomplish all of that. We will need to establish priorities."

"I know," Amala agreed. "I've been considering that."

"And there's something else you must take into consideration as well," Glea went on. "Semle believed that there exists a strong force between men and women, a very powerful attraction."

Amala and Felis stared at her, then at each other. They had all been taught from childhood that mating was an unpleasant, primitive behavior that was thankfully no longer necessary to perpetuate their species. They knew it was both painful and degrading, something to be engaged in only by animals.

"I know what we were all taught, but Semle wrote otherwise. She believed that men and women want to mate with each other, that some force must exist between them that overwhelms all else."

Felis shivered. "But how could we possibly want to be touched by such monsters?"

"We have only our teachings to confirm that they really are ugly monsters," Glea pointed out.

Amala was silent for a moment, then spoke in a low, bemused tone. "Every time I've looked at the male babies, I've found it nearly impossible to believe that they could grow up into the misshapen, hairy monsters we were told about. Semle may have been right—at least about their appearance—but they're still monsters."

The trio was silent for a few moments as each of them considered that mystery. Then Amala spoke again.

"We must insist upon staying together and being apart from the men as well. If Semle was right about this force, then we cannot afford to be near them, at least until the laws are to our liking."

The other two agreed wholeheartedly, although none of them could begin to imagine such a strange force.

The next morning, Amala and Felis, together with three Semlians, crowded into the jepsa and drove off in search of the precious herbs. There had been no more tremors, and the day had dawned in serene beauty.

The valley where the herbs grew was a delightful surprise, an oasis of lush beauty in the midst of barrenness. It was protected on all sides by steep rock walls. Amala and Felis stared in wonder at a small stand of beautiful trees with fine golden fronds. They'd never seen such lovely trees before.

One of the Semlians joined them. "Glea says they're called kodans and that they're very rare even on the mainland. She said they grow only on her ancestral lands."

Amala continued to stare at them, but then she remembered that Glea's ancestral lands were Jorlan's lands now. She turned away quickly, her pleasure destroyed. Jorlan seemed to lurk always at the edges of her mind.

The Semlians showed Amala and Felis the herbs, and they all gathered them until they had filled the jepsa's storage compartment. They also carefully dug up entire plants and put them into pots so that they could ensure a future supply. The work in the warm sun that filled this lush place had a beneficial effect upon them all. The future seemed, if not entirely hopeful, at least far less threatening.

Early the next morning, Amala and Felis set out for home. Glea told them that preparing the herbs would take no more than three days. Amala wanted them to come back to the main colony as quickly as possible, so they agreed that she and Felis would return in three days' time with both jepsas to begin carrying the women and their belongings across the island.

Many trips would be necessary, but they calculated that if the jepsas held out, the Semlian colony could be abandoned within two weeks.

They were nearly across the sulphurous, scarred land when a sudden tremor shook the jepsa so hard that it very nearly overturned. Both women clung to their seats and held their breath as they waited for it to end. It seemed to go on forever, although it could have lasted for no more than a minute. The earth actually growled and shrieked, and when those terrible sounds finally subsided, there was a loud rumble behind them. They turned and saw huge boulders hurtling down the hillside they had just descended, obliterating the path they had driven only moments before.

Both of them stared in horror at what might have been. Then Amala lifted her gaze to the distant volcano.

"Do we have two weeks?" she asked into the sudden, menacing silence.

Jorlan turned away from the big viewscreen and walked out of the observatory, his fists clenched in frustration. She wasn't there; she hadn't been to the mountain for more than a week.

His thoughts now weren't on his child that she might be carrying but on Amala herself. What if she had been killed? They had no way of knowing just how much damage the continuing tremors were causing.

He climbed into his airsled and took off, pushing it to its limits. He'd never felt so frustrated in his life. All the rescue plans had been made. They could leave for the island on a moment's notice. Crews were standing by 24 hours a day with high-speed boats, airsleds, larger boats equipped as hospitals and the big airlifters.

The mist continued to recede but at no faster a rate than before. He didn't know how he could manage to wait for another ten days, the time they calculated it would take for the mist to disappear completely.

The Council was meeting daily now, as they all began to face up to their very much changed future. New issues were being raised at each meeting, interlaced with the everpresent fear that they would not be able to save the women. Throughout the land, men were fearful, wary, defiant, sullen, eager—often all at the same time.

Theirs was a well-ordered society, so the details of preparing for a doubling of their population were proceeding smoothly. Doctors were busy studying obstetrics and gynecology, subjects for which they'd heretofore had no use. Factories were operating 24 hours a day, turning out women's clothing. Foodstuffs were piling up in warehouses on the edge of the city and in the outlying villages and farming communes. Merchants of every kind were eyeing their stocks, trying to gauge what would appeal to the new customers they eagerly awaited.

At yesterday's Council meeting, Zakton had proposed that the women be allowed to stay at Savleen for as long as they chose. Jorland had arrived late, in the midst of the heated debate, and ended it quickly by stating his agreement with Zakton. Never had Jorlan's power on the Council been more obvious.

The truth was that he had decided he preferred things that way, at least for a while. For a man who could plunge headlong into situations that would frighten any other man, Jorlan had become very cautious.

The reason for that caution he kept secret, even from Zakton. He had reread the diaries of his ancestor that had been kept within the family, and those outpourings of a man brought to weakness by a woman troubled him greatly. He didn't understand it, but he had no intention of letting history repeat itself.

Amala awoke in the gray light of predawn, that time when night hasn't yet quite given up its hold and the sun has only tentatively hinted at its reappearance. She was instantly alert. All of them slept lightly these days.

Had there been another quake? She stared at the small pots of herbal creams on her ancient dresser. They had rounded bottoms, and several had fallen to the floor during past quakes. Nothing had moved, and the colorful datera wall-hanging hadn't shifted. She relaxed and burrowed deeper under the covers. Perhaps she'd only been dreaming again. Strange, frightening dreams plagued her almost nightly now. Troubled sleep was common among them as well.

But her thoughts went briefly to the Semlians. If there *had* been another quake . . . Today was the day they would be starting the evacuation of the Semlian colony. She planned to invite Glea to stay with her, since her mother was now staying at Verta's isolated cottage, keeping what they all knew was a death watch.

Sleep teased her, stealing close and then backing off again. She tried to grab it, then gave up with a sigh. She would have to get up soon in any event to begin the long journey to the Semlian colony. They hoped to make two trips a day with the jepsas, and one of them was already parked just outside her cottage.

She sat up and stretched. Perhaps she'd awaken Felis so they could get an early start. By the time they actually set out, it should be full light.

The night breeze from the nearby sea was always cool, so the window was shuttered. As always, her first act upon getting out of bed was to throw open the shutters. She did so now, then stood there for a moment, staring at the sea through the growing light. We all see what we expect to see, and Amala was no exception. Even when the difference finally did register, more seconds passed before she could accept what her eyes saw.

The mist was gone! Not a trace remained. Even in the pale light, she could see the dark smudge along the distant horizon that was her ancestral homeland, the land of the men.

A chill played along her spine and prickled her skin. It should not have happened this quickly! They'd been sure they would have weeks yet, and many even had believed it would stop diminishing at some point. Now it had vanished overnight. What did it mean? She paused only long enough to scan the sea for signs of approaching boats, then after reassuring herself that none were there yet, she turned away quickly to grab her clothes.

The precious herbs! She had to reach the Semlians before the men could, so that they could find some way to hide them and carry them to the mainland. She had no doubt that the men would be here very quickly now.

She had just reached the front door of the cottage when she was halted by a series of loud, terrifying sounds, rather like giant branches being snapped by some unbelievably powerful force. The men! Could they be here already? Cold terror washed over her.

When all became silent once more, she opened the door cautiously.

After reassuring herself that no monsters lurked out there, she stepped out, her head turned toward the sacred mountain. The mist was gone from there, too, and in its place was a dull red glow. Disbelief piled upon disbelief as she stared at it, realizing that the sounds must have come from there. Then there was a bone-shaking explosion, and she saw dark objects being flung heavenward from the glowing top of the mountain. The sky was becoming pale with the dawn, but the color at the peak only brightened with it.

Amala paused again, weighing her options. Felis lived at the far end of the settlement, her mother and Verta were even farther away at the other end. Already other women were stumbling sleepily from nearby cottages, then stopping to stare in awe at the red-crowned mountain.

Then there was yet another explosion, and Amala ran for the jepsa. Her decision was made. Nothing could take precedence over those precious herbs. There was little she could do here in any event. The Semlians had small boats and could get away, but she was sure the boats couldn't carry the entire population plus the herbs. The herbs had to be brought back here, where they could be hidden among other things the women would want to take with them.

As she started the jepsa, several women turned from the mountain and called out to her, but she ignored them. She had no time to explain, and Felis would know where she'd gone.

She pushed the jepsa to its limits while she still had decent road beneath her and quickly left the village behind. Behind her, the sun rose above the land of the men, its ruddy disc mimicking the fiery glow from the volcano. When she crested the first ridge, she slowed down enough to turn and stare at the scene.

The mountain continued to glow as a dark haze settled over its peak. The rising sun bathed the sea in a reddish gold and silhouetted the land at the horizon. She still couldn't see any boats or flying machines, but her mind produced a horrifying image of a sea and sky filled with them. She shuddered and drove on, forcing herself to think only of her all-important mission.

When she finally reached the barren, blasted interior of the island, she was actually reassured by its vapor-filled bleakness. It looked no worse than on her previous trip. If any new fissures had opened up, they weren't large enough to be obvious.

There would surely be enough time for her to reach the Semlian colony, fill the jepsa's storage compartment with the herbs and return to the main colony. She had no doubt that the men would have arrived by that time, but all would surely be chaos and the herbs could be hidden.

The Semlians could remain where they were until the men came for them, or they could leave on their own boats. Amala thought they would choose the latter course.

She climbed the next to last hill in the hellish center of the island, then paused at the top. The eastern sea was still visible from here, and now she thought she could make out small, dark specks moving with amazing swiftness across the water. Then she scanned the sky and thought that perhaps she saw moving black dots there as well. The men were coming! Myth was about to become reality.

For one moment as she began the tortuous descent from the hilltop, Amala felt a pang of guilt for having abandoned the women at such a time. But they were no less safe for her absence, and she had to think of the future now facing them.

She was about halfway down the hillside when the next explosion came—a deep, booming sound that filled her entire world. The jepsa began to shake violently, and she struggled to hold onto the steering wheel as the ground beneath her started to heave.

"No!" she shouted as the jepsa was suddenly lifted into the air and the wheel was wrenched from her grasp. It slammed back to earth, then began to tumble down the hillside. In those final few seconds, she recalled her nightmare of being trapped out here with the ghosts, but the nightmare was mercifully cut short.

By the time the next explosion shook the land, the jepsa had come to rest at the bottom of a ravine, a twisted pile of bright blue metal.

Jorlan also slept lightly these nights. When he awoke in the opulent master suite of his great house on the edge of the city, he too listened for a moment, wondering what might have awakened him. In the garden just outside his window, a lone bird was calling to the as yet unseen sun. Pearly gray light bathed the room.

Like Amala, he settled down beneath the covers again, seeking a few more hours of sleep before rising to face another tedious day of waiting. But before he had quite found that oblivion, a softly insistent bell drew him up sharply. He fumbled for the bedside audio, knowing what he would hear before the harbor watch commander's voice came out of the speaker.

"The mist has vanished, and the volcano is erupting!"

He bolted from bed and pulled on his clothes as adrenalin surged through his system. He ran from the house and raced to the airsled parked on its pad at the far side of the gardens.

He was quickly airborne in the lightening sky, joining several other airsleds that were streaking toward the harbor. By the time he reached it, the first of the small, swift boats were already casting off from the docks. Over the sled's speakers came crisp assurances that the plan was proceeding with all due speed.

Far out on the western horizon that had not yet been touched by the rising sun, he saw a pinpoint of glowing red. He longed to follow the lead airsleds that were already carrying officers to the endangered island, but instead he put his sled into a wide arc and circled the harbor, checking on progress below.

Then, just as he was once more facing the island, he heard a distant, dull sound and watched in horror as roiling black smoke obliterated the red glow. After one last glance down at the harbor, he summoned full power and shot over the water toward the island.

A thick cloud of black smoke hung over the island like a negative image of the pale mist that had surrounded it for so long. Jorlan couldn't help thinking that while the mist had been lethal to men, this could well be deadly for the women. And all the while, the image of a golden-haired woman danced behind his horrified eyes.

She could not die! She belonged to him, not to her accursed goddess!

He circled the harbor, trying to see through the smoke, then flew over the ridge to where he knew the settlement should be. Another thunderous explosion shook the sled as he brought it down slowly, seeking a landing spot. Only after the sled had touched down did he realize that he had managed to find the square in the center of the village. Several other airsleds were already parked there, but their drivers were nowhere to be seen. In fact, there was little of anything to be seen through the unnatural darkness.

When he climbed out of the sled, he could hear shouts of male voices mixing with female cries. He started in that direction, assuming that the voices must be coming from somewhere near the harbor, then stopped in his tracks as an incredible sight greeted him, coming suddenly out of the semidarkness.

A jepsa! He hadn't seen one of them in years, not since his last visit to the technology museum. He was so shocked to see the ancient vehicle bearing down on him that he was nearly run over before the driver spotted him and braked hard.

The passengers were all elderly women, their faces nearly covered by the cloths they had pressed to their noses and mouths. His eyes had already begun to sting as he stared at the driver. She was young, perhaps in her mid-twenties, with short, curly auburn hair and huge, dark eyes that streamed with tears as she stared back at him.

"Get them down to the harbor," he ordered. "The boats should be here in a few minutes, and two of them are equipped as temporary hospitals."

For a moment, he thought she couldn't understand him, but then she nodded briefly and accelerated without a word, disappearing quickly into the acrid smoke.

Felis drove toward the harbor with the image of the man burned into her brain. Jorlan! She was sure it had been him. There'd been a noticeable likeness to his kinswoman, Glea.

The old stories had been wrong, after all. Men

weren't ugly monsters—but they *were* huge and hairy and misshapen. And that deep, commanding voice did indeed bear a resemblance to the old myths. In the midst of the lie had been some truth.

The harbor was a chaotic mass of humanity. Women milled about or sat on the ground. Some clutched bundles while other held babies. Children were crying and darting about through the crowds.

And there were more men. Felis brought the jepsa to a halt and told her frail passengers to wait there. Several of them looked ready to pass out. She got out of the jepsa, seeking some of the younger, stronger women to help her, but the first to approach her were three men.

The one in the lead peered at the elderly women, then shouted for assistance. Immediately two other young men appeared with strange equipment. Felis stared at it fearfully as they approached the terrified, gray-faced women. Then the first man turned to her briefly.

"It's oxygen. It will help them breathe until we can get them onto the hospital ship. I'm a doctor, by the way."

Relieved, Felis looked about to see if her help was required elsewhere. But then she saw the other men staring at the jepsa in disbelief. One of them gestured to it.

"How have you kept it running all these years?"

Felis drew herself up proudly. "I made some

of the parts myself and took others from ones that had stopped running."

The men stared from her to the jepsa and back again, and it was in that moment that Felis finally began to let herself believe in the future. What she saw in the eyes of these young men was respect.

She turned back to the gray-haired doctor. "Can these women be moved from the jepsa? I need to go back for several more."

The men immediately helped the women from the jepsa, their movements hesitant and careful. For their part, the women were too sick to notice that they were being touched by the dreaded men.

When Felis climbed back into the jepsa, the doctor and another man got in as well.

"Have there been any deaths?" the doctor inquired.

"I don't know. It all happened so fast. The explosions have damaged a number of houses, but I think everyone was already outside by then. The two women I have to pick up now were all right when I last saw them."

The doctor nodded soberly. "But shock can be as dangerous for the elderly as physical injury."

Felis turned briefly to him. He was far less frightening than the other men. His voice was gentle, and his face had an aura of kindliness to it.

By the time they reached the square, the

breeze had begun to dissipate the smoke, and they all stared at the distant, glowing mountain. It was a spectacular sight, awesome in its beauty despite the horror it was bringing. Molten lava had begun to edge slowly down the side. Felis guessed that it had already reached the level spot where they had once danced for the goddess.

Then, just as she began to turn toward the house where she'd left the two women, the jepsa was jolted by a quake that was accompanied by a deep, rumbling sound from the bowels of the earth. Even in the midst of her own fear, Felis felt a certain satisfaction to see both the men clutch the jepsa tightly.

"Aleala's balls!" the man in back shouted. "The whole damned island's going to go up!"

When Felis turned to stare at him, not understanding the strange curse, the man looked embarrassed and quickly mumbled an apology. The doctor threw him a sternly disapproving look. She might have asked what he'd meant, but her attention was suddenly drawn away by a strange whining sort of sound coming from above them. She looked up and gasped. A huge craft was approaching them, and even as she stared open-mouthed, it came to a halt over the square and a door slid open in its underside. A sort of staircase dropped down, and before it had even touched ground, more men were scrambling down the steps.

The doctor turned to his companion. "Go

help them, Disten. Some of the women can be brought up from the harbor."

Felis continued to stare at the incredible craft, wondering if any of the women could be persuaded to climb up there. The doctor must have seen her doubtful expression.

"Don't worry, it's safe. Safer than this, I'd say." He chuckled and thumped the side of the jepsa. "Now, where are those other women?"

Felis drove through the deserted village, ignoring the small aftershocks that rocked them every few seconds. They were nearly to the house where she'd left the two women when she saw a lone figure walking slowly toward them.

"Lady Mava!" She gasped as they drew alongside the woman. It was Amala's mother, and the significance of her being alone struck Felis even as she spoke.

"Verta has gone to the goddess," the older woman said quietly, her gaze flicking from Felis to the doctor.

Then yet another quake struck, toppling the elegant, gray-haired woman. The doctor immediately leapt from the jepsa and helped her to her feet and then into the jepsa. They set off quickly and found the two elderly women they'd been seeking. Both were white-faced and trembling.

"Back to the harbor," the doctor ordered. "The hospital ships should be there by now."

More tremors rocked the jepsa as they made their way back toward the harbor. Felis noted with a grim smile that no one paid them any heed by now. The angry rippling of the land was becoming too routine. She glanced at Lady Mava, who sat silently beside her, wondering if she were in shock. But then the older woman suddenly turned to her and asked the question Felis dreaded most.

"Where is Amala? I expected her to come to me."

Felis cringed. The woman had already received two shocks this day—Verta's death and the eruption. What would a third do to her? She also noticed that the doctor had leaned forward attentively, as though the question interested him as well. It brought back to her Amala's statement about the men's attitude toward her.

"She took the other jepsa across the island," Felis said finally, carefully not divulging the purpose of Amala's mission and hoping that Lady Mava would also be discreet.

Lady Mava gasped but said nothing. The doctor, however, continued to display his interest.

"What's on the other side of the island?"

"A group of women live there. Amala went to assist them." Felis shuddered as she thought about what might have happened there. The tremors had always been much worse in that area.

By this time they had reached the village square, and a long line of women were waiting nervously to climb up to the hovering craft. The doctor suggested to Lady Mava that she join them, but she said that she preferred to wait for news of her daughter. So they drove on to the harbor, where two larger ships had now joined the smaller craft. Women and children were just beginning to board them as well.

"There is Lord Jorlan," the doctor exclaimed. "I must tell him about the women on the other side of the island, in case they haven't been rescued yet. Perhaps he will have news of Amala as well, Lady Mava."

But before the man could climb from the jepsa, Jorlan spotted them and strode over. Felis stared at him. He still frightened her more than the others, although she could not have said why. Certainly part of it was his size—he was the biggest man she'd yet seen—but she knew there was more to it than that.

"Lord Jorlan, there are women living on the other side of the island. Have they been rescued yet?" the doctor asked.

Jorlan's dark eyes flicked over Felis, then rested on Lady Mava. "I wasn't aware that anyone lived over there."

He raised a big hand, and a younger man came running. "How many are there?" he asked Felis.

"About fifty, I think. They have boats, so they might have set out in them already." She paused, then added quietly, "If they're still alive. The tremors are always worse over there."

Jorlan's response to that was a grim look that

spoke eloquently of his contempt for the foolishness that had put them in danger. Then he turned and issued orders to his aide to send sleds and lifters over there immediately.

Felis decided then and there that this arrogant and obviously powerful man represented the worst possible threat to them. Amala had good reason to fear and hate him.

Then, when the aide had run off to carry out his order, Jorlan turned his dark gaze to Lady Mava. The doctor started to introduce them, but Jorlan cut him off in mid-sentence.

"Where is your daughter, Lady Mava?"

Felis saw the older woman draw herself up imperiously, obviously affronted by his peremptory tone.

"She has taken the other jepsa to assist the women in the other settlement," she replied, unable to keep the fear from her voice.

Jorlan cursed loudly and colorfully, and Felis saw his face darken. "She drove through that?" He waved a hand toward the center of the island, where a pall of smoke still hung in the air.

Felis felt compelled to defend her friend. "She makes the journey often."

His dark, glittering gaze rested on her only briefly before a thunderous explosion shook them violently. They all looked up to see huge boulders being propelled from the mouth of the volcano. Even as they watched in stunned silence, one large, dark rock smashed into the ancient Great Family boat the women used for the monthly exchanges. It was docked at the far end of the harbor, some distance from them, and it now began to sink before their horrified eyes.

Lady Mava cried out, and Felis put a sympathetic hand on her arm. The boat had belonged to her family and was the last of the boats that had brought them to the island.

Then the quakes began again, and the doctor insisted that they get to the last of the big ships in the harbor. But Lady Mava refused his assistance as she watched the boat sink through tear-filled eyes.

"Amala," she whispered. "Where is my daughter?"

Jorlan opened the jepsa's door and took Lady Mava's arm.

"I will find her," he said as he urged her toward the dock.

Felis, who had hung back slightly, stared at him as she heard the certainty in his voice. For one sickening moment, she wondered if her friend might not be better off dead. Then he saw her lingering and gestured impatiently.

"Go with her. There is nothing more you can do here."

She nodded and hurried to catch up to the doctor and Lady Mava, but just before she started up the ramp onto the boat, she stopped and looked back. Thick, dark smoke was once more descending from the mountain, and she caught only a quick glimpse of Jorlan as he ran back toward the village.

Jorlan was half-blinded and choking by the time he reached his airsled. He climbed in quickly and started the engine, shutting down the fresh air intake to keep out the smoke. Then he took off quickly, lifting the sled above the murkiness and heading across the island.

As soon as he was airborne, he called the commander of the group sent to the far side of the island and learned that they had just spotted a group of women in small boats.

"Find out if Lady Amala is with them," he ordered, "and get them onto a lifter. If the island blows, their boats will be swamped."

He stayed high above the smoke as he flew westward, and he had just reached the small cluster of cottages when the speaker came alive again.

"They say that Lady Amala is not with them, Lord Jorlan. They haven't seen her. The lifter's moving into place now, and we'll be bringing them up in a few minutes."

Not with them? Jorlan tensed as shards of ice ripped through him. He brought the sled around so that it was once more facing the smoke-covered center of the island. Then she must be out there somewhere. A dull ache began inside him. Thus far, it appeared that not one life had been lost, making the rescue mission a great success. But in that moment, he would have traded the lives of every last woman and even his own men for the one who might not have survived.

She had to be alive! He refused to accept that she could be lost to him before he had ever had her, but he felt the metallic taste of fear in his mouth as he brought the sled down into the thick smoke. A tormenting image danced before his eyes—a golden-haired woman who stayed forever just beyond his reach.

He stayed close to the ground, dangerously close considering the terrain. He had to switch off the sled's automatic collision-avoidance system because the alarm sounded steadily. Then, when he saw the faint outline of a road that was little more than a dirt path, he slowed the sled to just above stall-speed.

A few moments later the track disappeared completely in a land that was filled with big ugly fissures and jagged rocks. He crisscrossed the hellish terrain several times, seeking a patch of bright blue amidst the blacks, grays and browns. He saw with increasing horror that several of the fissures were large enough to have swallowed a jepsa.

Then the Chairman's voice startled him as it came over the open speaker. He demanded to know what Jorlan was doing out there and urged him to leave the island immediately. They were all certain that an even worse explosion was imminent.

Jorlan ignored the question and the warning, then switched off the speaker when the Chairman continued. He liked and respected the

Chairman and had never before in his life disobeyed an order, but he would not leave this island without her. Although he would never acknowledge having had such a thought, some deep part of him had decided that if she were dead, he would end his own life here as well.

He continued to crisscross the blasted land, growing more desperate with every slow pass. And then he thought he saw something! He had brought the sled up slightly to clear a hilltop, and in the shifting pall of smoke he thought he'd glimpsed a patch of blue. Trembling now, he brought the sled down bumpily on a ledge just below the crest of the ridge.

The moment he jumped from the sled, the thick, hot air nearly choked him, but he paid it no heed as he began to scramble down the hillside, his heart pounding.

And there it was, lying upside down at the bottom of the ravine. He rushed toward it, realizing how miraculous it was that he'd found it, considering its position.

But there was no sign of her. That gnawing pain began again as he approached the vehicle. She might have abandoned it, or she might be trapped beneath it. He didn't know which was worse, since there were fissures all around that could easily have claimed a body.

As he walked around the jepsa, his foot struck something, and he looked down to see a worn, handmade sandal. He bent quickly and picked it up as more pain shot through him, and it was then that he saw the small, pale foot and part of a leg protruding from beneath the overturned jepsa. Several seconds had passed before he could bring himself to reach out and grasp that slender ankle.

Half-expecting to find the cold stiffness of death, he cried out with relief when his fingers closed around warm, pliant flesh. Still holding onto her, he got down and peered beneath the jepsa. Then he felt his first true exhilaration as he saw that the ground was somewhat hollowed out where she lay, so that the weight of the vehicle wasn't touching her. He let her go reluctantly, then stood up and pushed the jepsa off her, the act requiring considerable effort and care since it rested on a slight incline.

When he'd freed her, he stood there for a moment, staring. She lay face down and very still, her pale hair spilled around her face and shoulders. She was wearing that same shapeless outfit he'd seen on her at the dances, but up close now, the body beneath was far more evident. He knelt beside her and reached out to brush away that silken hair, then curved his fingers about her neck until he reached the pulse point at the base of her throat.

His own blood was hammering through his veins, so it took a few seconds before he was sure that what he felt was indeed her pulse and not just his own. It felt surprisingly strong and steady, and his hopes now truly soared.

Then he slid his hands carefully over her body, searching for broken bones even as he tried to quell the surge of heat that rushed through him. She was so small, almost childlike, but no child had those lush curves.

Reasonably certain that nothing was broken, he gently rolled her over and then sank back on his haunches to see for the first time the face of the woman who had haunted him all these years. In the distance, there were sharp cracks and dull explosions, but he barely heard them.

Her face was streaked with dirt, but nothing could mar the perfection of her beauty. She was, he thought, even more beautiful than her infamous ancestress. There was something softer about her, although he realized it might be merely the slackness of unconsciousness. He recalled the haughtiness he'd seen through the camera.

He tore his gaze away from her face and let it travel instead over her body. Beneath the light clothing, her full breasts rose and fell with her breathing, and the torn trousers revealed a smooth, curved thigh.

How long he might have stayed there, just staring at her, he'd never know. Suddenly the ground started to heave once more, and she made a small sound and lifted a hand briefly before letting it drop again. Her eyelids fluttered for a moment, then were still.

Jorlan stood up and then bent to pick her up carefully. She weighed next to nothing, but it still required considerable effort to carry her up the steep hillside that trembled beneath his feet. The sled itself was rocking from the force of the tremors as he put her inside, strapping her securely into the passenger seat before climbing in himself.

In the second before he switched on the ignition, Jorlan feared that the sled might have been damaged by the quakes. He held his breath until the panel showed that all systems were operational. A light flashed to tell him that someone was trying to contact him, but he continued to ignore it. The tremors seemed to be growing worse and were now accompanied by tortured sounds as the land was ripped asunder.

He put the craft into a steep, swift climb through the smoky air, gulping gratefully the cool, unfouled atmosphere inside the sled. Beside him she coughed weakly a few times, then lay still. He glanced at her pale face and wondered if there might be injuries he'd missed. She could be bleeding internally.

Then, after he had set an easterly course, he turned to stare at her flat belly. Could she be carrying his child? Anger surged through him that he should be forced to wonder about such a thing, but surely she wouldn't have risked her life if she were pregnant.

Then the anger drained away, and instead he smiled with satisfaction. It didn't matter now. She would be his, and he would get children with her the way nature had intended.

They passed over what remained of her home. Most of the houses had been destroyed and the wharf was on fire, probably the result of debris from the last explosion. Off to the far side of the harbor, only the tip of a bow remained of her family's old boat. He felt pleasure once more at the sight. The boat had been used for years in the women's nefarious scheme to perpetuate their race. No more babies would be sent to their fathers that way. It was over.

He could see the two hospital ships about two kilometers out to sea. The smaller boats would already have reached the mainland, as well as the other sleds and the lifters.

Finally, he switched on the speaker, catching the Chairman's aide in the midst of calling his name. This time he responded, telling him that he had found Amala and they were now enroute to the mainland. He knew he'd have to account for himself to the Chairman, but it mattered little to him. Disobeying an order was a serious offense, but he knew his own power. Besides, as head of the rescue mission, he could justifiably claim that he should be the last one to leave the island.

He was about to switch frequencies and check on the harbor operations when the final explosion came. The resulting shock wave buffeted the sled, sending it briefly into an uncontrolled spin until he wrestled it back under control. It was the best model made and Jorlan was a first-rate pilot; otherwise, they might well have crashed into the sea.

Below him, the two hospital ships weren't quite so fortunate. He knew they wouldn't capsize, but from his bird's-eye view, he could also guess that there would be injuries.

He turned the sled in a wide arc to face the island once more. Nothing was visible behind a thick curtain of black smoke, but he knew the island no longer existed. They would be saved the trouble of blasting it out of existence.

Then he headed for the mainland, pausing only to glance at his still-unconscious passenger to reassure himself that all that had mattered on that accursed island had been saved.

Felis moved about the deck of the big ship, checking on various women and children. Many of them—in fact, most of them—seemed too dazed to speak coherently. Others crowded together, drawing comfort from familiar presences as they tried to avoid the men.

The few men on the deck were also moving about, checking to see who might require medical attention. Their presence, however, far outweighed their actual numbers. The little girls shrank from them, hiding behind their mothers as the men sought to check on them.

Felis stopped for a while and watched the men. They were certainly easy to spot in the crowd. They all towered over the women, and they wore tan uniforms that made them even more obvious amidst the women's brightly colored clothing.

Their voices were different as well—deep and booming, much like the monsters of their mythology—and many of them had hair, either above their mouths or covering the entire lower portion of their faces.

But for all that, they didn't behave like monsters. They were polite and gentle with the women and occasionally paused to smile at the babies and young girls. Felis thought that the only truly frightening man she had yet seen was Jorlan—and that brought a spasm of fear for Amala. Had he found her? Certainly he had looked as though he would move heaven and earth to accomplish that.

Her fears for Amala were still uppermost in her mind as she suddenly spotted Lady Mava, standing alone in a narrow recess. Felis knew that Amala's mother had never really cared for her daughter's friendship with one so lowly born, but now she went to her anyway. Tending her best friend's mother was the only thing she could do for her now.

When she reached the older woman, Felis was stunned to see how terrible she looked. Her fair skin had an ashen cast to it, and her lips looked faintly bluish. She raised a hand to push her hair from her face, and Felis saw that she was trembling.

"Lady Mava, you must see the doctors," Felis said, reaching out impulsively to take her hand. "Let me take you to them."

The older woman gripped her hand tightly but didn't move. "Amala," she whispered. "Is she safe?"

"I don't know yet," Felis admitted, "but I'm

sure Jor . . . Lord Jorlan will find her."

When their eyes met, Felis was sure that Lady Mava was having the same thoughts she herself had had, but she felt compelled to put the older woman's mind at peace.

"Please don't worry about her, Lady Mava. He seemed quite concerned about her. Surely that old rivalry between your two families died long ago."

"I hope so," Lady Mava whispered uncertainly. Then suddenly, she cried out and pressed a hand to her breast.

Felis caught her as she began to stagger, at the same time shouting for help. Within seconds, two young men appeared. One of them immediately lifted Lady Mava from her feet, and the other cleared a path as she was carried down a stairwell. Felis hurried after them.

The men ran through a narrow corridor, then into a larger room where there were all sorts of strange equipment. Just then, the doctor Felis had met on the island appeared. He looked from Lady Mava to Felis.

"Does she have a heart problem?"

Felis nodded. "I think so. Amala said she was worried about her heart."

"In here," the doctor ordered, and the man carried her into a small room and deposited her on a cloth-covered table. Someone else wheeled in a large cylinder and quickly attached a mask on the end of a hose to Lady Mava's mouth. The doctor pressed a strange instrument to her chest and bent over her. Felis moved into a corner to stay out of the way.

Then the doctor barked an order to one of the young men who quickly brought a small cylinder with a long needle attached to one end. Felis could not help crying out as the needle was plunged into Lady Mava's pale, lifeless arm. Her cry drew the doctor's attention.

"She'll be fine," he said. "We'll run a scan as soon as we get her to the hospital, but whatever the problem is, it can be fixed."

Felis just nodded. He then asked her if there was any news of Amala. When she shook her head, he suggested she go talk to the ship's captain to see if they could find out. He then turned his attention back to his patient, but one of the other men told Felis how to find the captain and she left the room quickly, trusting that the doctor would take good care of Lady Mava.

She hurried back down the corridor, seeking the thing called an elevator. The word was vaguely familiar from old books, but Felis couldn't recall what it was. She hoped she'd find a sign.

Then some doors slid open ahead of her, and she recalled what an elevator was—a little room that moved up and down. As soon as the man inside stepped out, Felis stepped in. She'd been told to take it to the top so she pushed the highest numbered button, and the doors closed and the room began to move.

But it had only moved for a few seconds before there was a thunderous explosion. She was thrown against a wall as the elevator suddenly became very dark, darker than anything she had ever experienced before. With her heart thudding noisily in her chest, Felis sank to the floor. The elevator was swaying back and forth sickeningly. Had something happened to the ship, or had there been another explosion on the island?

She huddled in the darkness, listening to shouts and cries beyond the walls. She had no idea how much time passed before the lights came back on and the elevator began to move upward again. Then it stopped, and before she could scramble to her feet, the doors opened and two men stood there.

"Are you hurt?" One of them asked her as she shakily regained her feet.

When she shook her head, they both stepped inside and pushed one of the buttons. "Good. Then you can come with us and help with the women on deck. Some of them are injured."

"What happened?" Felis asked, rubbing a bruised elbow and keeping as far from the men as possible in the small space.

"The whole damned island must have gone up this time," the man replied.

"Saves us the trouble of doing it ourselves," the other man stated, then shut up quickly at a look from his companion.

Felis backed farther still into the corner. Is

that what they'd planned to do? She struggled to keep her composure as all her fears came flooding back. Then she remembered Amala. If she hadn't gotten off the island before the explosion . . . .

The doors opened onto the deck, where cries and moans and male shouts greeted her. For the next half-hour, she did what she could for the bruised and bleeding women. Small boats were put into the water to rescue those who had been thrown overboard by the explosion. Several wet, terrified women were brought back, but she feared that some were still unaccounted for.

Then the ship glided into a huge harbor. By now the injured had been dealt with, and Felis had a few moments to stare in awe at the city beyond the harbor. How could they have built buildings so high? They seemed to reach higher than the sacred mountain. The men, she thought suddenly, had built their own gods.

On the docks vehicles of all sorts awaited them. She started to work her way through the stunned crowd of women to check on Lady Mava, but by the time she got below deck, no one was there. A man she met in the corridor informed her that all the injured women were being airlifted to the hospital directly from the ship.

When she returned to the deck, the women already were being led down ramps to a huge vehicle that had many comfortable seats in rows along each side. Someone said they'd been told they were being taken to a place called Savleen, but no one knew what it was.

The vehicle moved with such smoothness that Felis at first thought it must be airborne, but when she looked out the windows, she saw a smooth gray road beneath them. They passed large buildings where men poured forth to watch the procession. Felis saw the curiosity on their faces but nothing more. Her fears began to recede once again.

The vehicle carried them to a large open area where another of those huge flying machines awaited them. Within moments, they were airborne, but this time, to Felis' disappointment, there were no windows. They sat on hard benches along the walls, held in place by straps the men had shown them how to use.

A few of the women began to cry, fearful of what might be about to happen to them.

"Nothing will happen," Felis stated firmly. "If they had wanted to hurt us, they would already have done so. They put themselves at risk to save us. Besides, they need us."

Somewhat to her surprise, the women listened to her and calmed down. Felis had never been one to speak up, preferring to remain in the background and use her mechanical talents.

After what seemed like an hour had passed, they felt the craft begin to descend. There was a small bump, and then the barely perceptible whining sound stopped. Wherever Savleen was, they had obviously arrived.

The two young men who had helped them aboard reappeared and opened the huge door. The staircase unfolded again, and they motioned the women out. Felis was the first to step through the door.

Another group of uniformed men awaited them. Felis felt her heart sink and at the same time heard the nervous sounds of the women behind her. It looked like a prison, even though there were big tubs of flowers and shrubs in the huge courtyard where they'd landed. Great stone walls rose all around them. The place was obviously very ancient.

Then one man stepped forward, and Felis' attention was drawn to him. She was stunned to find herself staring into the bluest eyes she'd ever seen, save for Amala's. Could it be?

The man smiled, directing his attention to her since she was in the lead. "I'm Lord Zakton, and I welcome you to Savleen."

Emboldened by the knowledge that this was Amala's brother, Felis swept an arm about her. "Are you welcoming us to a prison?"

He smiled again, and Felis had to stifle a sob as she recalled Amala's having said once that her brother couldn't possibly be a monster. This man had the kindest, gentlest face she'd yet seen.

"I know it must look like a prison to you," he said, "but it's just an old fortress. We've done our best to make it comfortable for you, but there wasn't much time."

Then he turned to the men with him. "Show them to their quarters and see that they have everything they need."

Felis started to follow with the other women, then stopped and turned back to Zakton. He had started off in another direction, but he stopped when he saw her.

"Amala," she said fearfully. "Is there any word of her? She's my friend—my best friend."

His face lost its pleasant expression and turned grim with worry. "She's my sister, and I was just about to see if there's any word of her."

"She was still on the island when I left, and Lord Jorlan was searching for her."

He nodded gravely. "And Lord Jorlan is *my* best friend, so I have two people to worry about. But I'm sure he found her and got her away before the explosion."

"How can you know that?" Felis asked, startled and yet hopeful at the certainty in his voice.

His mouth curved briefly into a sad smile. "I know it because I cannot bear the thought of losing them both. And I've waited so long to meet Amala."

Then he drew himself together quickly. "What is your name? I'll let you know as soon as I receive word."

"My name is Felis. Thank you."

She hurried away then, running to catch up with the others. Zakton stared after her for a moment. Amala's best friend! And what an attractive woman she was. She hadn't given her family name, but he was sure she must be Great Family.

He started toward the communications room, trying to hold onto the faith he had projected to her. They must have made it! The alternative was inconceivable.

before. The brilliance of the colors alone nearly hurt her eyes. There were two dressers of strange design in a bright, shiny yellow and a thick rug of yellow and green stripes.

The bed in which she lay was huge, at least twice the size of her own bed, and of a material that managed to be both soft and firm. The cover was the same bright yellow as the dressers, and on a small yellow table next to the bed were several strange objects. One she was reasonably sure was a lamp, although it bore no resemblance to any lamp she'd ever seen before. The other squarish object with letters and numbers she couldn't begin to identify.

Tentatively, she began to move her limbs, and it was the resulting pain that brought back the memories. The jepsa had overturned! With that sudden recollection, all the rest of it poured forth, inundating her in a tidal wave of sheer horror—the disappearance of the mist, the eruption, her desperate flight across the island!

She sat up quickly, then cried out as a sharp pain shot through her chest and back and shoulders. Her throat hurt, and she swallowed painfully as she tried to focus her thoughts.

Obviously she was no longer on the island. That meant she must have been rescued by the men, and that meant there must be some of them close by. But where were the other women? She strained her ears but could hear nothing. The utter silence terrified her.

Then she thought about the reason for her desperate trip across the island. She'd failed!

Had Glea and the other Semlians managed to save the herbs? Where was everybody?

Moving very quietly and cautiously, she climbed out of bed, then stared down at herself in dismay. She ran her hand slowly over the fabric of the long, bright red shirt she wore, enjoying its luxurious softness for a few seconds before she began to wonder how she'd come to be wearing it.

There were two doors leading from the room, one of which stood slightly ajar. She walked to it, gritting her teeth against the pain each movement brought. She ached all over, but she was reasonably certain that it was nothing more than bruises and strained muscles.

A bathroom. She recognized it, although the fixtures, like the furnishings of the bedroom, were strange. She used the toilet, then fumbled for a moment with the faucets until she figured out how to adjust the temperature. Then she quickly splashed water on her face and dried it with a wonderfully thick, soft towel.

She stared at herself in the big mirror over the sink. The clarity of her reflection shocked her; she'd never really seen herself so clearly before. She touched a small lump on her forehead. There were several scratches as well, but nothing serious.

She continued to peer at herself as she thought about the accident. The place where the jepsa had overturned was covered with a powdery black dirt, yet she was clean. She pulled up the shirt and examined the rest of herself. There were a few bruises but no dirt.

Revulsion washed over her, leaving her shaky and nauseous. Had one of them touched her, bathed her and put this shirt on her? She wanted to leap out of her body. What else might have happened to her while she lay unconscious? Her skin crawled.

Then the revulsion gave way abruptly to anger. Blue fire flashed in the eyes that stared back at her from the mirror. Propelled by a need to demand some answers, she hurried out of the bathroom, paying no attention now to her aches and pains. Just as she stepped back into the bedroom, the other door opened, and her short-lived rage turned to horror.

Amala clutched the doorframe as she stared at him. All the nightmares she'd ever had coalesced into the monster who now stood there staring back at her. He was head and shoulders taller than her, even though he stood in a slight crouch, as though he might spring at her any moment. His entire body was covered with thick, coarse, dark brown hair.

She stumbled back into the bathroom and slammed the door, fumbling away precious seconds as she tried to figure out how to work the lock. At any instant she expected him to fling it open and attack her, but nothing happened. Breathing raggedly, she pressed her ear to the door, trying to listen over the pounding of her heart. There were strange, muffled sounds, but no words.

When she had heard nothing at all for a few

moments, she backed away from the door and tried to think. He hadn't attacked her—that gave her some small degree of confidence—but who was he?

Two possibilities, each equally awful, came to mind. He could be her brother Zakton, or he could be Jorlan. She hoped it was Zakton, even though the thought of having something like that as a brother nearly reduced her to tears.

Then, just as she was trying to decide what to do next, the monster spoke, his deep voice booming through the closed door in yet another part of the nightmare come true.

"Amala! Are you all right? Come out here!"

She held her breath and said nothing, but she thought he sounded more worried than angry—or was that only wishful thinking? Was it Zakton? She was about to ask when the door handle began to turn. She hadn't been sure it was locked, but it must be, because it didn't open.

"Amala, open the door. You're safe. No one will harm you."

"Wh . . . who are you?" she asked, her voice raspy.

"It's Jorlan. Dammit, Amala, open the door or I'll break it down!"

She didn't respond. A fresh wave of revulsion engulfed her. If it had been Zakton, she might have risked it. Monster or not, he was still her brother. But Jorlan? She felt sick as she thought about how close she had come to bearing a child to that hideous creature, perhaps giving birth to another one like it.

She turned and ran over to the open window. It was a long drop to the ground, but there was a big tree whose branches nearly touched the window. Her tree-climbing days were far behind her, but she climbed quickly onto the wide sill, then crawled out onto the heavy limb just as there was a thudding sound and another shout behind her.

She began to crawl as fast as she could along the limb, hoping only to be lost in the dense foliage by the time he broke into the bathroom.

Jorlan stumbled into the room when the door gave way, then stared around in surprise. He had just turned his attention to the open window when he caught a flash of red disappearing into the foliage of the tree. Then he paused just long enough to close the window and cut off that escape route before running through the house to the garden. His Feloth servant huddled in a corner, making nervous, mewling sounds, but he had no time to calm it now.

Amala reached the trunk of the huge tree and began to work her way down quickly. She had to get out of the tree and into a better hiding place before he figured out where she'd gone. She could see now that the house was very large, so perhaps it would take him some time to get out here.

Just as she leapt to the ground, she saw movement beyond the pendulous branches. Her strained muscles refused to hold her up, and she fell painfully to the ground, biting her tongue to keep from crying out. And at that moment, he burst through the leaves.

Amala was too stunned to try to regain her feet. It wasn't the monster! He was in fact much bigger than the monster—but at least recognizably human. The thick, black hair was confined to his head, although there was a thinner covering on his bare legs and arms. He wore a shirt and shorts, and muscles bulged all over.

"Dammit, are you trying to kill yourself?" he said in that deep voice. "You're supposed to be resting."

As he spoke, he came closer, then squatted down in front of her. She saw the Great Family ring on his huge hand.

"*You're* Jorlan?" she croaked, her voice not much more than a hoarse whisper.

"Yes, I told you that." His dark eyes bored into her. "And you're not supposed to be talking, either. You inhaled too much smoke."

But she ignored him and shifted her gaze briefly back toward the window. "Then who was *that*"

He frowned uncomprehendingly for a moment, then to her astonishment began to laugh. He sank back to sit opposite her as his laughter died away into chuckles.

"That was Shebba. She's a Feloth."

"What is . . . ?"

"Feloths are animals—highly intelligent animals. They were trained to be servants long before . . ." Then he stopped and shook his head in bemusement.

"You thought she was me? Haven't you ever even seen a picture of a man?"

Amala shook her head, which by now was thumping with a pain that matched the rest of her body. It was all too much for her. She wanted to curl up on the soft grass and go to sleep until it began to make sense, but it was obvious he wanted some answers.

"What lies were you told? How could you have believed men look like that?"

She fumbled for something to say, but before she could think of anything, he waved a hand in abrupt dismissal and got to his feet.

"Forget it. You can satisfy my curiosity later. You need to get back to bed. I have some spray for your throat. You can have something to drink if you want it, but no solid food until tomorrow morning."

She began to struggle to her feet, but he quickly lifted her into his arms. The sudden contact terrified her.

"Put me down!" she croaked.

"No. You've caused yourself enough trouble."

It was plain even to her befuddled brain that she couldn't break free, so she let him carry her back into the house. Everything about him felt so alien—his rocklike strength, his bristly arms. He even smelled strange—not unpleasant, but definitely different.

"Where am I?" she whispered.

"At my house in the mountains. Just stay quiet until I get you back into bed, then I'll tell you what happened."

His voice was so harsh and abrupt that it was difficult for her to tell whether or not he was angry. Maybe men always talked like that.

He deposited her onto the bed, then went into the bathroom and returned a moment later with a bottle.

"Open your mouth. It won't hurt, but it doesn't taste good, either."

She did as told, and he sprayed a bitter substance into her mouth. She swallowed and grimaced, but the hot dryness in her throat lessened. He turned and called out.

"Shebba! Come here!"

A moment later, the monster came into the room, scurrying on all four feet now and acting very frightened. Jorlan reached out to pet the creature.

"It's all right, Shebba," he said in a much gentler tone than he'd used before. "She's not afraid of you now. Bring her some tea."

The creature paused only long enough to give her a wary look, then scurried out of the room.

"Feloths are never vicious," he said. "Some are brighter than others—or more trainable. Shebba's one of them. She understands simple sentences quite well, and she can even communicate with me after a fashion."

Amala said nothing. She was still thinking about the gentleness he'd shown the creature. Then she tried her voice once more and discovered it was nearly normal.

"Tell me what happened. Where are the

others? My mother . . . ?"

When he sat down on the edge of the bed, she quickly slid to the far side.

"Your mother is in the hospital. She suffered a minor heart attack on the way over, but she'll be fine. They've diagnosed the problem and are treating it. The other women are either in the hospital or at Savleen." He saw her frown and went on.

"It's an old fortress in the mountains. They'll be staying there until we can sort things out. Zak had it fixed up, so they'll be comfortable enough, certainly more comfortable than on the island, which, by the way, no longer exists."

"Zak? The island is gone?" She'd heard that triumphant note in his voice.

"Zakton—your brother. And yes, the island's gone. It blew up less than ten minutes after we left. The explosion nearly blew us out of the air and injured and killed some women on one of the boats. We don't know how many died yet, but we should have a count by tomorrow."

"Does my brother know where I am?" Amala suddenly wondered if the old feud between their families could have erupted again. Could he be holding her hostage here for some reason?

"Yes, I spoke with him just a while ago."

But he must have read something in her expression because he shook his head. "No, the feud died a long time ago. Zak is my best friend. He's in charge of Savleen, so he's very busy, but I'll see to it that you talk to him tomorrow."

So her brother and Jorlan were best friends.

Amala knew that discovery required some thought, but there was so much to think about just now.

Shebba returned at that moment with a cup of tea and held it out tentatively to her, making strange little noises. Amala took it from her, then put out her hand to pet the creature's head as she'd seen him do. The sounds changed to a low rumble, and Amala would have sworn that there was a smile hidden in that furry face. She watched the Feloth scurry away, then turned back to Jorlan to see a very definite smile on his face. Their eyes met, but she looked away quickly, concentrating on her tea.

"Why am I here, instead of at Savleen?"

"Because the doctor said you needed a few days of rest. You had a slight concussion and a cracked rib, and you inhaled a lot of smoke. But it wasn't serious enough to keep you in the hospital when the beds are needed for more serious cases. Zak and I agreed that things are too chaotic at Savleen right now for you to get any rest there."

Amala thought that his explanation sounded very glib, but she was too tired to question it now. Besides, she sensed a very fragile sort of balance between them. She set down the cup and slipped beneath the covers. Then something he'd said struck her.

"You saved my life."

He nodded and got up from the bed, his dark eyes fixed upon her with a strange intensity. She closed her eyes to that piercing gaze.

"Thank you," she murmured, then abruptly opened her eyes again. He was still standing there staring at her.

"Felis! I have a friend named Felis Sauken. Could you find out if she's safe?"

"I'll check."

"And Glea? She's your kinswoman."

"I've already made inquiries about my kinswomen. There's no word on Glea yet."

Jorlan poured himself a goblet of the dark, heavy wine made in his family's own famed winery. He needed it, although he certainly didn't need to muddle his brain.

He was grateful that she'd gone back to sleep. He didn't like the way she made him feel. He didn't like it because he didn't understand it, and he was always suspicious of things he couldn't understand.

There was something inherently alien about women. Not only were their bodies different, but their minds were as well. He'd obviously been foolish to have believed that she'd be much like Asroth and the other Bethusan women—passive and easy to please.

She'd risked her life to reach the women on the other side of the island and then, even in her present condition, had managed to escape from his house. Those were definitely not the actions of a passive woman.

Furthermore, there was something in those blue eyes that suggested a powerful will even in her present condition. He thought about that time at the observatory when she'd stared directly into the camera with an angry defiance that would have done credit to a warrior.

He wondered how long he could keep her here, then wondered if he should even try. Perhaps it would be better if she went to Savleen for a while.

On the other hand, Zak was there, and given his obsession with her, that could be the worst possible thing to do. Who knew what hold she could gain over him?

But then there wasn't much either of them could do to thwart his plans.

When Amala awoke again, the room was dark. Her brain felt far less muddled this time, although she still ached all over and her throat was burning again. She picked up the bottle of spray he'd left and used it again. Then she got out of bed and searched the closets, hoping to find something to wear over the thin shirt. Finding both closets empty, she picked up the bedcover and wrapped it around herself to ward off the cool night air.

Moving soundlessly on bare feet, she opened the door cautiously and peeked out into the dimly lit hallway. A large dark shape was huddled on the thickly carpeted floor just beyond her door. Perhaps Shebba was a guard as well as a servant. She edged her way carefully past the softly snoring creature and set off to explore the house, confident that its owner must also be asleep.

She roamed about in the semidarkness, examining everything and wondering if this were a large house by the men's standards. Certainly it was the largest house she'd ever seen, but since it was his mountain home, it might actually be small.

Finally, just as her stomach began to rumble ominously, she found the kitchen. Such wonders! She knew what a refrigerator was, since there were a few left working on the island, but everything else was beyond her imagining.

She opened the refrigerator and found it well-stocked, so she began to take things out and examine them, sniffing and poking. There were some fruits and vegetables she recognized, so she decided to make a small meal of them. Then she sniffed at a hard block of something that was pale yellow in color. It smelled quite interesting. Surely if it was in there it must be edible.

Carrying her meal with her, she opened the big glass doors and went outside. The view was breathtaking. Beyond the stone terrace was a steep cliff. The heavens were bright enough that she could see deep valleys and very high mountains beyond. There appeared to be no other dwelling or building of any kind in sight.

She sat down on the low wall at the edge of the terrace and began to eat the fruit and the yellow substance. It was amazingly good, whatever it was.

Suddenly she thought about the island, and a deep, cold loneliness came over her. Gone— and with it the only way of life she'd ever known. She wished that Felis were here as well as Glea, and she wondered if Jorlan had told her the truth about her mother. Could she really be dead and he didn't want to tell her yet? Would he do such a thing?

And what were they to do now? She was glad that the women were being kept together, but now she wondered why. Was it possible that the men too were nervous about this great change, this abrupt transformation of their lives?

She chewed on the fruit and thought about that possibility. It was impossible to guess what men were really like when she'd talked to only one of them. But he definitely had seemed uneasy around her, she thought now.

It was essential that she understand how men thought. Much as she wanted to be with the others at the old fortress, might it not be better to stay here a while longer so she could observe one of them closely?

And especially this particular man. He would be a member of the Council and his family name virtually guaranteed that his would be a powerful voice even in that group.

But could she trust him? It occurred to her that she'd simply accepted everything he'd told her, save possibly his statement about her mother, but he could easily be lying.

On the other hand, he'd saved her life; that seemed clear enough. And he'd been both kind and polite toward her.

She was weighing these thoughts and trying to decide if she should insist upon going to Savleen when a sound drew her around sharply.

He strode across the terrace, a huge, shadowy figure clad in a dark robe. She drew the blanket more tightly around herself.

"Come back inside. It's too cold out here," he said in that deep, gruff voice that still fell strangely on her ears. "I see you found something to eat."

She nodded as he came to a stop too close to her. "It was very good. What is this?" She held up the remaining piece of the yellow substance.

"Cheese. It's made from yelat milk. They're . . ."

"I know what they are. I've seen pictures of them." Her tone was abrupt. She disliked having him think she was totally ignorant.

"But you never saw a picture of a man," he said, shaking his head with a chuckle she found annoying.

"No." She picked up the remnants of her meal, wrapped the blanket more tightly around herself and walked back into the house.

"Let me get you something warm to wear," he offered as he went over to the fireplace and lit a fire with some strange metal rod.

As soon as he'd left the room, she picked up the fire-starter and examined it. There was so much she had to learn. Tears welled up as she thought about the lost simplicity of life on the island.

Then she angrily brushed away the tears. She could not afford to let herself wallow in the past, not when the future was so very threatening.

He came back with a thick robe much like the one he was wearing, but instead of handing it to her, he opened it and held it for her to put on. She hesitated for a moment, then let the blanket fall away and slipped into it. His hands remained on her shoulders for a moment, then fell away. The sensation lingered much longer.

"Have you found out anything about Felis and Glea?" she asked, not really certain how long she'd slept.

"Felis is fine. She's at Savleen and knows you're safe here, but there's still no word on Glea."

Then he told her about the rescue of the women from the Semlian colony. "Is Glea a friend also?"

"Yes," she replied, taking a seat in a comfortable chair before the fire. He sat down across from her as she stared into the fire. Deep down inside, she was sure that Glea was dead. How they needed her strength and leadership now!

"Why were those women living on the other side of the island? Surely they would have been more comfortable in the main settlement."

Amala hesitated. The truth would probably come out at some point, so perhaps she could soften it a bit. "They preferred to live there. Their beliefs were different from ours, but we got along well enough."

"What do you mean their beliefs were different?"

"They didn't believe in Aleala."

"But you did?"

She regarded him silently for a moment, thinking that he was gaining more information from her than she was from him at this point. But if she wanted to pry into his thoughts, she should probably feed his curiosity a bit.

"Most of us do, although some are more fervent in their beliefs than others."

"But what about you personally? You must believe, since you danced on the mountain."

The moment the words were out of his mouth, Jorlan realized his mistake. She gave him a puzzled look.

"How could you know that?"

So he told her about the camera, certain that he was about to have a very angry woman on his hands and equally certain that he didn't know what to do about it. To be at such a loss was a totally new experience for him and a very uncomfortable one, but to his complete astonishment, she actually began to smile.

"So you *were* spying on us. Felis and I once talked of that possibility, but we never told the others." Then she turned away and her voice dropped to a near-whisper.

"There were times when I thought I could feel someone watching."

He remained silent, thinking about that time when she'd stared so defiantly into the camera.

"I danced because it was as much a social activity as a religious one, and I enjoyed the dancing. My faith in Aleala was never all that strong, but I worry now about those who placed all their faith in her."

He merely nodded, afraid that anything he might say would only get him into the trouble he'd somehow managed to avoid.

"Of course," she continued, "one could speculate that Aleala decided that it was time for us to return."

He thought he heard some unspoken words there and decided to risk a question. "Had *you* decided that it was time?"

The question clearly caught her by surprise, but after a moment's hesitation, she nodded. "I think so. Life on the island lacked challenges. There was no opportunity for us to advance, and of course, we knew that you must have made many advances."

Jorlan had to make a serious effort to conceal his shock. A woman seeking challenges? He'd been certain that must be the exclusive province of men. She was making him more and more uneasy, and he wished he'd taken her to Savleen or left her at the hospital.

"Do the men really want us back?"

"Of course. If we'd been able to get through that damned mist, you'd have been back long ago."

"If you'd been able to get through the mist, we would never have gotten there in the first place," she pointed out. "And if you hadn't been so terrible, we would never have wanted to leave here."

Her accusatory tone made him angry.

"Dammit, Amala, you've been fed lies all your life. Can't you see that? Things were never that bad."

"From a man's perspective, I'm sure they weren't," she replied with an infuriating calm. "But I've studied our laws, and women were treated little better than slaves. That must change!"

He stood there staring at her, and she met his gaze squarely. She knew perfectly well that he was trying to intimidate her, but despite his size and her tenuous situation at present, she refused to let that happen.

"You have the power." Verta's strange words came back to her. She didn't know yet just what that power was, but she felt it at this moment.

"Most of us agree that there must be some changes," he said finally.

"Do you mean a majority of your Council?"

"Yes, I think so," he replied abruptly, wanting to end this discussion. He had envisioned the Council granting the women some rights, not the women demanding them.

"That's welcome news. As soon as we can get our Council together, we can begin negotiations. I've studied our laws very carefully and spent a considerable amount of time deciding what changes must be made."

"You have?" He didn't even try to hide his surprise this time.

"Yes. Many of the laws will have to be rewritten."

"I see," he said carefully. "Well, Zak and I

agree that women should be allowed to own property."

"That's only a beginning. Among the first issues we must deal with are the marriage laws. There can be no forced marriages, and just because a woman has chosen a man to father her children doesn't mean that she will be willing to have him as a husband."

He stared at her silently for a long moment, as though seeking some hidden meaning in her words. Then he chuckled.

"I think I can safely say that most of the men would agree with you."

She decided that it was time to end this discussion. If they continued, they were bound to get into an argument, and it was too soon for that. So she got up and announced that she was tired again. He stood, too, and for a very long moment they simply stared at each other in the flickering firelight. She could sense his uneasiness, but it gave her little pleasure because she too was uneasy. There was something strangely compelling about this man.

Suddenly, she recalled Glea's warning about the unknown forces that operated between men and women. Could those forces be at work here?

She said good night and quickly left the room.

Jorlan watched her go, then felt his body begin to relax when she had disappeared. She fascinated him; there was no other word for it, although he wished fervently that he could find one. With Asroth and the other women on Bethusa, there'd been only sexual desire, a pleasure taken and then forgotten until the next time. This was different.

The thought that this woman could actually exert such power over him truly frightened him, so much so that if she had offered herself to him, he might well have run in the opposite direction.

He very much wanted to get her out of here so he could regain some sense of perspective, but he also desperately needed to know something only she could tell him.

Savleen teemed with activity. Airlifters arrived with more supplies and also women who were deemed well enough to leave the crowded hospital. The small contingent of men at the old fortress kept to themselves under orders from Zakton, but they managed to push those restrictions to the limits in their efforts to catch glimpses of the women.

The women reacted to their dramatically changed situation in various ways. Those whose faith in Aleala's protection had been strongest withdrew into small groups or sat in isolation, often staring dazedly about them, unable to believe their goddess had deserted them.

Others, like Felis, kept their fears at bay by undertaking various projects, rooting themselves firmly in the here and now in order to avoid both past and future.

The women's Council had been decimated.

Two members had lost their lives at sea. Three more, including Mava, were hospitalized. Several others were among the faithful who could not yet reconcile themselves to the loss of their goddess' protection. And Amala, the one who might have drawn them all together, was not at Savleen, nor was Glea, whose followers also continued to hold themselves apart.

Felis had recruited several other women to help her with the task of recording the names of all present and obtaining the names of the fathers of children and babes-in-wombs. All their records had perished on the island. The men would presumably have their records of the children, since information on girl babies had always been sent across. But given the low value they placed on female children, Felis decided to include them just in case.

She wasn't really surprised to find that many of the women refused to name the fathers of their daughters. After all, most of them had never expected to have to confront them. Fathers or sons might well be among the men now at Savleen, a possibility that made them even more wary.

Zakton had expressed a particular interest in the names of men who had fathered unborn children, though he gave no reason for this concern. However, when Felis passed this information along to the women who were pregnant, not one of them would name the father. Most professed not to know—they'd simply allowed the keepers of the lists to choose—and those women who were among the faithful were disinclined to talk of anything.

Felis was not altogether displeased at this lack of cooperation. She sensed that this information the women alone possessed could be a formidable weapon to hold over the men, especially the Great Families and the lesser nobility who placed great store in bloodlines.

She was sitting quietly in the courtyard of the fortress, thinking about their future and wishing that Amala were with her, when a young man she recognized by now as being Zakton's aide approached her in his hesitant fashion.

"Lord Zakton wishes to speak with you, Felis Sauken."

Felis followed him across the courtyard to the building that housed the men, hoping that he had more news of Amala. Since their brief meeting upon her arrival, she'd spoken to Amala's brother several times. As he'd promised, he'd told her of Amala's rescue and said that she was well but had to rest for a few days before coming to Savleen. Felis' own relief hadn't prevented her from seeing the happiness in his own eyes, and she'd decided in that moment that she liked Zakton.

He seemed far less formidable than most of the other men and more at ease around her, too. Certainly he was very different from his friend Jorlan. Felis had wanted to ask him where Jorlan was and if it had been he who'd rescued Amala, but she'd never had the opportunity.

Zakton's aide led her into the men's building,

and as they approached the room where she'd spoken to him before, she heard a voice that drove all thoughts about Jorlan from her mind. Amala! She was here at last! Felis' heart leapt with joy.

Amala had awakened a short time earlier to find a breakfast of fresh fruits and tea awaiting her and a closetful of brightly colored clothing. She devoured the meal, bathed and then began to examine the clothing. There were many dresses, but they were all of the same style—long with close-fitting bodies and high necks. They looked uncomfortable. On the island the women had worn simple, loose clothing, and most of the younger ones, like Amala, had chosen to wear loose trousers rather than skirts.

But the colors and the fabrics were wonderful. Given the limitations of their lives, they could do little to create beauty other than embroidering the plain fabric they wove, and Amala was not one of those who was handy with a needle.

She took out a gown that was a perfect match for her eyes and admired the fine, soft fabric. Then she opened the dresser drawers and discovered underclothing of an even finer fabric, so light that it weighed nothing and was nearly transparent.

Finally she searched the room for shoes but could find none. Was there a reason for that? She couldn't very well escape barefoot. She was just contemplating that when the door opened and the Feloth shuffled in. The creature managed to make it plain that Amala was to follow her and she did so, but she decided she must find a way to make the furry servant understand that she should knock before entering her room.

Shebba led her through the house and into another bedroom, this one at least twice the size of her room and far more luxurious. Obviously this must be Jorlan's room, and even though he was nowhere to be seen at the moment, Amala felt a twinge of uneasiness.

"Where is Lord Jorlan?" she asked the Feloth, speaking slowly and distinctly.

Shebba regarded her silently for a moment, then abruptly dropped to all fours and hurried away. Amala assumed that she had gone off to find her master. But why had she been brought here?

As she awaited an answer, she walked about the room. The bed dwarfed even the huge bed in her own room, but then he was very much bigger than she was. Still, she found such hugeness rather daunting. No doubt her ancestors had lived this way once, but she'd known only the small, cramped cottages on the island. All this space made her feel exposed and vulnerable.

She walked over to an open doorway on the far side of the big room, assuming she'd find a larger version of the bathroom in her own quarters, but she stopped and stared in renewed amazement.

Parts of two walls were glass, and set before them was a huge tub, certainly larger than even a man his size could possibly need. An array of unknown fixtures gleamed against the smooth border of the tub. It was filled, and she dipped in a finger to find that it was pleasantly warm.

"I thought you might enjoy it," said that familiar voice behind her, "and it should ease the aches and pains."

Amala straightened quickly and turned to face him. How much more time would she have to spend in his presence before she could rid herself of that uneasiness? He'd been nothing but kind to her, and yet . . .

"Why is it so large?" she asked curiously.

He glanced from her to the tub and back again as a smile came and went, a smile she couldn't quite interpret.

"No doubt everything seems large to you. Your homes on the island were very small." Then his gaze traveled slowly over her. "I hope the clothing meets with your approval. I'm afraid it's the best we could do for now. The color suits you well."

"Thank you," she said, feeling increasingly uncomfortable under his scrutiny. "But why did Shebba bring me in here? There is a tub in my own bathroom."

"But not like this." He moved past her to bend over the fixtures.

She gasped as the water suddenly began to swirl about madly. He turned to her with a smile.

"The movement of the water should soothe your muscles."

She thought that it did indeed look inviting, although she had some reservations about using it when it was surrounded by all those windows. However, after he had left her there, she peered out and saw that the land dropped away quickly on this side of the house, and beyond the window was nothing but endless forest.

The swirling waters felt wonderful. In fact, she remained in the tub until Shebba once again put in an appearance. Amala hadn't quite settled her mind about this creature. Should she regard her as being human? Her tendency to walk in unannounced probably indicated that she was accustomed to behaving this way with Jorlan, but Amala still felt slightly uneasy. It seemed to her that Shebba was closer to being human than animal.

The Feloth was clearly urging her to follow her somewhere, so Amala dried off and dressed hurriedly. Her body felt wonderfully free of pain and tingling with energy. Shebba then led her through the house to a door that had been locked when Amala had done her nighttime explorations. She now saw that it contained some strange machinery.

Jorlan was seated before one of these machines. He turned and saw her staring at the array of unfamiliar devices.

"This is a computer," he said, his dark eyes glittering with amusement. "Perhaps you've heard of them."

Amala could not mistake the irony in his tone. So this was the machine whose secrets her ancestress had learned, the machine that had enabled them to escape from the men. Now she understood why the door had been locked.

"Yes, but there were no pictures of them." She walked closer and began to examine the machines. Finally, she looked at him.

"She could never have learned to operate this without help."

"She didn't. He taught her," was the tight reply.

"But why? Surely he must have known that it would put all kinds of information at her disposal. Besides, we were taught that women received almost no education."

"He underestimated her abilities," Jorlan replied in the same tone.

Amala smiled, thoroughly enjoying his obvious discomfort. "He certainly did. My admiration for her is even greater, after seeing this."

Their eyes met in silence, but Amala heard the unspoken words: *I* will never make that mistake.

"I promised you you could talk to Zak today. I'll get him now."

He began to press various buttons and the large square of glass in front of him lit up. Amala was excited but also disappointed. She'd hoped to see her brother, not just talk to him.

Suddenly, a face appeared on the screen. Amala cried out in surprise, but she knew immediately this was not her brother. He was far too young. It took her several seconds to realize that the man in the glass could see Jorlan and speak to him. Jorlan asked for her brother, and the face disappeared. When another face filled the screen, she drew in her breath sharply.

"Zakton!" There was no mistaking the likeness to herself, even in his very male face. He was smiling broadly, and she could see the excitement in his blue eyes that were so like her own.

Jorlan greeted him, then got up from his seat and gestured for her to sit down. "Then he'll be able to see you, too."

She did as told, her eyes never leaving the screen. Neither of them said a word for a very long time. Amala felt tears welling up in her eyes. She hadn't expected to feel like this, and she certainly hadn't expected to see the same reaction from him.

"Are you feeling better, Sister?" he asked in a husky voice.

"Yes, much better. I . . ." She faltered, then let her heart speak for her. "Oh, Zakton, I'm so happy to see you. But when will I meet you?"

"Soon, I hope. The doctor wants you to rest for a few days, and you wouldn't get much rest up here, believe me."

"Have you seen our mother?" she asked.

"No." The light seemed to go out of his eyes briefly. "She's still in the hospital, but I've been assured that she's doing well. I've been very busy here."

The smile returned quickly. "You look so much like her, even more than I'd thought. I know Jor told you about our spying."

"Yes, but I think it might be wise to keep that from the other women for now. Some of them would be very upset about it, and they already must be suffering."

"We've done our best to make them comfortable, Amala, and I've been keeping the men here away from them."

"Thank you for that," she replied, thinking that she would definitely have an ally in him. There was a gentleness and essential kindness in Zakton that was lacking in Jorlan, and yet they were best friends.

Zakton turned momentarily away from the screen, then faced her again. "I thought you might want to speak to your friend Felis, so I sent for her and she's here now."

And then Felis' dear and familiar face filled the screen, and Amala felt the tears begin anew. After expressing their pleasure at finding each other alive and well, the two women began to talk about the condition of the others. Felis told her that in addition to everything else, some of the women and girls had become sick since their arrival. They were suffering from dizzy spells and muscle cramps, and the nurse-midwives had no idea what it was.

Then, perhaps forgetting about the presence of the men, Felis told her about her attempts to make lists.

"They don't want to give names, Amala, because they're afraid the men will come and claim them. I need you up here to help me."

Amala was about to reply when she was jolted

into an awareness of Jorlan's presence behind her.

"We keep all the birth lists, so the only ones we'd need are the mates of the pregnant women."

Amala saw the stunned look on Felis' face and realized that she must not have known he was there. "Jorlan is here with me, Felis. I'm staying at his house."

The two women stared at each other in silence, Felis full of concern and Amala trying to reassure her. She could well imagine what Felis must be thinking. She changed the subject quickly.

"Have you heard anything about Glea?"

Felis shook her head sadly. "She must have drowned. She was in the last boat that left the island, and after the explosion, the others saw it overturned. They told me that she'd insisted upon taking the oldest and smallest of the boats."

Amala lowered her head sadly. How they would miss Glea and her strength! Then she raised her face to the screen again, trying to find a way to ask about the herbs. Could they have brought at least some of them with them in their boats?

The two women stared at each other in silent communication, and then Felis nodded slightly. Amala could barely restrain herself. They *had* brought them!

There was much more they both wanted to say, but the presence of the men prevented it.

Amala told Felis she would be there within a day or so and they said good-bye. Then Zakton came back on and said his good-byes to both her and Jorlan.

"I had intended to tell you about Glea," Jorlan said as he turned to her. "We've searched the entire area. I'm very sorry, Amala. She was the only close female relative I have, and I had hoped to meet her. Perhaps when we have time, you could tell me more about her."

Amala just nodded, thinking that he wasn't likely to care much for what he'd hear, but she had to admit that he sounded sincere. The blood ties were powerful in Great Families.

She had to get to Savleen quickly. The Council was shattered, and Felis obviously needed her.

She turned to Jorlan. "I must go to Savleen tomorrow. I'm feeling much better, and I'm needed there. But first, I would like to see my mother. Is that possible?"

Rather to her surprise, he agreed to both requests. Encouraged by his behavior, Amala put to him a question that had been troubling her.

"Zakton seems unconcerned about our mother. Why is that?"

Jorlan's gaze slid away as he shrugged his wide shoulders. "He's very busy, as he said, and he knows she's being well cared for."

No, she thought, that's not it. There's something else. But it was obvious she wouldn't have an answer until she could get to Savleen and talk to her brother in person.

In any event, she was heartened by Zakton's reaction to her. She was very sure she would have him on her side during the battles to come.

She was far less sure of Jorlan, however. Despite his kindness, he remained a mystery to her.

CHAPTER SIX

FELIS STARED AT ZAKTON IN UNDISGUISED DISBE-lief. "*You* are responsible for this?"

"Aleala's ba . . ." Zakton caught himself at the last possible moment. On top of everything else, her accusation had been too much.

"We may be responsible," he went on in a placating tone, "but you can't blame us for it."

"Then just who can we blame?" Felis persisted, her dark eyes flashing. "Three women and a two-year-old girl are already dead. At least two more are near death, and more are getting sick all the time." She paused to draw in a ragged breath, then continued.

"For all your bragging about your advances, how can you let a little bug kill us?"

Zakton slumped in his chair and closed his

eyes briefly. Why was he letting her criticism get to him this way? She was only a woman—and a lower class one at that. Then, ashamed of his ugly thoughts, he tried again.

"We're making the vaccine as fast as possible, and the medicine we already have is working for most of the victims. How could we possibly have known that a virus we became immune to years ago could harm you?"

Felis finally sighed and sank into a chair. She threw him an apologetic look. "I'm sorry, Zakton. It's just that after all we've been through, this is . . ." She shrugged.

Zakton stared at her. In the short time he'd known her, Felis had come to mean something to him. He remembered virtually every word they'd spoken to each other, every gesture, every smile, every time their eyes met. He wanted to believe that it was just because she was the only woman with whom he had regular contact, but some inner voice told him it was more than that.

"At least you haven't got it yet—and Amala is safe, too."

She ignored his remark about her, although she would remember it, just as she remembered everything he said. "Amala may be safe from the virus, but she won't be truly safe until she's here."

Ever since she'd discovered that Amala was with Jorlan, she'd been worried about her friend, despite the reassurances Amala had conveyed to her on the vidcom. Jorlan frightened her, as Zakton did not.

"Jor is my best friend. He'd never harm her."

"Perhaps we define 'harm' differently." She got up. "I must get back to the others."

Zakton watched her walk out of his office, amused that she still wore the rough, loose pants and shirt she'd been wearing when she came here. Apparently the only time she took them off was to wash them. He was sure she was making some sort of statement, just as he knew that beneath that feisty exterior was a vulnerable, scared woman.

What will happen to her, he wondered sadly. He knew now that she came from the lowest class of their society. He and Jor had talked at considerable length about the society the women had fashioned for themselves, a society where family and class distinctions appeared to be almost nonexistent. She would never give that up, and he couldn't blame her. They hadn't anticipated such a change, and now they didn't know what to do about it.

Both he and Jor had always championed improving the lot of the lower classes, and he thought they'd accomplished quite a lot. But now that he'd met Felis, he knew it wouldn't be enough.

Amala felt her strength returning almost hour by hour. She was eager to rejoin the other women, even though a tiny part of her wanted to stay here and observe this man who was so important to their future. It was for that reason that she'd allowed Jorlan to persuade her to remain another few days.

Jorlan and Zakton held the key; she was now sure of that. He'd told her a little about the other members of the Council, and she'd been able to read between the words quite easily. Her brother was clearly a powerful voice but also a radical one, and that, she knew, would make him less effective as an ally.

But implicit in Jorlan's words had been his own preeminent power on the Council. He stood somewhere in the middle, although she guessed that his friendship with Zakton probably moved him slightly to that side.

He was such a difficult man to understand—but then, perhaps all men were this way. How could she know at this point? He hid his emotions well, far more than Zakton, she thought, and yet she couldn't truly think of him as being cold. Something moved in the depths of those dark eyes.

She thought about all this as she walked along a path she'd discovered that began at the edge of the garden and meandered through the forest. As far as she knew, Jorlan was still on the vidcom with the other Council members, undoubtedly discussing their future. She'd tried listening outside the closed door, but before she'd heard more than a few words, Shebba had come shuffling up to her. Amala had no idea how well the Feloth could communicate with her master, so she'd hurried away. She had no desire to have Jorlan learn that she was spying on him.

It was a lovely day and she enjoyed being in the forest, listening to the birds and identifying the ones she'd known from the island. Birds had been the only other living creatures on the island, but there were obviously many different species here.

Thoughts of the island brought that familiar pang of sadness. So often these days, she would find herself longing for the peace and security she'd known there. Then at other times, she'd be filled with an eager determination to face the challenges of this new world.

She'd thought a few times about telling him of her vision for their future, but she'd kept prudently silent. She'd constructed a dream, but she knew that they'd have to settle for something between that dream and the nightmare their forebears' lives had been. The question was which parts of the dream they should refuse to surrender.

And through all these musings ran the ever-present fear that there might be forces working against them, those forces Glea had talked about. Hadn't she already stopped regarding Jorlan as an enemy, even if she didn't quite think of him as a friend?

She paused for a moment in the lush forest, thinking sadly how very much she would miss Glea's wise counsel. The other Semlians would be helpful, but none of them had Glea's intellect or her Great Family status.

The path ran along the edge of a steep ravine, at the bottom of which was a small stream. As she stood there looking down at it, four creatures suddenly emerged from the thick woods on the far side and began to drink. Amala stared at them, half in wonder and half in fear. They were lovely, graceful creatures with long, slender legs and soft, reddish brown fur. But they also had enormous, curling horns that grew in a backward angle from the tops of their heads.

Could they be dangerous? She was sure she'd seen a picture of them, but she couldn't recall what they were called or what had been written about them. Deciding to take no chances, she moved quietly to a nearby tree with some low branches and climbed up until she was sure she was out of reach of those horns. One of them lifted its head and looked up in her direction, but the others continued to drink.

Then several more joined the group at the stream's edge. Amala sat there watching them, totally fascinated but still wary. She couldn't bring herself to believe they could be dangerous, but she couldn't quite convince herself that they weren't, either.

Suddenly a sound below her drew her attention away from the creatures. She peered down through the branches and saw Jorlan just below her. He had stopped just beneath the tree and now squatted down as he too watched the animals. Something that looked like a weapon dangled from his belt. She was barely able to stop from crying out.

Surely he wouldn't kill them! Her stomach curdled at the memory of the meat he'd eaten. At the time, she'd been too repulsed by the sight and smell of it to think all that much about where it had come from. Now, having seen how beautiful animals could be, she simply could not imagine killing and eating them.

Somehow the creatures now sensed that they were being watched. One bolted for the woods and the others followed quickly. Amala looked down again and saw Jorlan straighten up. He hadn't touched the weapon.

He started back to the path, and it suddenly occurred to her that there could be other creatures around. She'd been very foolish to have gone off alone like this in a land she didn't know. She called his name, and he stopped abruptly, turning around with a frown.

"I'm up here," she called, then began to work her way back down the tree.

By the time she reached the lowest branch, he was there. She prepared to jump to the ground, but he caught her instead and swung her to the ground. His arms continued to encircle her waist as he frowned at her.

"I thought you were back at the house. Don't come out here alone again, Amala. The carelas aren't dangerous, but there are some other animals that could attack you."

Then his frown vanished as he smiled at her. "You seem to have a fondness for tree-climbing."

His arms remained around her, bringing them close—too close—but even though his closeness made her nervous, she still felt a strange warmth spreading through her. He was so very big and powerful, and yet he could be so gentle, both with his touch and in his tone.

She backed off slightly, gesturing at the same time to the weapon he carried. "Is that why you have that weapon?"

He nodded. "It's a stunner. It wouldn't kill them. There are many rare species of animals and birds here that have been hunted almost to extinction everywhere else. I don't allow hunting here."

"But you eat meat?" she asked, confused.

"Of course, but that comes from animals that are raised for food."

"I don't understand the difference."

Rather to her surprise, he laughed. "Well, don't expect me to explain it to you, because I'm not sure I do, either. But I can't give up meat, so I do my best to ignore the contradictions."

Amala smiled. This was not the first time he'd given evidence of a self-deprecating humour. In such moments, she found herself actually liking this man she'd hated for so long.

He asked her if she'd like to walk a bit farther and she agreed, so they continued along the path as he described some of the other animals that inhabited the forest. Then he told her about his first—and last—hunting trip.

She felt, rather than heard, the difference in

him. He seemed more relaxed than she'd yet seen him. She asked questions about his childhood and about his father.

"He spent much of his time trying to find ways to best your father on the Council," Jorlan said with a smile. "The blood feud had died long before, but they weren't exactly friends, either. Between the two of them, they managed to tie up the Council for years.

"In a way, I think that's why Zak and I came to be friends. We met at the academy, and by that time both of us had seen what they were doing. We wanted it to be different for us."

"And has it been different? You said that you don't always think alike."

"We don't, but we don't let our disagreements paralyze the Council, either."

"I remember your mother," she said. "She died when I was still very young, but I know that she and my mother were close."

He was suddenly very silent, and she glanced at him. He met her gaze quickly, then looked away.

"I think I saw her, but I was never sure."

Amala heard the anger he was trying to conceal. She thought about him as a young boy, watching the women and trying to guess which one was his mother. For the first time, she began to understand what had been done to them. She knew that the women had had no choice, but she now began to think about the price.

She wanted to tell him what she was thinking, but before she could find the words, she heard a low, roaring sound ahead of them.

"What is that?" she asked, half-fearing that some animal was about to attack them.

"It's what I brought you here to see," he said, taking her arm and urging her on.

A few minutes later, the path ended abruptly. Amala gasped. Ahead of them was a sheer rock wall where some small shrubs and clusters of flowers clung precariously to ledges. Water gushed from an opening about two-thirds of the way up and tumbled noisily down to form the stream. The air smelled wondrously of cool, damp earth and the pale pink flowers that bordered the spot.

"I've never seen anything so beautiful," she murmured, sinking into a cross-legged position on a big, flat rock just beyond the reach of the spray.

He sat down beside her. "It's my favorite place. I often come here to read or just to think."

She cast him a quick sidelong glance. He seemed so filled with an impatient energy that it was difficult for her to imagine him doing such a thing, but she was almost growing used to these surprises.

They were both silent for a while as they both stared at the waterfall. Then she gradually became aware of a tension in him. Finally, he stood up.

"I can't take you to Savleen tomorrow."

"Why not?" Her pleasure in the beauty of the place vanished, and so did the pleasure she had begun to find in his company.

He told her about the virus. She had known that some of the women were sick, but she hadn't known the extent of the illness.

"We had a similar problem when we first landed on Bethusa," he went on. "A virus that we'd long since built up immunity to spread through the Bethusans and killed some of them before we realized what was happening."

"Then someone should have anticipated this," she said angrily, thinking of the lost lives and the impact this latest tragedy would be having on the women.

"I agree. We should have, but we didn't. There wasn't much time to think about such things, and besides, you aren't a different race."

"Then there could be other viruses that may strike later?"

He nodded. "We're preparing for that. We won't be caught like this again, but it means that you'll have to stay here for a while longer. And we can't risk going to see your mother, either."

"I agree that it could be risky, but I don't see why I can't go to Savleen. After all, I've been exposed to you with no ill effects, and besides, I'm healthy and you said it's only dangerous for the elderly and young children."

He frowned slightly and searched her face carefully. "But it *is* risky for you now."

"Don't be ridiculous, Jorlan! I've recovered completely from the accident."

He continued to scrutinize her closely, and when he spoke again, his voice was very soft.

"You don't know, do you? I thought you did."

"Know what? What are you talking about?"

"You're pregnant."

She stood up quickly. "No! That's impossible!"

"The doctor who examined you at the hospital confirmed it."

"He was a man! How could he possibly know?" She couldn't be pregnant! She hadn't been inseminated again after her last monthly. She knew that it occasionally happened that way, but such situations were rare.

"He may have been male, but he's also a doctor," Jorlan went on. "The test is a very simple one that was in use long before the women left. Just as a precaution, the doctors tested all the women who were brought in for treatment."

Amala turned away from him, her fists clenched helplessly at her sides. For one moment, she was tempted to think that the goddess had done this to her as punishment for her disbelief. Why now—the worst possible time? It wasn't fair.

"You really had no idea?" he asked. It wasn't the question he wanted to ask, but he couldn't face the humiliation of having to ask if it was his.

"No!" She started back to the path. "And this doesn't change anything. In fact, it's all the more reason I need to get to Savleen—to see the nurse-midwives."

Jorlan's frustration finally erupted as he followed after her. "You're not going to Savleen, and you're not going to be taken care of by some old women whose medical knowledge is a century out of date."

She ignored him and quickened her pace. He made no attempt to catch up to her because he knew he was too angry to be rational now.

He didn't understand her anger. She was the one who had decided to get pregnant, after all. Furthermore, he'd always thought that women eagerly anticipated motherhood, that it gave them a purpose in life.

He watched her stiff, awkward gait, so unlike her natural grace. Her fists were clenched at her sides. Obviously, he was wrong—again.

Then he began to worry that she might want to see the midwives for another reason. A chill shook him as he recalled that midwives had once been known to help women get rid of babies they didn't want. Back in the old days, some of them had been executed for that practice.

Amala went back to her room and slammed the door behind her. She didn't know what made her angrier—the fact that she was pregnant or the fact that he had known before she did. It felt almost like a return to the old days, when men impregnated women as they chose.

But she was too rational to cling to that kind of thinking for long. She was the one who had decided to have a baby, not him. She'd made the mistake.

She too was aware of the fact that midwives

had once helped women get rid of unwanted babies. That particular skill hadn't been needed for a long time now, but she supposed that they could still do it.

No, she couldn't do it. She understood why women had done it in the old days, when they'd been worn out by too much child-bearing and when many of them couldn't afford to feed the children they had. But inconvenience seemed like a poor excuse to her. Pregnancy might be annoying, but it wasn't debilitating. She could still accomplish her goals.

Then her thoughts turned to Jorlan and his insistence that she be cared for by the doctors. He couldn't possibly know that the child was his. The records had been destroyed on the island, and even if the midwives had been persuaded to talk, they'd never name her as being pregnant, since she'd told them that her monthly had come.

He couldn't know, but he had undoubtedly guessed.

Should she tell him? She knew how important it would be to him. He needed an heir. She pressed a hand to her belly, hoping it was a girl. But what if it was a boy?

Her thoughts were interrupted by a hesitant knock at the door.

"Go away, Jorlan! I don't want to talk now."

But he opened the door anyway, although he didn't enter the room. He looked very worried. "I just wanted to tell you that Zak knows you're pregnant, too, and he agrees that you should stay here until the virus is gone."

When she said nothing, he withdrew, closing the door after him.

She stared at the closed door. Only a few short moments ago, she'd been thinking that she truly liked this man. Was it fair for her to begin regarding him as her enemy again? Or had she been wrong to have let herself like him?

Jorlan shut off the vidcom and cursed. He'd been hoping that Zak would find a way to get the truth out of the midwives, but they'd refused to talk to him. He was more frustrated than he'd ever been in his life. He was sure that the baby must be his, but though he needed to hear it from her, he didn't dare risk upsetting her. The doctor had warned him that trauma, especially in the early stages of pregnancy, could cause a miscarriage.

But what if it wasn't his? She belonged to him, but he could scarcely go out and kill the father, when the man had had nothing to do with it.

And neither could he give her up. He wanted her, and he was confident that at some point, she would realize that she wanted him, too. Already he'd seen that she was more comfortable with him.

There was also the larger issue that the Council was even now grappling with. There was agreement that no man should be forced to take a wife he hadn't chosen, but no one knew yet what to do about the situation.

Zak was urging a sort of middle ground that would permit the male children to remain with their fathers and the females to stay with their mothers, with each of them then free to marry whom they chose. It made sense, but it would also allow her to refuse to marry him.

He leaned back in his chair, thinking about what he'd told her about his mother. Perhaps he shouldn't have said that; thoughts of the woman who had borne him and then abandoned him still made him angry. It wasn't natural.

Marriage and family were the natural way, as they'd always been until the women's treachery. There'd always been some illegitimacy and even divorce in fact, if not in law, among the lower classes, but among the Great Families, marriage was sacred.

Surely she wouldn't go against so many centuries of tradition. Or would she?

Dinnertime came and he ate alone, then told Shebba to take food to her. After dinner he returned to the comroom, intending to work on some engineering problems, but instead, he just sat there, drumming his fingers restlessly against the table.

Perhaps some sort of peace offering was in order. He hadn't done or said anything wrong, but he guessed that scarcely mattered to a woman. Besides, women always liked gifts. However different she might be in many ways, he doubted she was different in that regard. He thought about it for a few minutes, then called his aide down in the city.

Earlier, Amala had discovered a book about Jorlan's infamous ancestor, written by a man whose name she'd seen in old books on the island where there certainly had been no books about Jorlan.

After picking at the dinner Shebba had brought her, she turned to the book now. She needed something to take her mind off her problems, and besides, she was quite curious about the man.

Unfortunately, she quickly discovered that most of the book was devoted to accounts of his many battles. She paged through it with little interest until she came to a description of the Battle of Savleen. Since she certainly had an interest in that place, she decided to read about it.

From the date, she saw that the battle had taken place less than a year after the women's exodus, and by the time she had finished the chapter, she understood more clearly than ever before the reason her ancestress had left him.

The man had been a bloodthirsty monster, willing to sacrifice nearly a quarter of the male population to satisfy his sick quest for glory.

Why did men have this need to kill? She pondered that for a while, then found her thoughts drifting back to that moment in the forest when Jorlan had told her about turning this place into a wildlife refuge and about his own dislike of hunting. Well, perhaps men just preferred to kill other men. As far as she was concerned, that was preferable to their killing animals.

She was pulled from her thoughts by a strange whining sound that grew louder, then stopped abruptly. A few moments later, as she resumed reading, she heard it again, loud at first and then dying away quickly.

She paid it little attention because she'd discovered that here, in the last few chapters, she began to get small glimpses of the man, not just his victories in battle. Quotations from his own writings were used, and Amala discovered that there was a beguiling sense of fairness to Jorlan —beguiling, that is, until one remembered that this man, through his enormous power on the Council, had kept even the most basic rights from the women.

She paused for a moment, thinking about how she'd observed that same sense of fairness on the part of the present Jorlan and in Zakton as well. Her hopes of having them both as allies began to dim. Perhaps their sense of fairness, too, was limited to men.

When she came to the final few pages, she read with increasing disbelief. The historian couched everything in vague terms, but there was a strong suggestion that the family had withheld portions of Jorlan's diaries. One sentence in particular caught her attention:

"Some even suggested that the great Jorlan died proclaiming his willingness to give up all he had achieved for the return of his perfidious wife."

Amala set the book aside and stared into space. Could it have been true? Surely not. Yet why would an historian who had spent an entire book detailing the man's greatness then end it by including something like this, something that surely detracted from that greatness in the eyes of his all-male readers?

Among the treasures lost on the island had been Amala's diary. She felt its loss keenly now, and she also thought about that sense she'd had that it was incomplete. The pages had never been numbered, and some pages were clearly not the originals, but she'd been told that time had damaged them and forced others to copy them.

She recalled how she'd always come away from reading it with an overwhelming sense of sadness, even though she'd never been able to give a reason for that feeling.

There'd been virtually nothing about Jorlan in the diaries, not even at the beginning when she was still his wife. She'd mentioned him then only in connection with her plans or to complain about his callousness toward the women's needs. And after she'd arrived on the island, she'd never mentioned him again.

As she thought about it anew, it seemed to her that Amala had been a woman struggling with an iron-willed determination against pain, a pain she'd never named.

She had just begun to think about those forces

Glea had warned about when she heard a scratching at her door. Knowing it must be Shebba, who had finally been taught to knock before entering, Amala called out to her to come in.

The Feloth shuffled into the room, bearing in one hairy hand a lovely vase filled with the most exquisite flowers Amala had ever seen. In the other, she carried a small, silvery box. Amala could see a toothy imitation of a grin beneath all that hair as Shebba thrust them at her. She took them and murmured her thanks, but Shebba had already dropped to all fours and rushed out the door.

Not only were the flowers wondrous to behold, but they also quickly filled the room with a beautiful fragrance. She inhaled the heady scent for a few moments, then set them aside to see what the box contained.

The aroma that filled her nostrils when she opened the box was very different from the flowers, but just as marvelous. It came from small cubes of something she couldn't identify, but her nose told her it was definitely edible. She picked one up and bit cautiously into it to discover the most delicious food she'd ever tasted. So she gobbled down the rest of the cube then ate two more before deciding that something so rich should probably be eaten in moderation.

With the wonderful taste still lingering in her mouth, she sniffed the bouquet again. It was a safe bet that the gifts had not been Shebba's idea. She recalled that sound she'd heard earlier and wondered if it might have been an airsled.

She continued to stare at the flowers and allowed herself one more of the little cubes as she thought about Jorlan—the current bearer of that name, not his ancestor. Perhaps he'd intended the gifts to be a peace offering, but she knew there was no reason for that. He'd done nothing wrong.

The truth was that the man had done nothing wrong since she'd met him. If anyone was in the wrong here, it was she, for withholding information that must be important to him.

Still, she sat there for a few moments longer, once again lost in thought about their common ancestors.

Jorlan had given up trying to work on a redesign for the thrusters of the new starship, something at which he could normally spend many happy hours.

Apparently the gifts weren't going to produce the desired result. He glanced with increasing self-disgust at the ornately carved wooden box that sat on his worktable. Maybe he should send Shebba in with that or take it himself.

No, dammit, he'd made enough of a fool of himself already. For all he knew, she could be sitting in there now laughing at him. Who could possibly understand the mind of a woman, let alone this particular woman?

With a sound of disgust, he flung himself out of his chair and went out to the great room, where he poured himself a large goblet of wine. Maybe he ought to drink himself into a stupor, something he hadn't done since his foolish youth. If he didn't, he just might find himself crawling on his hands and knees to her door, begging forgiveness for something he hadn't done.

Just as the first taste of the wine slid down his throat, he heard a sound and turned to find her standing there. She was wearing one of the gowns he'd had sent up for her—long and loose with a high neck that covered everything. He wondered angrily who had designed the damned things. The dress was a deeper blue than her eyes, but it seemed only to enhance that remarkable shade.

She had far more than beauty, he thought admiringly; she had presence. There was even that same defiantly upward tilt to her chin that he'd seen on the screen that time, the same look her ancestress wore in the portrait that Zak persisted in displaying in his home.

For one brief moment, Jorlan longed for the simplicity of the past, when she'd been only a dream and not this overwhelming reality. He even tried to summon up an image of his Bethusan lover, Asroth, but discovered that she simply no longer existed.

"Thank you for the gifts," she said formally as she advanced slowly into the room.

Aha! Despite that attempt at defiance, she was nervous. He immediately began to feel much more in control.

"You're welcome," he replied, mimicking her formal tone.

She walked over to the terrace doors, saw that a fine mist was falling and returned to take a seat. He was feeling better and better.

"I've been reading that book about Jorlan."

He slid quickly down to a cautious neutrality. Was she about to begin haranguing him about his ancestor?

She stared hard at him. "He was a bloodthirsty monster. How could such a man be honored?"

"The same way a woman could be honored who betrayed her husband and abandoned her son," he replied coolly.

"She had no choice; she was married to an inhuman monster."

Then she gave him a considering look. "Would you have done what he did at Savleen?"

If there was one question about his ancestor Jorlan had no desire to answer, that was it. She obviously had an instinct for such things. He remained silent.

"Well? Would you have?"

"It was a necessary battle," he said shortly, then gulped some more wine.

"Why? From what I read, Jorlan could simply have waited them out. Victory could have been his without any loss of life."

"There are always losses in battle."

Now she gave him a bitter smile. "But not so many anymore, are there? If we have accomplished one thing, it's that you now understand the value of life."

"We have no real enemies anymore. There's no need to make war."

"Not here, but you look for them out there." She waved an arm upward.

"It's a man's nature to seek new challenges," he replied, then recalled what she'd said about not having any challenges on the island. Damn, but this woman confused him.

"And what is a woman's nature, do you think?"

He knew a loaded question when he heard one. "How could I possibly know? I haven't met any, except for you. And the Bethusans," he added as an afterthought.

"Who are the Bethusans?"

"They're our nearest neighbors in space." Why had he mentioned them?

"Tell me about them. Are they human?"

So he told her, taking great care to let her know about all the benefits they'd heaped upon the primitive, childlike people. She listened carefully, and when he had finished, she once again asked the question he least wanted to answer now.

"Have you mated with them?"

"There are no half-breed children out there," he stated coldly.

She decided not to press the issue for now, but she was very curious. She didn't doubt his statement that there were no interracial children, but that didn't necessarily mean that they hadn't mated with these Bethusans. Perhaps the men had developed some method of birth control themselves.

Jorlan poured himself some more wine, then stared at it thoughtfully. She might never have had wine before. He turned to her.

"Would you like some of this?"

She nodded distractedly, and he filled a goblet and brought it to her. She reached up to take it, and their eyes met briefly. He could see that she was struggling with something and braced himself for more questions he didn't want to answer. But once again, she surprised him.

"The baby is yours."

For one brief moment, he was sure he'd imagined those soft words. He stared at her, but she'd turned away. When he said nothing, she finally looked up at him, tossing her golden hair over her shoulders and once more lifting her chin.

"I hope it's a girl."

Now, finally, he believed it! He tried to restrain himself, but just couldn't manage it. He grinned like a damned fool even as she watched him with a slight frown.

"Surely you must have guessed that it was yours."

His pleasure was briefly submerged beneath that old anger. "I didn't know any such thing. I have no idea how you make those decisions."

"We can choose our mates when we're twelve, just the way men once chose us. But most women simply leave it to the keepers of the lists."

"But you didn't?"

"No, I chose you. Some of the older women didn't like it much. They thought it was a bad omen."

She paused, then went on softly. "Perhaps they were right. I became pregnant just before the goddess deserted us."

Now that he knew the baby was his, Jorlan was more than ever worried that she might try to get rid of it, and her words did little to allay those fears.

"Don't you want this baby?"

She hesitated, then sighed. "Not now. This just isn't the best time."

His alarm grew. "Yes, it is," he said hurriedly. "It's the perfect time. Our people are reunited, and . . ."

"And what, Jorlan? Back to the same old ways? That's not going to happen! We will not be turned into slaves again!"

"You weren't slaves before," he said defensively, "and it'll be different this time."

"It certainly will!" she stated as she drank some more of the wine. "I've drawn up a whole new set of laws for our society."

He stared at her in disbelief. She'd alluded to something like this before, but he hadn't thought it had gone this far.

"It started out as nothing more than a mental exercise," she went on, "but it's very serious now."

He sank into a chair opposite her. A woman

rewriting their laws? But curiosity won out over disbelief. "Just what did you have in mind?"

She shook her head. "I can't tell you that. We'll discuss it when we begin the negotiations. Will that be soon?"

Negotiations? He now recalled that she'd mentioned that before as well. "Just what do you have to negotiate with?" he asked, suspended between amusement and uneasiness.

"What do you mean?"

He leaned forward to emphasize his point. "When two parties negotiate, each has some weapon to bring to the negotiations, and you no longer have your damned mist to protect you."

"No," she replied coolly. "But we do have weapons, as you put it."

"What weapons?" he scoffed.

"I'm not foolish enough to disclose that now."

He stared at her. Her face was flushed, and nearly half the wine was gone. Before she finished the other half, he could have the information he wanted—and have her in his bed as well. He allowed himself to savor those prospects. Then, regretfully, he began to consider the aftermath. She would hate him and undoubtedly refuse to marry him, and she even might be able to persuade Zak to go along with that. He got up and took the goblet from her hand.

"You've had enough of this. It's very potent, and you can't be used to it."

"I've had wine before. We made it on the island."

But she didn't argue with him. Maybe he was right; her head did feel a bit fuzzy. And she hadn't intended to bring up the subject of her plans for their society. She stared at him, wondering why he hadn't just let her get drunk so he could gain more information.

"You're a very strange man, Jorlan," she said, more to herself than to him.

He leaned back in his chair and smiled at her. "Of course, you're speaking from wide experience of men."

She laughed. "No, I just meant that what I've seen of you doesn't fit with what we were taught."

"I don't doubt that," he responded drily. "She made it very clear that she'd prevent women from ever wanting men again."

"She? You mean Amala?"

He nodded. "It was in her diary. Surely you had a copy on the island."

"There's a copy here, too?" she asked. "That's wonderful! I thought we had lost it."

"She left it in the computer. Zak had a copy printed as well."

Seeing her pleasure in this news, he went on. "There's a portrait of her, too. The likeness is remarkable."

"Yes, I know. We have . . . had a portrait of her, done by an artist on the island. Do you have any portraits of Jorlan?"

He nodded. "Several. They're at my home in the city." He paused, then added in a quieter tone, "Actually, I have a portrait of Amala as well. Families always commissioned portraits at the time of weddings. It's been in storage for years."

"Do you look like him?"

"Yes—almost as much as you look like her."

Their eyes met, and this time they both quickly looked away. Each of them was uncomfortable with those comparisons, without truly understanding why.

"The book I was reading hints at the possibility that your family withheld portions of Jorlan's diaries. Is that true?"

"There have always been rumours to that effect," he said noncommittally, then quickly got to his feet. "I have something else for you."

He returned a moment later, bearing a large ornate wooden box that he set on the table before her.

"This should be yours."

Amala opened it, then gasped in astonishment. They had very little jewelry on the island, since the first women had chosen to leave most of it behind. Amala's diary had said that men often bestowed such gifts upon women, as though such frivolities could make up for their lack of freedom.

On top of the glittering pile were two wide bands of intricately woven gold threads, studded with precious jewels. She picked them up and admired them, then suddenly realized what they must be.

"Men gave them to women when they married. The women wore them always."

She hastily put them down again. They might be beautiful, but they represented the slavery into which women had been given. She ignored them and sorted through the other pieces.

Jorlan sat silently, watching the light reflect off her pale, shining hair and the jewelry she was examining piece by piece. Strange feelings came over him. He wanted her now more than ever, but he knew that what he felt wasn't merely lust. He was suddenly afraid to examine it further.

"Tomorrow, if you like, I'll take you for a ride in the airsled and show you the city and your family's lands as well."

She looked up with a smile that only increased that strange feeling in him.

"I would like that. Could I see Savleen as well?"

"You can see it—but only from the air. I'm not trying to hold you prisoner here, Amala. Surely you understand that." But he didn't want to let her go, either. He still worried that she might rid herself of his child.

She merely nodded, but she was determined not to remain here a day longer than necessary. She was still intensely curious about this man, but that curiosity was finally being tempered by caution. Something *was* happening between them.

He sat there, his face hidden as he stared into his wine goblet. She sensed that something was troubling him and waited uneasily to learn what it was. After a few moments, when he looked up at her, she was shocked to see fear in those dark eyes.

"Amala," he said slowly, "I know you don't want the baby, but you wouldn't do anything to . . . get rid of it, would you?"

She was shocked, then frightened because she had considered doing just that. Were they already to the point where they could feel each other's thoughts?

She shook her head. "I wouldn't do that."

She saw the true extent of his fear when he relaxed. If he'd truly been this worried, couldn't he have simply held her prisoner here until the child was born? She doubted that even Zak could have withstood this man's power. But his fear seemed to prove that he'd had no intention of doing that.

She got up, wanting only to lose her confusion in sleep, but she cried out as she tottered slightly on unsteady legs. The wine! She'd drunk more despite his warning.

He shot out of his chair and circled her waist before she could protest.

"You were right to have warned me about that wine," she said, a bit breathlessly. "I shouldn't have had more, and it's probably not good for the baby, either."

Then he picked her up and carried her back to

her bedroom, ignoring her protest that she was able to walk. His big, hard body still felt alien to her, but she was no longer repulsed by it. When he set her down carefully on the bed, she even felt a small regret.

"I admire your honesty," he said as he stood there looking down at her. "So I'm going to be honest, too. I almost didn't warn you about the wine. Getting you drunk could have been very . . . interesting. Perhaps you should think of that as a warning itself."

She searched his face, certain that he was talking about more than just getting information out of her.

"You wanted to mate with me," she stated. "But why? I'm already carrying your child."

He backed off a few steps and groaned as he ran a hand through his thick, black hair. Then he moved back to her and cupped his hand beneath her chin.

"Pleasure, Amala, the pleasure a man and woman can give to each other."

She lifted her chin from his hand and wrinkled her nose in distaste. "I don't find that idea very pleasurable."

Then suddenly, she narrowed her eyes. "And how do *you* know it's pleasurable?"

He backed off with a muttered oath. "All right, we *have* had Bethusan women. What did you expect? They were there, and they were willing—unlike our own women."

"But you said there were no children."

"Of course not. We can prevent that."

"I see. Well, good night, Jorlan. Thank you again for the gifts."

He knew a dismissal when he heard one, and in any event, he didn't dare remain there one minute longer.

Chapter Seven

Jorlan glanced sideways at Amala as she leaned forward, looking at his heavily forested lands spread out beneath them. Despite his constant, aching need for her, he was also oddly content just to be with her. Perhaps it was the knowledge that she carried his child, or perhaps it was more than that.

Never before in his life had he focused so intently upon one person—except, perhaps, on his father when he'd been a child. But his father had been a relatively uncomplicated man; Amala was a different matter altogether.

She could be as easy to read as a child like she was now, eager and excited over her first time aloft. Or she could be coldly imperious, as she'd been when she'd dismissed him last night. And sometimes she could amaze him with her intelligence and boldness, as she'd done when she'd told him about her plan for their society.

How, he wondered, could all those things—and perhaps even more—be contained in one small body? And was there still room in there for an as yet unawakened passion?

"Kodans!" she exclaimed suddenly. "I saw them on the island. They're very rare, aren't they?"

He looked down at the golden trees that he'd so often likened to her pale hair. When he turned back to her, he felt a sudden jolt of awareness of her reality that forced him to look away quickly.

"I didn't know there were any on the island. I've always thought that these are the only ones."

"They are now," she said wistfully. "There was just the one little grove, growing in a tiny valley not far from the Semlian settlement. They're so beautiful. Glea said there were more here on her family's lands, but I'd forgotten."

Jorlan recalled the discussions he'd had with Zak about that strange group. Zak seemed to be awed by their discipline and their muscular bodies.

"Tell me more about the Semlians," he asked. "Zak says they're unusual."

She cast him a sidelong glance, wondering what her brother had actually said. "I'm not really familiar with all their beliefs," she lied. "They're very secretive."

"But Zak said you were some sort of ambassador to them and that's where you were headed when you had your accident. So you must have been close to them."

She wondered just who Zakton was getting his information from. She needed to get to Savleen. He might be her brother, but as far as she was concerned, he still couldn't be considered completely trustworthy.

"As I told you, they don't believe in Aleala. They weren't actually banished from the colony for that, though; they chose to leave years ago. And they follow a strict routine of mental and physical fitness that I find rather admirable."

"Zak says they train like warriors."

"Mmm, well, I suppose it might be something like that. I went there that morning to warn them about the volcano and to help bring them back to safety—or what I thought would be safety. It all happened so fast."

He didn't believe her. He was sure that the volcano was visible on that side of the island as well, so they hadn't needed to be warned. And how could one jepsa be of any value in getting them anywhere? She was hiding something, but he was disinclined to make an issue of it. In any event, they were now passing over the border between his lands and Zak's. Below them were the ancient stone pillars that marked each mile of the boundary.

"What are those pillars?" she asked before he could explain.

"They're called tuthens. They were built centuries ago to mark the borders between our lands."

"Our lands? You mean your family and mine?" she asked eagerly.

He nodded. "There was a time when anyone crossing that boundary from either direction could expect to meet instant death. Zak and I started to walk that border regularly years ago—a kind of ritual between us, I guess."

She thought that he seemed almost embarrassed to be admitting it, even though it was a wonderful ritual. Did peace actually make him uncomfortable? No, more than likely it was talking about feelings that embarrassed him. She'd noticed that before.

She stared down at the narrow valleys and steep hills that were her ancestral lands, lands that had been in her family for countless centuries. She felt a fierce swelling of pride in her heritage, but then it dimmed quickly. These were Zak's lands, not hers. Amala had written that property was power, and the men had denied them that right of ownership.

She looked hungrily at the lush forest beneath her, finally understanding what it meant to own land. She'd never quite understood that before, since ownership of property hadn't been important on the island. They'd all believed the island belonged to the goddess.

Was it possible, she wondered, that she might persuade her brother to give her a piece of that land?

"That's a gold mining village," Jorlan said before she could inquire about the cluster of small houses below them now. "There are more on Zak's land and on mine as well, and we both have diamond mines, too. Some of the worst wars between our families were fought over those mines."

Then he put the sled into a slight dip and she saw a house, nearly hidden beneath its leafy canopy. "That's Zak's home."

She decided that she too wanted a home like that, out here in this beautiful green land. Surely Zak could be persuaded to give her a plot of land. Then, once she'd learned how to fly an airsled . . .

She glanced over at Jorlan as he set the sled back on its original course. Airsleds didn't look all that difficult to fly. She'd been surreptitiously studying it ever since they'd taken off and was fascinated by the freedom it offered.

They flew on, and when she saw the distant object high on a mountaintop, she knew what it must be even before Jorlan confirmed it.

"That's Savleen," he said as he reached for the audiocom.

Amala peered at the old fortress as he identified himself to someone down there. He brought the airsled very low, and she could now see women in the great courtyard, their faces upturned as the sled passed over very slowly. Then a male figure emerged from a building, his golden head tilted up and his arms waving broadly.

Jorlan chuckled. "That's Zak. He knows you're with me."

Amala felt a thrill of pure happiness. She had to get down there. Not only did she want to meet him in the flesh, but she knew that the women needed her.

Then she saw one of the female figures separate from the small group and run toward Zak. A moment later, she too was waving.

"Felis!" Amala cried, now recognizing that dark head.

Jorlan was also peering down as he circled the courtyard one more time. "Yes, I think so. Zak's mentioned her several times. Her family are share-miners on my land."

As they left the fortress behind, Amala wondered if Felis knew that yet. She recalled that look on Felis' face when she'd discovered that she was staying with Jorlan. Perhaps she did know, and that was why she feared him. Her family was virtually in thrall to Jorlan.

Then she thought about how Felis had run to Zakton, and Jorlan had said her brother had mentioned her as well. Was that where Zakton was getting his information? Felis was certainly too smart to give much away, but she might also trust Zakton too much just because he was her best friend's brother. Besides, Felis was still too much aware of class differences, and Zakton could probably intimidate her quite easily.

Jorlan swept away from Savleen as she looked back at the forbidding fortress one last time. Then she turned her attention to the controls and kept it there until the city came into view.

After that, she was simply too astounded to pay any attention to the operation of the airsled. Until now, she'd seen only rural land that hadn't been all that more modern in appearance than the island, though much larger and more varied, but the sight ahead of her now was nearly beyond her comprehension.

Jorlan pointed out various sights to her even as he paid closer attention to the piloting. Many other airsleds dipped and soared over the huge city.

"That's my family compound," he told her, pointing out a large, sprawling collection of stone buildings behind a low wall. "Zak's is on the other side of the city."

She saw wide streets with sleek little vehicles rolling along them, and buildings many stories high, all in a luminous white material. There were fountains and parks and a large number of shops. When she commented on the shops, he laughed.

"If there's one group that will welcome the women back without reservation, it's the shopkeepers. Of course, it will take a while for the factories to produce things women want."

She said nothing, but she definitely detected a patronizing tone in his voice. Luxurious goods weren't going to placate them this time.

We will have the right to own those shops and factories, she thought, *not just buy the things men produce with money they give us.*

"That's the sports complex," he stated, indicating a huge circular structure just ahead. "There's a dome covering for bad weather, and the building beside it is for indoor sports. I doubt if women would find it very interesting, though."

"We have sports," she said defensively. Then she thought of the rigorous dancing she had so loved. Could they ever dance again? Although she enjoyed it for its own sake, she suspected that some of the women would be offended if it continued merely as a sport.

"Then we will build a place for women as well," he said expansively. He was thinking about her dancing. "You dance very well, by the way. It looked difficult."

In spite of herself, Amala warmed to his compliment. "Thank you. I enjoyed it. But for most of the women, the dances were associated with the worship of Aleala, so I'm not sure it can continue." She paused for a moment, then went on in a thoughtful tone.

"But perhaps we could build a place as a monument to Aleala, who protected us all those years. That might make it more acceptable."

Jorlan said nothing. He didn't know if even he could persuade the Council to erect a monument to their accursed goddess. On the other hand, if it made them happy, what was the harm? The island was gone and with it that infernal mist.

"That's the Council building," he said as he pointed to a large, curved structure atop the highest hill.

Amala stared at it. There was power! And there was where she would be one day soon. Of course, she said none of this to Jorlan, but merely remarked upon its beauty and exclaimed over the unusual fountain in the plaza before it.

"When you see the fountain from the ground, you'll appreciate it even more," he assured her. "Zak and I commissioned it jointly some years ago as a gift to the Council. The creator, surprisingly, is a man from the lowest class, but then, so are some of the best athletes—and some good spacemen as well."

His casual air of noblesse oblige irritated her. She thought again about Felis and her fears for her future. Things had to change.

They had left the city proper behind and were traveling now over less densely populated land. Jorlan pointed out Zak's compound. She saw that it was much like Jorlan's—red-roofed stone buildings set within walls that also contained gardens and forests. She could see figures in the gardens including several men and some Feloths and a smaller figure as well.

"That's your nephew, Levyan," Jorlan said. "He's a fine boy. He already wants to become a starship commander."

She looked down but said nothing, which surprised him. Then she asked about the large cluster of buildings ahead of them.

"That's the Space Command Academy. Both Zak and I went to school there. In fact, that's where we first met. The boys who are selected start there at the age of ten. We both work there when we're grounded."

She heard the slight irritation in his voice when he spoke that last word and looked at him curiously.

"Do you dislike being grounded?"

He looked surprised. "Of course. Space is where we all want to be. I don't mind coming back for a short time, of course. In any event, I had no choice this time. My ship is in for major repairs. We ran into a bad meteorite shower."

He had talked of space before, but she still had no understanding of what it would be like to be out there among the stars. Her world had expanded greatly but not that far—not yet, anyway.

Then he brought the sled around to head back across the city toward the distant mountains. They had to return to his mountain home so he could take part in the Council meeting by vidcom.

Jorlan's mind drifted, not an unusual occurrence for him at these interminable debates. There were those on the Council, chiefly members of the least powerful Great Families, who perceived their roles as being ones of opposition to everything. The Chairman was tolerant of them—too tolerant, in Jorlan's opinion.

Images of Amala kept intruding into his attempts to focus on the debate about marriage. Amala and the future were now inextricably linked. Somewhere in the dark corners of his mind, he knew that he was becoming as obsessed with her as his ancestor had been with her infamous forebear, but since he was also a man of boundless self-confidence, he ignored that knowledge. Perhaps the first Jorlan had allowed himself to be brought to weakness; he would not.

A consensus finally seemed to be emerging. Some sort of special status would be granted to children born from the unnatural unions that had characterized their society for so long. Fathers would be required to recognize and support the children of these unions, but not to marry the mothers.

Then Zak, who was also attending via vidcom, brought up the point that men from the lower classes could scarcely be expected to support two families and therefore would be unable to marry. He suggested public support in such cases.

That set off another debate. Zak was easily the most liberal among them, so any spending plan of his was bound to antagonize the Council's conservatives. One of them stated that their society had never supported bastards and this would be setting a dangerous precedent. Zak pointed out calmly that if poor children born from these unions were to be considered bastards, then so were they all.

It went on in this vein for another ten minutes, and then Jorlan lost patience.

"I agree with Zak," he stated as all eyes turned to him through the vidcom. "This is a special situation and can be presented as such.

We can make it quite clear that no precedent is being set."

A few of them grumbled, but most now nodded in agreement. A vote was taken, and Zak's proposal carried easily. Jorlan was known to be a moderate who sometimes voted with his friend and sometimes against. When they were of like mind, the results were virtually guaranteed. The Chairman then instructed the Minister of State, who sat with the other ministers and their aides along the walls, to draw up a proclamation to that effect.

It was then that Jorlan noticed the Chairman's haggard look. His health had been deteriorating slowly over the past year, but he was only 56. At the moment, though, Jorlan thought he looked at least ten years older. Quite apart from the fact that he truly liked and respected the man, Jorlan also worried that any premature retirement would cause him problems. They all knew, as Jorlan himself did, that he would become the next chairman. When that day came, he would be forced to give up space exploration forever.

Then thoughts of Amala intruded once more, and for one brief moment he wondered if he really could give up space.

Amala listened carefully at the closed door, knowing that Shebba couldn't catch her this time. The Feloth had been taken back to the city for the day by one of Jorlan's aides. Jorlan had explained that Feloth families were always kept together and that Shebba was always sent back to visit if he kept her up here very long.

She had heard most of the debate, and it had been very instructive. Not only was the result to her liking, but it had now become clear to her that her brother would be an ally. Jorlan's role was less clear, however, since he'd taken only a limited part in the debate. But if his position wasn't yet clear, his power certainly was. She knew she would need him, perhaps even more than Zakton.

Still, she chafed inwardly at having to learn their decisions in such a manner. She was more than ever determined to have seats on the Council for the women, herself certainly among them.

Then the discussion turned to the condition of the women at Savleen, and Amala clenched her teeth as she heard derisive remarks from a few of the men, though not from Zakton or Jorlan. Some of them spoke with the tone of self-indulgence used toward children.

One member asked if the women had any leadership "other than her", and it took Amala several seconds to realize that he meant *her*. Was he refusing even to speak her name? But her anger was cut off as Zakton responded.

"Their Council isn't functioning at the moment. The only woman other than my sister who seems to be a leader is Felis Sauken."

Amala smiled as she heard the unsubtle emphasis on the words "my sister", as though

Zakton were reminding the questioner of that fact. She was also pleased to hear Felis referred to as a leader, even though she knew that role had been thrust upon Felis unwillingly.

"Sauken?" the questioner scoffed. "What about Great Family women? Who is this Sauken woman?"

"Her family are share-miners on my land," Jorlan put in in an amused tone.

"The only other Great Family women who might be leaders were Jor's kinswoman, Glea, who is dead, and Lady Mava, who is ill."

"Well, then as long as we keep her away from them, there should be no problems."

That did it! So it *was* a conspiracy to keep her apart from the women. She had foolishly trusted both Jorlan and her brother. Amala didn't bother to wait for either man to reply. She ran from the house through the garden to the landing pad where the airsled sat.

She was angry, as angry as she'd ever been in her life! But the worst of her anger was directed at herself, for having trusted men. She was going to Savleen—now!

She climbed into the pilot's seat and then willed herself to be calm. She had time; he would be busy with the meeting for a while longer. So she went over all the instruments, making sure she understood their purposes. The airsled was in fact not that much more complicated to operate than the jepsa, and she'd mastered it quickly enough.

Of course, she reminded herself, if she had problems with the jepsa, she could just stop. That was rather more difficult to do in the air.

Then, satisfied that she knew all she needed to know, Amala murmured a prayer to the goddess she didn't believe in and pressed the ignition button.

Inside the house, Jorlan's attention had begun to waver once more as the Minister of Finance began a sonorous accounting of the cost of the women's return. Then he straightened up sharply as a sound outside thrust the man's voice completely from his mind.

He lost precious seconds suspended in disbelief. An airsled? He wasn't expecting anyone, and he had never encouraged casual visitors here. Awareness dawned slowly, and then he leapt from his seat and ran outside. But he knew he was too late. As soon as he'd emerged from the house, he saw his blue and silver sled ascending at a steep angle.

For the first time in his life, Jorlan felt utterly helpless as he watched the craft disappear into the heavens, leveling out in an awkward fashion and then wobbling for a few seconds before heading northwest. Moments later, it was gone.

Helplessness gave way briefly to anger and finally to icy fear. She would die; she couldn't possibly operate the sled.

But she already is, he reminded himself in desperation, and they weren't really all that difficult to operate. Obviously, she'd watched him earlier, and she'd remembered the direction to Savleen as well.

He ran back into the house, where his reappearance on the screen drew questioning looks from his fellow council members. He interrupted the Finance Minister.

"Zak, I must speak to you privately—now!"

A moment later, the two men had switched to a private channel. Jorlan told him what had happened, and they stared at each other in horror.

"Can she make it?" Zak asked in a taut voice.

"Well, she knew how to get it airborne. I think she'll make it to Savleen without problems, but I'm worried about the landing. How are the winds up there now?"

"Hang on a minute."

Jorlan waited impatiently. Landing up there was often tricky. The winds in the high mountains could be ferocious and often shifted without warning.

Zakton returned, his face grim. "Moderate at the moment, but shifting. They often do at this time of day."

"She should be there in a little more than an hour if she knows her way. You'll have to talk her down, unless you can convince her to return here."

Both of them knew that would be impossible.

"We could send someone up to lead her in, just in case she gets lost," Zakton suggested.

"No, that might scare her. She knows the way."

"Then there's nothing we can do but wait," Zakton stated grimly. "Should we tell the others?"

"No, wait until she gets there."

Both men then returned to the meeting, ignoring the questioning looks. Behind their masks of imperturbability were two terrified men.

And both were already thinking about the ancient historian who had said that those who ignored history are condemned to repeat it. Another Amala had escaped, and might be lost to them forever.

Amala didn't think about switching on the audiocom until she had been airborne for nearly an hour. Operating the sled had proved to be remarkably easy; it very nearly flew itself. Her anger with the men lessened as she thoroughly enjoyed her illicit ride. She even began to wish that she had stayed a few moments longer to hear Jorlan and Zakton's response. Perhaps she'd been wrong to have assumed that it was a conspiracy. Nevertheless, she didn't regret her hasty departure. Conspiracy or not, she needed to be at Savleen. With the men making important decisions about their lives, she had to rally the women.

It took her a few minutes to figure out the audiocom, since she hadn't paid close attention to it when Jorlan had used it. Then, just as she finally spotted the old fortress in the distance, she heard an unfamiliar male voice calling her name.

She ignored it for the moment, then swiveled her head in all directions to see if anyone might be following her. The skies were empty.

The voice was still calling her when suddenly the sled was buffeted violently. She grasped the wheel more tightly and finally succeeded in leveling out once more. She hadn't noticed anything like this when Jorlan had brought her up here, but he was an experienced pilot and, in any event, she'd been staring at the fortress.

The violent winds came at her, then receded just as quickly. Worst of all, their direction shifted from one gust to the next. But Amala was beginning to get a feel for the craft and its limitations, and each new gust caused fewer problems.

Savleen was now clearly visible in the distance, and the voice was still calling her name over and over. Now that she had the sled more or less under control, Amala began to think about the landing. The first thing that occurred to her was that landing might not be quite so easy as taking off had been, especially up here. She knew she would have to cut power to land, and once she did that, she would be even more at the mercy of the winds. For the first time, she began to doubt the wisdom of her actions and wondered if she might not be better off returning to Jorlan's home.

No, she decided, I will not go back and admit failure.

Just then, the voice that had been repeatedly calling her changed to a very familiar one.

"Amala, it's Zakton. We have you on our screen. To answer me, just pick up the microphone."

She hesitated, then reached for it as Savleen loomed ever larger.

"I'm here, Zakton, and don't try to talk me into going back. Just tell me what I need to know to land this thing."

To his credit, he made no attempt to dissuade her. Instead, he went over the landing instructions with her, explaining what she would feel and what she should do in various circumstances.

He then suggested that she fly over the fortress a few times before attempting to land. She did so and saw that the big courtyard was empty except for a small group of men who stood near one end with equipment she couldn't identify.

Finally, she took a deep breath and began her descent. As soon as she cut back on the power, the sled became much more difficult to control. The world beyond the window tilted, then righted itself, then tilted again. A bell sounded urgently, a light flashed on the panel, and she gave it more power, as Zakton had instructed her.

The stone pavement rushed up at her, and the sled itself seemed to be fighting contact. Then it bucked and rocked wildly with a loud screeching sound. She'd made it! She could scarcely believe her eyes as she stared out the window and rubbed a bruised elbow.

At that moment, a familiar figure rushed across the courtyard as Amala began to fumble with the door lock. Her legs were shaky, but she still managed to run the few steps into Felis' arms.

The two women clutched each other and laughed in relief. They still had their arms around each other and Felis was telling her how terrified Zakton had been, when Amala saw him approaching. Felis turned and saw him, too, then released Amala and stepped away.

For one very brief moment, Amala wondered if her brother had been part of a conspiracy to keep her away from here, but her anger dissolved completely as she stared into those blue eyes so like her own. He smiled at her and stopped a few meters away.

"Welcome to Savleen, Sister. For the past hour, I thought I might never get to say those words."

They stared at each other for a moment longer, then he slowly held out his arms. With a cry, Amala ran into them.

That surge of affection she'd felt on the vidcom now returned even stronger. She wrapped her arms tightly around him as her legs continued to tremble. He kissed her brow and ran a soothing hand through her hair.

"You're safe now," he murmured. "And

you've certainly lived up to your name."

She frowned at him, and then comprehension slowly dawned. A smile replaced the frown, until she remembered Jorlan.

"Does he know I'm here?"

Zakton nodded. "I just told him."

She didn't bother to ask what Jorlan had said; it probably wasn't repeatable. She glanced back at the sled, which she now saw had a damaged wing and a jagged hole in its undercarriage.

"I doubt if he's going to be concerned about that," Zakton said drily as he followed her gaze. "Come inside and I'll pour you some of our family wine, which is better than his and not so strong."

She wondered just how much time the two men had spent talking about her. It wouldn't do for her to forget that these two were best friends.

They both turned to Felis and Zakton invited her as well, but Felis declined.

"I'm sure you have much to say to each other." She took Amala's hand and squeezed it briefly. "We'll talk later. I'll see that quarters are prepared for you."

Across the courtyard, Amala saw other women beginning to emerge from the main building. She raised her hand in a wave, then turned back to her brother, who caught her hand and held onto it.

When they drew near the building at the far end of the courtyard, other men appeared. Amala fought down her uneasiness as they stared unabashedly at her. She feared that she would see hostility on their faces, but instead all she saw was curiosity and awe.

Zakton led her into his private quarters, apologizing for its austerity. "You'll feel more comfortable when I can take you home. Jor said he'd showed it to you."

She smiled. "I'm not accustomed to luxury, Zakton. It may take some getting used to."

They had stopped in the middle of the small sitting room, hands still clasped. Zakton leaned forward and kissed her cheek, then backed off and shook his head with a bemused expression.

"You look so much like her, and Jor says that the resemblance is much more than skin deep. Now I believe him."

But Amala didn't care what Jorlan thought. Right now, all she wanted was to be here with her brother, to bask in the affection she saw in his eyes.

He poured them both some wine, which she agreed was better than Jorlan's, and they began to talk. There was no formality between them and no hesitations. She might have known this man all her life. There was also none of that charged atmosphere that seemed always to surround Jorlan and herself.

At first, though, she couldn't help making comparisons between the only two men she yet knew. Although much taller and heavier than her, Zak was also much smaller than Jorlan. Where Jorlan seemed filled with a restless energy and surrounded by an aura of power, Zak was a quiet man who exuded a gentle sort of charm.

They talked of their family. Zakton had already met the other two women of their extended family and had informed them that they would have homes in the family compound when they could leave here. When Amala asked about news of their mother, he said that she was progressing well but would have to remain in the hospital for a while longer. Amala noted once again an absence of emotion in his voice, and this time she couldn't let it pass unremarked.

"Zak, I don't understand. Why do you sound so . . . so cold when you talk about Mother?"

His gaze lowered to his goblet, and he shifted about nervously for a moment. Then, finally, he looked up at her again, his expression a plea for understanding.

"Amala, this is difficult to talk about. All of us feel that way, I think. Our mothers abandoned us when we were babies, and that just isn't natural."

"But you couldn't have remained on the island. The mist would have . . ."

"I know that. We all know that, but it doesn't help. I want to love Mother, and I'm sure I will in time. But it's probably for the best that I won't have to face her for a while yet."

Amala sat there silently, trying to see it from his point of view and recalling Jorlan's brief mention of his mother. Unconsciously, her hand went briefly to her stomach. If they were still on the island and her baby were a boy, he too would have hated her.

Then she thought about the tendency of women to become quiet and withdrawn following the birth of a boy. She'd always assumed it was because they'd wanted a girl. They'd been taught that giving up a boy meant nothing, since he would soon turn into a man.

Zakton had seen her gesture and smiled again. "At least your son—if it is a son, of course—won't have to face that. Jor's very happy, by the way, just in case he hasn't let you know that."

"He'll be happy if it's a boy," she stated disgustedly.

"Well, he'll be happier if it's a boy, but then, you'll be happier if it's a girl."

She nodded. "At least I won't have to marry him."

"So you *did* overhear the council's discussion. We both guessed that was what happened."

"Did either of you have any part in the conspiracy to keep me away from here?" she asked, fixing him with a steady gaze.

He shook his head. "There was no conspiracy. It's true that some of the Council members were happy you weren't up here, but Jor and I were thinking only of your safety."

She nodded her acceptance, and he regarded her quizzically. "What do you think of Jorlan?"

The question caught her off-guard. "I don't

know. I don't hate him as I'd expected to, but he's very complicated. And he makes me uncomfortable."

Zakton hid a smile. "He makes a lot of men uncomfortable as well. Jor *is* complex; most truly brilliant men are. He's always restless and often impatient and sometimes arrogant, but he's also fair and basically a good man. There's no doubt that he'll be the next Chairman of the Council." And perhaps sooner than he thinks, Zakton thought unhappily.

"But some of what you've seen in him is just the difference between men and women, I think. Men don't show their emotions as much as women do, and they don't talk much about feelings, either."

"You're very different from him," Amala observed. "It's hard to understand how you could be such good friends."

Zakton laughed. "Maybe it's because we're so different, but we both respect those differences. And our families' history has a bit to do with it, too."

A young man brought some food to them, and they ate and talked a while longer. By the time Amala went off to join the women, she knew she had far more than an ally; she had a friend.

Jorlan roamed about his mountain home. Another airsled had been brought up to him, and though he intended to return to the city, he was reluctant to leave. Her presence lingered on here.

He stopped in the doorway of the bedroom she'd used. The flowers were beginning to wilt and the empty box of candy sat on a table next to the jewelry chest. All the clothes he'd given her were still there, too.

He stood there, thinking about his last conversation with Zak, less than an hour ago. Zak was so damned happy to have her up there. Jorlan knew it was absurd to be jealous of him, but he was. He wanted her back—badly. Zak said he should be patient. "She doesn't hate you."

Patience? He'd been born without it, and no one had ever been able to teach it to him, either. He thought he'd already been as patient as he could. He hadn't taken advantage of an innocence that gave a whole new dimension to the word. Not only had she never had a man, she didn't even know she wanted one.

Maybe she doesn't want one, he thought with frustration. Maybe she never will. Maybe her ancestress' threat had come true.

Then he thought about Zak's teasing remark that he made her "uncomfortable." There might be hope, after all.

Amala knew he would come at some point, but she tried to avoid thinking about him. The subject of Jorlan was one she found very difficult. Felis questioned her about him, and she'd had to struggle to describe her feelings. She liked him, but he disturbed her. He fascinated her, but she'd had to get away from him. Felis, being a true friend, had refrained from pointing out the glaring contradictions.

She was able to avoid dwelling on him because her days were very busy. She gathered together the remnants of the Council and succeeded in having both Felis and Shatra, the Semlian closest to Glea, elected to fill the vacancies left by death.

They'd had many meetings, but it was difficult to get the women to focus on any one issue, since there were so very many clamoring for their attention. Their sense of rootlessness didn't help, either. They all knew that Savleen was only a temporary home. They mourned the past, largely ignored the present and feared for the future.

The sickness passed, and most women had now left the hospital, although Amala's mother remained. Doctors came to inoculate them all against various diseases. Most of the women refused to see them, so the doctors showed the nurse-midwives how to give the injections.

And then Jorlan arrived. A young guard passed the word through the women's quarters that Lord Jorlan wished to see Lady Amala. At the time, she was busy writing out again her new set of laws for their society, the original copy having been lost on the island. Zak had offered to show her how to use the computer for her work, but knowing that computers passed things to other computers, Amala refused the offer.

She considered refusing Jorlan's request to

see her, then decided that she could ill afford to antagonize him further. Zak had already told her that the Chairman was in poor health and Jorlan might ascend to that all-important position at any time.

So she reluctantly set her work aside and followed the aide across the courtyard. She hoped that Zak would also be present, since she was already feeling that familiar discomfort.

Her wish was granted when she walked into Zak's quarters and found both men waiting for her, but their grave expressions caused her to stop in the doorway.

"What is it?" she asked as her eyes darted from one man to the other.

It was Zak who spoke. "The Chairman has just announced his intention to resign."

Her eyes slid from Zak to the big, dark man beside him, and she felt again that odd weakness inside. Why did he do this to her? Then she realized that some sort of remark was required.

"I'm sorry. I realize that such a change must be very difficult at a time like this."

When neither man said anything, she inquired about the election of a new Chairman. Zak told her they would be meeting the next day, then he excused himself and left the room before she could say anything more. After the door had closed behind him, she turned reluctantly to Jorlan, who had remained silent all the while.

The silence grew between them. He watched her with that unreadable black gaze. Zak had said he wasn't angry over her abrupt departure and the damage she'd done to his sled, but she wondered now if he might be. In any event, she had to say something.

"I apologize for the damage to your airsled."

His expression didn't change. "And what about the damage to my sanity?"

"I . . . don't understand."

"You took that sled and flew it to the most dangerous area on Volas, and you don't understand that I might have been worried?" His dark brows raised in mock surprise.

"Well, I didn't know that at the time, although it wouldn't have made any difference. I need to be here."

"Doesn't the life of our child mean anything at all to you?"

His use of the phrase "our child" had a strange effect upon her, but she ignored it. "Of course it does. Don't be ridiculous, Jorlan."

But the simple truth was that she hadn't even considered the baby and still didn't think about it. She'd consulted the nurse-midwives and confirmed the pregnancy, but that was all. Pregnancy was a natural part of life. Perhaps he just didn't understand that.

"Jorlan, I don't intend to harm the baby, but neither is pregnancy going to alter my life. That's our way, and you're just going to have to understand that."

"I want you to see the doctors."

"Why? I have the nurse-midwives here."

He waved a hand in dismissal. "They know nothing."

In spite of herself, she smiled. "Oh really? Who do you think has been tending pregnant women and delivering babies for the past hundred years?"

"I insist that you see a doctor. I'll take you to the hospital."

"You are not in a position to insist upon anything," she replied angrily. "And if you continue to bother me like this, I'll deny that the baby is yours."

"You can't deny it. There are others who know."

"They won't admit it unless I agree. I know you had Zak ask them before I came here, and they wouldn't say anything."

He ran a hand through his thick, black hair, and she saw that it was shaking slightly.

"I didn't come here to argue with you," he said distractedly.

"Then why did you come?"

He looked away, shifting his stance slightly. "I just wanted to see you, to be certain you're well and comfortable."

"Thank you for your thoughtfulness. I'm fine and quite comfortable." She paused, then asked, "Will you be the next Chairman?"

Once again, he ran a hand through his hair. "I will be if I want to be."

She gave him a surprised look. "Aren't you sure?"

"If I become Chairman, I'll have to give up my starship command. The Chairman has to remain on Volas."

"I see."

"No, you *don't* see," he said with a trace of anger. "You couldn't possibly see. I knew I'd have to give up space someday, but I never expected it to be this soon. Too damned much is changing right now."

She took a seat, hoping he would do the same. He was pacing about the room like a man possessed. She knew he wasn't angry with her, but she also knew he was showing more emotion than she'd yet seen in him.

"I think maybe I do understand—at least a little. I knew even before the volcano erupted that I would have to leave the island someday, but when it happened, I still wasn't prepared."

He finally did take a seat as he stared at her. "How could you have known that?"

She shrugged. "I don't know, but I did. Some others did, too, but it didn't make it any easier to face. Of course, we didn't have a choice—and you do."

"No, I don't," he said in a quieter tone. "If I don't accept, it could mean problems for all of you. The man who wanted you to be kept away from here would probably become Chairman."

Their eyes met and held. "Please accept it then, Jorlan. It's not just important for us; it's important for all of you, too."

He finally nodded. "I know that."

"We must begin negotiations soon. The women need some stability, some hope in their lives. I know we're not really prisoners here, but it still feels like it."

"And I suppose you'll be the one doing the negotiating," he said with a slight smile.

"That hasn't really been decided—but yes, I assume I will be."

He laughed and shook his head. "If there was ever a reason for me to refuse the chairmanship . . ."

"I don't understand. I thought we've gotten along rather well, all things considered."

His smile remained. "That's just the problem. You haven't considered *all* things."

She felt as though he were toying with her, and she didn't like it. "Jorlan, I don't understand what you're saying."

He stood up. "I know you don't. If I thought you did, I'd be tempted to wring your beautiful neck."

She frowned at him, still not understanding, and he bent toward her. "Just answer one question for me. Are you as comfortable in my presence as you are in Zak's? You've spent about the same amount of time with each of us."

She lowered her gaze and shook her head slowly. He must have already known the answer—no doubt Zak had told him what she'd said—but she couldn't afford to let him think he could intimidate her.

"You're very different. And Zak is my brother."

He extended a hand to her, and she got to her feet. Then, when she tried to withdraw it, he held on. She looked up at him questioningly.

He raised his other hand and cupped it beneath her chin, drawing her face up to meet his. She felt that terrible melting sensation inside again, but she didn't pull away.

He brushed his lips lightly against her cheek, then hovered there, his breath warm against her skin as he spoke.

"Tell me what that discomfort feels like," he murmured, "and tell me if it's worse now."

It was—much worse. She braced a hand against his chest. He was toying with her. He knew exactly what she was feeling.

He backed off slightly, but both arms were encircling her waist. "She failed," he said with satisfaction.

"Who failed?"

"Your damnable ancestress. She tried to make sure women would never want men again, but it didn't work."

Then he drew her against him and lowered his face to hers once more, but this time his mouth brushed against hers, moving softly, teasing her lips open.

Amala heard the echo of his last words as her world spun about her. Her whole body came alive with sensations. His tongue began to probe hers, and she stiffened and tried to draw away from the strangeness. But he wrapped a hand around the back of her head and held her in place until she no longer wanted to get away.

She didn't even know she'd moved her own hand until she felt her fingers threading their way through his hair. From somewhere deep inside her, a moan pushed its way into her throat.

He released her slowly then, as though that sound had been his goal all along. She looked up at him, certain she would see triumph on his face, but what she saw instead was a tenderness that very nearly brought another cry from her. She would never have believed this man capable of such an expression.

"Jorlan . . ." she began, then couldn't quite think what she should say.

"I know," he said with a smile. "Now you're *really* uncomfortable."

She was still trying to gather her scattered wits when he left the room.

Chapter Eight

"We appreciate all your efforts, dear, but the men will do with us as they wish. Aleala so willed it."

Amala fought down her anger. Only the sympathy she saw in Felis' and Shatra's eyes kept her voice calm and reasonable.

"Aleala willed that we should leave the island, but she did not will that men should rule us again. Verta said that we have the power, and we do!"

She certainly had their attention now. All eyes stared at her in shock and wonder.

"Did Verta actually say that?"

"Why did we not know of this?"

"Mava said nothing about any prediction."

Amala stared hard at each of them in turn. "My mother doesn't know. Verta said this to me alone." She paused, then added, "She also said that I am the leader."

The women looked quickly from one to the other, none of them yet willing to speak. Amala just sat there waiting. She felt no guilt at all for having changed Verta's one statement to suit her purposes. After all, if she had the power and she was the leader, then they all had the power.

"I propose that we officially declare Amala to be our Chairman," Shatra stated, breaking the silence.

"But Thurzia is . . ."

Felis interrupted her quietly but firmly. "Thurzia is in the hospital and won't be strong even after she returns to us. Besides, her term is nearly finished in any event."

So Amala was declared to be the new Chairman—or Chair*woman*, as she insisted upon being called. She was pleased to have that status, but she was even more pleased to find that both Felis and Shatra were going to be strong voices on the Council.

"Jorlan has informed me through my brother that the negotiations will begin in one week, when he returns from inspecting his starship. So we have one week to get our priorities straight. That's why I've given you each copies of the proposed changes to our laws. We cannot hope to get all we ask for, but neither will they."

"Amala," asked one of the older members, "how do you expect to force them into giving us anything we ask for? After all, we're virtually prisoners here."

"I honestly believe that a majority of the men do not want to return to the old ways, either. They may have their faults, but they're scarcely the monsters we had believed them to be. They too have changed."

"You're basing that assumption on very limited evidence," Shatra pointed out.

"That's true, but Jorlan and Zakton are the leaders of the two most powerful families, and Jorlan is now Chairman." She made herself sound far more certain than she felt. Zakton she could count on, but Jorlan remained a mystery, perhaps because she couldn't think about him rationally.

"Besides, we still control the population, thanks to you and the Semlians for bringing the herbs."

"But they don't know that," someone pointed out.

"No," Amala admitted. "But I think that I have conveyed the message that we do not come to this negotiation without power. Let them try to guess what it might be."

"We're only safe as long as they don't find them and destroy them," Shatra stated grimly.

They moved on to other matters, but when the meeting was over, Amala sought out Shatra. Something in her tone when she'd made that remark about the herbs had troubled Amala. Felis joined them, and the three women returned to Amala's quarters.

"Shatra, what makes you think the men might discover the herbs? They never come into our quarters, and they wouldn't know what they were in any event."

Shatra gnawed on her lower lip for a moment. "Well, I overheard a conversation just this morning that leads me to believe at least one of the women may be getting friendly with the men."

Both Amala and Felis stared at her in disbelief. "Who?"

She named a girl in her late teens known to both Amala and Felis. They exchanged disgusted looks.

"She hasn't a brain in her head," Felis said with a grimace. "I know she spends a lot of time out in the courtyard, and she has on a different dress every time. It wouldn't surprise me."

"From what I've heard, she's claiming that this man is a kinsman and that she's not doing anything you don't do, Amala, but the women who were talking don't believe her."

"Who is this man?" Amala asked. "Zak has given strict orders that they're to stay away from us, and I'll insist that he get rid of him immediately."

"They didn't mention his name, but it doesn't matter. It will happen. If it's not her, it'll be someone else."

"I think we should hide the herbs in a place known only to the three of us," Felis proposed.

Amala agreed, but her thoughts remained on Shatra's prediction. What would they think if they knew what had happened between Jorlan and her? She'd told no one, not even Felis. How could she? In the moments after he'd left and she'd regained her senses, all their teachings had flooded back, leaving her awash in guilt and shame.

They decided to hide the herbs in an old tunnel that Shatra had discovered during her wanderings about the fortress. It was dank and dusty and obviously hadn't been used in many years. They all agreed that its accidental discovery was unlikely to be repeated by anyone else.

After that, they began the long, difficult task of ordering their demands. More than once, Amala went out into the courtyard at night to stare up at the moon, Ethera, and think about the man she would soon face.

Zakton had brought her not only a copy of the portion of Amala's diary that had been made public via the computer but also another diary, begun when she was still in her early teens. She'd read the version that had been in the computer, which was nothing more than a detailed account of her plans, together with a warning to the men that she would make sure women never wanted them again.

But she hadn't yet read the older diary that covered her marriage to Jorlan and their early years together. Zak had said it was important for her to read it, that it might help her to understand some things.

She had a very uneasy feeling about what she'd find in that diary.

* * *

"Shatra thinks we're being foolish and frivolous," Felis said as she watched Amala admiring herself in the long mirror.

"And I'm worried about the men's reaction to *that.*" She gestured to Amala's pale, silk-clad legs.

"I don't care about their reaction," Amala stated, then turned from the mirror. "No, that's wrong. I want them to react; that's just the point. I want them to see that we're different."

Felis grinned and shook her head. "I think that's going to be very apparent."

Amala drew Felis to her side, and they both stared into the mirror a moment longer. Amala was pleased with what she saw. Felis wore a long, split skirt that just grazed her ankles, topped off with a full, silken shirt and a matching sleeveless jacket. The skirt and jacket were a rich wine shade that set off her short, sleek, dark red hair and dark eyes.

Amala herself wore blue, always her best color. Her dress was full-skirted and high-necked, and over it she too wore a sleeveless jacket, beautifully embroidered in gold and multicolored threads. Zak had brought the jacket to her, saying it was among clothing he'd discovered in a storeroom trunk when he was a child. She preferred to think that it might have belonged to the other Amala, although it could have been anyone's.

But what had drawn Felis' concern was the length of her skirt. It ended just below the knees, leaving her legs bare except for the nearly transparent covering woven for her by a team of women who had worked night and day to have it ready.

Amala was making a statement. It was clear from the clothing they'd quickly manufactured for the women that the men expected them to dress in the long gowns worn by their ancestors. Therefore, Amala was determined they would dress differently.

There was a knock on the door and Shatra came in, wearing loose trousers and high, polished boots with a severe white shirt and a leather jacket. She saw Amala and her initial frown changed slowly to a grin that transformed her rather plain features into a striking handsomeness.

"Zakton will never allow you out of here dressed like that," she said, shaking her head.

"Then the Council will just have to come up here," Amala replied as she picked up the leather case Zakton had given her.

The three women left Amala's rooms and made their way through the building, pausing to acknowledge the astonishment and admiration of the other women. Amala could feel all their hopes closing in on her and prayed silently that she could make good her promises to them.

She'd already won a victory of sorts when Zak had finally agreed that she could pilot her own airsled to the Council headquarters. He'd had a sled brought up in the family's colors of gold and white, then made her practice takeoffs and landings until he was satisfied she could manage.

They walked into the courtyard to find Zakton awaiting them beside the sleds. Amala thought he looked very handsome in his formal white uniform, adorned with their family's crest. Other men had gathered around but remained at a discreet distance. Amala could actually feel the shock in the air as they walked toward the sleds.

"I take it that a statement is being made," Zakton drawled as his blue eyes traveled over the three of them in turn, ending with raised brows as he looked at her legs.

"Very perceptive of you." Amala smiled.

Zakton shook his head with a chuckle. "I feel sorry for Jor."

She wasn't quite sure what he meant, but she shook her head. "I don't. Feeling sorry for one's opponent is a serious mistake."

She climbed into the pilot's seat, Shatra folded her long limbs into one of the two rear seats, but Felis allowed Zakton to help her into the other front seat as she gave him a nervous smile. He bent close to her for a moment and said something Amala couldn't hear. Then he strode off to his own sled, and as Amala waited for him to take off, she turned to Felis with arched brows.

"I couldn't very well refuse his assistance," Felis muttered.

"Did you want to?" Amala asked.

Felis looked away. "He's been very kind to

me. I like him."

"So do I. He's clearly the best of the lot, if I do say so myself."

Amala stared at her friend for a moment, noting the slight flush to her olive skin, and she thought of the other times when she'd seen the two of them together. Could something be happening to Felis as well? The thought frightened her, but she had no time to dwell on it as Zak took off and she started her airsled and followed him.

The women were mostly silent during the journey, each lost in her own thoughts. Their solemnity suited the occasion. All were fully aware of the responsibilities they shared.

Amala's mind drifted back to that other lifetime when she'd sat in the island's small library, studying their laws and laboring over changes. Could she have known even then that it was more than just an exercise born of intellectual boredom?

They'd all worked so hard during the past week, refining the proposed changes, struggling to find exactly the right words. As a result, all but the most religious among them were now suffused with hope.

Amala had told them about the men's elite Space Academy and their sports complex and about her idea for a similar, combined facility for the women with a place of honor for Aleala. Although her faith in the goddess had been shaky at best, she was willing to acknowledge that Aleala represented the protection afforded them all those years. Now they must protect themselves.

The city rose in the distance and Felis and Shatra became animated as they gazed at it. Amala, remembering Zak's warning, paid it no attention as she kept an eye out for other air traffic. There seemed to be far less of it this day, and nothing came close to them as she followed Zak's sled to the far hill where the Council building gleamed in the bright sunlight.

Jorlan paced back and forth across the plaza in front of the Council building, his eyes constantly scanning the skies over the city. The ceremonial sword of the Council Chairman slapped annoyingly against his thigh. He hated the damned thing and wasn't entirely comfortable with what it represented, either.

He'd finally agreed to assume the post of Chairman until this matter with the women was settled. After that, he would reconsider the matter.

What would they demand? Even Zak, who saw his sister regularly, hadn't a clue, except to say that it was certain to be far more than the men were prepared to concede.

He knew he lacked the patience and the diplomacy required of the Chairman, who ruled the Council by persuasion rather than fiat. The Council, he'd told Zak, was nothing more than a collection of over-inflated egos, and yet, this one time, he *had* to persuade them.

Jorlan's feelings about the women were

mixed. He certainly favored some of the changes they were bound to demand—fairness required that—but he knew Zak was right. They would make impossible demands. The situation was already bad enough without *her* role in it. If she wasn't satisfied, he didn't have a chance.

Then he saw two sleds traveling in a direct line over the city, heading in his direction. As they closed that distance, he could see the gold markings.

Under normal circumstances, he probably wouldn't have spotted them until they were about to land, because the skies would have been filled with other sleds, but he'd issued an order grounding all but emergency flights until they arrived. Despite Zak's confidence in her piloting skills, he wasn't taking any chances.

The sleds landed—so perfectly that he couldn't tell which one she piloted—and he hurried toward the pads, eager to see her again but wishing it were anywhere but here.

Before he could reach them, the door to the nearer sled opened and she stepped out. He nearly stumbled as he stared at her. But by the time her eyes met his, he had somehow managed to regain at least some of his aplomb.

Amala climbed out of the sled, then stopped when she saw him. She hadn't expected to find him out here. Behind her, she heard Felis and Shatra getting out and sensed their sudden awareness, too.

She'd never seen him dressed formally before, and the effect was very nearly overwhelming. He wore the same white, close-fitting uniform that Zak wore, but on him the effect was very different.

The fabric clung to his big, hard body, and thick golden braids crisscrossed his broad shoulders. His family's crest was embroidered in gold and silver on his chest and a jeweled sword hung at his side.

Amala was so struck by his appearance that for a moment she forgot her own, but he reminded her quickly as his dark eyes swept over her, pausing for an inordinately long period of time on her legs. By the time he stopped before her, his eyes were glittering with amusement.

"You learn very quickly," he said in a low voice clearly meant for her alone. Then he took her hand and raised it briefly to his lips.

She pulled her hand away, trying to ignore the tingling sensation at the same time she was forcing herself to meet his eyes. Neither was easy.

She introduced him to Shatra and reintroduced him to Felis, whom he acknowledged politely. Then he took her arm and gestured toward the building.

"The Council awaits us, Ladies."

Amala wanted to pull free of him but knew she couldn't do that now. Perhaps he too knew that. Drawing herself up to her full height (which unfortunately wasn't exactly impressive next to him) she made no attempt to match her stride to his, and he quickly slowed down. She decided to count that a victory. On this day, she was very much aware of victories of any kind.

When they reached the Council meeting room, absolute silence greeted them. Amala was sure that sentences must have been left hanging in the suddenly charged atmosphere.

She surveyed the room in dismay. According to law, the Council should number twelve, with the Chairman being the thirteenth member, but there were more than twice that many men in the room.

"Who are all these men?" she asked Jorlan in a low voice.

"The Council members plus the various ministers and their aides. They're the ones who implement our decisions, so they always attend the meetings unless we declare a closed session. I can do that if you wish."

Amala hesitated, flicking a glance toward Felis and Shatra, who obviously shared her dismay. Then she shook her head. To demand that they leave might indicate that she felt intimidated.

Some men had already been seated at the big round table, while others were standing around in small groups. Now, as though at some unseen signal, the paralysis that had affected them all vanished, and they began to move to their seats. The ministers and their aides sat in rows of chairs along the walls.

Jorlan's chair was conspicuous because of its ornateness, and Amala assumed that the empty one beside him was for Zakton. Opposite those two chairs were three empty chairs, both smaller and somewhat less elegant than the members' chairs. She wondered if it were a deliberate choice, or whether they simply didn't have any more of the other chairs.

Zak went to his seat, and Jorlan began to make the introductions after he'd led them to their chairs. He stood behind her as he introduced the members, one hand resting lightly on her shoulder. Inclined as she was to read hidden meaning into every gesture and word, Amala wondered what sort of signal his gesture was sending.

She didn't bother to memorize their names, since she was far more interested in their reactions. She carefully made eye contact with each man as he was introduced, and she hoped that Felis and Shatra, who sat on either side of her, were doing the same. She'd warned them that such things were very important—even more so for them, since alone among this group, they weren't from Great Families.

But as the lengthy introductions proceeded, Amala realized that Felis and Shatra might as well not be there for all the attention they were receiving. She and she alone was the unwavering focus of the members' attention. Some of them didn't even appear to be blinking.

"You are the leader. You have the power."

Verta's words hung there in her mind, more prophetic than ever. She felt that power now, even though she still didn't fully understand it.

Then Jorlan's hand squeezed her shoulder lightly in a gesture she assumed was meant to be reassuring, and he went to his chair. He gestured to a man sitting directly behind him with a small machine of some sort on his lap.

"Official records of Council meetings are kept in two ways," he explained. "Jasso is the Council Secretary and keeps a written record. This provides an oral record." He gestured to a dome-shaped object in the center of the table.

Amala merely nodded as she opened her case and withdrew some papers. She was conscious of the fact that her every movement was being closely followed by all eyes. Some of them, she thought, seemed almost in shock, while others betrayed a wariness and a few wore looks of steely determination. Certainly none looked apathetic.

"Do you have an opening statement, Lady Amala?" Jorlan asked formally, his own expression, as usual, totally unreadable.

"Yes, I do," she replied in a calm, clear voice. She had a written copy of it before her, but she had also memorized it. She began to speak, her eyes deliberately moving over all of them in turn.

Jorlan sat there trying to maintain a neutral expression. In truth, he was reeling from shock that only grew greater as she spoke. She was magnificent; there was no other word for it. If she'd been born male, he suspected he might not be sitting where he was now. He was certainly no politician himself, but he recognized a master of the process—even if this particular master had the most beautiful legs he'd ever seen.

He stifled a smile as he thought about those legs, now unfortunately (or perhaps thankfully) hidden from his view. He realized he'd been wrong to have assumed she'd dressed that way to be seductive. She knew nothing of seduction. If women in the old days had worn short skirts, she would now be wearing a long one.

Her speech was brief but eloquent. She struck the right note at the beginning by thanking the men for their assistance when the volcano erupted and for their forethought in preparing such comfortable quarters at Savleen.

Then, with only a brief mention of the old days, she went on to speak of the opportunity now before them to transform their society. The women, she said, were fully prepared to shoulder their portion of the burden for furthering progress, and they understood completely that with rights come responsibilities.

Then she told them a bit about life on the island and admitted their ignorance regarding men. With a quick glance at Jorlan, she related the tale of her awakening in his home to the belief that his Feloth servant was a man.

When she had finished telling that tale, there was genuine laughter in the room, followed by a visible relaxation.

Jorlan was caught somewhere between amazement and a respect that grew with each word. She claimed to know nothing of men, and yet no practiced seductress could have enchanted them more thoroughly.

By the time she concluded her speech with the story about her rewriting of their laws, Jorlan had come to the stunning realization that his idealized version of her—the one he'd clung to all these years—was gone. In its place was a growing certainty that this woman could never truly belong to him.

She passed typed copies of her proposals around the table. Jorlan knew that she'd refused to use the computer because she feared losing secrecy, so Zakton had borrowed an old typewriter from the technology museum and showed her how to use it.

There was silence in the room as the men read the pages, a silence broken occasionally by an indrawn breath or a muttered word. Amala continued to scan each member regularly, but it was Jorlan upon whom she now focused most of her attention. He frowned slightly a few times, but otherwise she couldn't begin to read his thoughts.

"At least no one is laughing," she whispered to Felis and Shatra. "That's a hopeful sign."

When they had finished, she spoke again. "None of these items is negotiable, but what *is* negotiable are the methods and the time frame for achieving them. We recognize that societies cannot be remade quickly, and we also recognize that given the limitations of our existence on the island, we must be educated to this world you've created."

Every brow in the place shot up at the beginning of her statement, and the men began to shift about in their seats and cast uneasy looks at each other. Only a few began to look decidedly hostile. Jorlan sat there in a relaxed posture, his dark eyes never leaving her face. She finally met his gaze squarely and held it until he was the one who looked away.

They'd all expected some sort of uproar at this point, but the men just sat there, glancing from the papers to her and back again.

"Are there questions?" Jorlan asked with what she thought was a trace of amusement.

So it finally began, although in a far less rancorous manner than she'd expected. Someone asked a sharp question about her proposal for the abolition of the class system, and Amala admitted that it could not be accomplished quickly or easily, but that it must be a stated goal.

"Why?" someone else asked. "The system has served us well for centuries."

"Then why is it that you've permitted men of the lower classes to attend the Space Academy and to be promoted to high rank? Aren't you admitting that exceptional abilities know no class distinctions? By limiting the opportunities of the lower classes, you're depriving our society of necessary talents."

Left unsaid was the fact that it was the women and their control over the population that had forced them to open such opportunities as now existed. There simply weren't enough Great Family men anymore.

Zakton spoke up for the first time. "I like your idea of creating a parliament whose members are elected from any and all classes. As my fellow members know, I've proposed that many times."

"Possibly that's where she got the idea," one member grumbled.

"No, it isn't," Amala stated. "None of this was discussed with any man—not even my brother."

"Marriage between the classes is shameful," an older member spat out.

"No one is suggesting that you or members of your family should do so," Amala responded mildly. "We're only saying that there should be no legal barriers to such unions. No one is to be forced into any kind of marriage."

And so it went. To her utter amazement, the one item that drew no questions at all was the admission of three women to Council membership. Amala didn't know how to interpret that. Did it mean they would accept it, or did it mean that they weren't even prepared to discuss it?

When the questions had finally ended, Jorlan made a brief closing statement in which he assured them that their requests would be given fair consideration, and that none of them wished to repeat the mistakes of the past. Amala thanked him formally, and the three women took their leave.

They were to stay that night at Zakton's home, and they all remained prudently silent as his aide carried them by airsled to the big walled compound at the city's edge. Zak would join them later, and brother and sister planned to visit their mother in the hospital.

Amala knew that Zak wasn't looking forward to this visit, but she'd pointed out that he could not avoid his mother much longer. She would be released within the week and would then be coming to Savleen, after which she would certainly come to live in the family compound.

They landed on a pad near the middle of the sprawling compound Amala had glimpsed only from the air. As soon as Zak's aide had departed, they all began talking at once. Felis and Shatra both seemed far more hopeful than they had before the session. Amala was somewhat less sanguine but could not bring herself to say so.

"Jorlan still scares me," Felis said, "even if he wasn't paying any attention at all to me."

Shatra laughed. "I think you shocked him, Amala. He wasn't expecting you to be so eloquent and forceful."

"I doubt that he'll make that mistake again," Amala replied with a smile. "And I still think he's our ally."

"You're probably right, although maybe not for the reason you think," Shatra stated. "I think if he helps us, it will only be because he's afraid of angering you."

Jorlan afraid of her? Amala smiled. "I'll take victory any way I can get it."

Then they finally turned their attention to the

magnificence surrounding them. There were large formal gardens with statuary and fountains and small, secluded seating arrangements. Thick woods surrounded the gardens and hid the smaller homes Amala had seen from the air.

The big house, where Zakton lived, was built of a mellow golden stone with a dark red, tiled roof. As she stared at it, Felis remarked that five or six of their little cottages on the island could fit inside it. Even the smaller houses were far bigger than anything on the island. Zak had told her that in recent years the old way of extended families living together inside these walled compounds had begun to change. Most of their relatives lived elsewhere, and many of the homes were now empty.

As the women walked through the gardens toward the big house, a Feloth suddenly appeared, pushing a wheelbarrow filled with plants. Both Felis and Shatra reacted with startled cries, even though they knew of the creatures' existence.

"You must have been terrified," Felis said as she stared at the creature, who paused to stare back before returning to its chore.

"I was. Jorlan found it very amusing." She remembered his laughter as they sat beneath the tree after she'd escaped from his house. The image was etched on her brain with startling clarity. Had she begun to change her opinion of him as early as that?

"I thought it was a good idea of yours to let

them know what we'd been taught about them by telling them that story," Shatra said as they resumed walking toward the house. "It may help them to understand, and if we're lucky, it might even force them to rethink what they've been taught about us."

"That was exactly my purpose," Amala agreed as they walked up to the ornately carved front door.

The splendor that greeted them as they stepped into the foyer silenced them all. Unlike the Council building and Jorlan's mountain home, the furnishings here were very old but wore their age beautifully. Gleaming dark woods and deep, rich colors vied for their attention, until they stepped from the foyer into the Great Room.

All three women gasped as they stared at the huge portrait that hung in a place of honor. Zak had told her about the portrait and Amala had been dimly aware of the fact that the first Amala had grown up here, but as she walked across the thick carpet to face the portrait, she truly felt it for the first time.

"This is where she grew up," Amala said softly. "She lived here until she married Jorlan."

"That must have been not long after this portrait was done," Felis said in the same low voice. "She looks like she must have been about eighteen."

The nearly life-sized figure stared down at

them, her Great Family ring seeming too heavy for the delicate hand that rested on an arm of a handsome chair.

Shatra looked from the portrait to the room, then took Amala's arm. "Look! I think that's the very chair!"

And so it was—or one exactly like it. The women were silent for a long time, staring at that near-mythic figure who seemed to be staring back in silent challenge.

We've come home, Amala told her silently, and I promise you it will be different this time.

Then they wandered through the rest of the house until they were too sated by its luxury to want to see more. Just as they returned to the Great Room, another Feloth appeared and through gestures managed to inquire if they wanted to eat. All three discovered they were indeed very hungry, and the creature led them to a shaded terrace, where several more carried out platters of fruits and cheeses. Their stay at Savleen had awakened an interest in all sorts of new foods, and they began to devour everything set before them.

"Are you going to marry Jorlan?" Shatra asked suddenly.

"No! I intend to marry no one! There is far too much work to be done, enough to last my lifetime. I plan to live here. Zak said I could either live in this house with him or choose one of the other houses."

"That could affect his decision about the

marriage laws," Felis pointed out quietly. "I don't doubt that he expects you to marry him."

"Yes, I've thought about that," Amala admitted. But she hadn't decided what to do about it yet.

Felis was right; Jorlan probably *did* expect her to marry him. It wasn't really fair for her to allow him to continue believing that, however convenient it might be for the women's goals.

They had just finished their meal when a young boy suddenly ran onto the terrace, followed by an elderly man. The boy's bright blue eyes and pale golden hair told Amala immediately who he must be. He had stopped a short distance away and was smiling at her shyly.

"Levyan!" she exclaimed, suddenly feeling a warmth she'd never felt toward any child. She'd seen him only as a tiny baby. His mother had never recovered from his birth, and Amala and her mother had cared for him until he was sent across.

She leapt from her seat and held out her arms, and the boy ran to her with a delighted laugh. "Aunt Amala! Father said you would be coming here."

Amala could scarcely bring herself to let him go, and she began to understand as she never had before how much they had all suffered—men as well as women. The elderly man introduced himself as her great-uncle and Levyan's tutor. In his eyes, too, she saw the meaning of family—a whole family.

Then she thought of her own baby and how he or she would never have to suffer such a loss.

Zakton arrived late in the afternoon, followed by Jorlan. Felis and Shatra had wandered off to explore the far corners of the compound, while Amala had remained behind in order to become better acquainted with her nephew.

When the sleds arrived, they were playing on a grassy area near the landing pads. Lev had a shiny red disc he called a freba, and Amala was trying to learn how to catch and throw it, not an easy task since it never sailed straight.

As soon as the men appeared, the boy sailed the freba in their direction. Jorlan caught it easily, then flicked it back into Lev's outstretched hands. Then he tossed it aside and instead launched himself at his father, who knelt to give him a big hug. After that, the boy ran to Jorlan, who swept him off his feet and whirled him around to the accompaniment of delighted squeals.

Amala stood there watching all this with speechless astonishment. Never would she have guessed that men would be so affectionate and playful with children. Jorlan continued to hold Lev, cradling him against his shoulder as they talked. Zak walked over to her, his smile very broad. He cupped her shoulders with both hands.

"I was very proud of you this morning. Not even your namesake could have done better."

Amala basked for a moment in the compliment, then turned serious. "But are they persuaded, Zak? I just couldn't tell."

He shrugged. "It's too soon to know. There's some resistance, but . . ."

"About what specifically?"

He glanced at Jorlan, then shook his head. "Jor and I both told the Council that we wouldn't discuss this with you out of their presence. Our situation is delicate, Sister."

She sighed in disappointment but nodded. "I can understand that. It's just that we hoped to gain some sense of their thinking."

Then she stared at Jorlan, who had just leapt high into the air with a surprising grace for such a big man. "I don't even know what he thinks," she muttered.

Zakton chuckled. "Perhaps that's because he doesn't know himself."

They were still standing there watching the freba game when Felis and Shatra returned. Both women made no attempt to hide their shock as they gaped at Jorlan. Zakton saw their reaction and laughed.

"Well, I guess that's the end of the monster myth."

Amala laughed. "But it still seems very strange to us."

"Well, in truth, if the boys had been raised by their mothers, perhaps we would never have learned to be good parents. That may be one bit of good that came from it."

Amala watched as Jorlan made a diving catch, rolled over on the grass and flung the disc back to Lev, who was laughing too hard to even try to catch it.

"I wouldn't have been surprised to see *you* play with him—but Jorlan?"

"I've been away so much of the time, and if Jorlan was home when I wasn't, he took Lev to his house. They're very close." Then he grinned at her.

"I wouldn't be surprised to find that this little game has been staged for your benefit, though."

If Zak was right, the performance had obviously worked, since Amala was still thinking about it as they all sat down to dinner later. In any event, she could scarcely forget it, since Jorlan's white uniform still bore a few grass stains.

They were joined at dinner by the great-uncle Amala had met earlier and by a cousin she hadn't yet met. Conversation flowed with surprising ease, owing largely to Zakton's gregarious nature, but even Jorlan made a special attempt to draw both Felis and Shatra into conversation. He lacked Zakton's easygoing charm, but he still exuded a powerful attraction of his own that Amala could see was having its effect upon the women.

Nevertheless, for all the attention he showered on the other two women, it was Amala who felt the full force of his powers. Each time their eyes met, she was transported back to those moments in Zak's quarters at Savleen. Shame vied with pleasure, and it was a stand-off.

After dinner, Amala and Zakton prepared to leave for the hospital, and Jorlan took his leave as well. Remembering her decision to discuss marriage with him, she told him that she needed to speak with him soon. He suggested that Zakton bring her to his home later.

The first meeting between mother and son was difficult, but not as tense as Amala had feared. Zakton was clearly uncomfortable and trying not to show it. Their mother, who looked healthier than Amala had seen her in years, was hesitant and shy toward her son.

In the end, it was Levyan who brought them together, as Amala explained her attempts to learn his games. Lady Mava asked many questions about her grandson, and his proud father went on at considerable length about his accomplishments.

When they were taking their leave, Lady Mava kissed her daughter, then extended her hand to her son. After a moment's hesitation, Zakton bent and kissed her cheek.

When they were back in the airsled, he took Amala's hand and squeezed it. "I'm glad you pushed me into this visit. We may never be truly mother and son, but I think we can become friends."

The evening skies were filled with sleds, and several times the warning bell sounded to indicate that other sleds were too close. After he had executed a sharp turn, Zakton cursed under his breath.

"Something is going to have to be done about all this damned traffic, particularly if the women are going to be flying, too."

"Are there many accidents?" Amala asked, staring at the crowded sky over the city.

"Surprisingly few, actually. The newer sleds are equipped with devices that automatically turn the sled if the pilot doesn't react in time. I think we'll have to ban those without that equipment. I'd been opposed to it because it would put poorer people at a disadvantage. The avoiders are an expensive option, but I'm afraid it will become necessary. Perhaps some sort of subsidy can be arranged for those who can't afford it, or since Jorlan has a controlling interest in the largest manufacturer of sleds, maybe he can be persuaded to do something about it."

"But surely the sleds aren't necessary to get around in the city?" Amala asked. "I saw ground vehicles."

"They aren't necessary, but everyone prefers them—and the rural folk must use them to get to the city."

He brought the sled down at Jorlan's compound, and Amala asked him to join them. She wasn't sure she wanted to face Jorlan alone after that last time, and she had no objection to her brother's hearing what she had to say to him.

But Zakton shook his head. "I've spent little time of late with Lev, and I want to get back before he goes to bed. Jor will bring you back."

Jorlan was waiting for her as she climbed

reluctantly out of the sled. A great stone house much like Zak's loomed behind him. As they walked toward it, he inquired about the meeting between mother and son. She told him it had gone better than she'd expected.

"I envy him," Jorlan said with a quiet sincerity.

She said nothing. She was learning that silence was best in such moments. Jorlan would never be as open about his feelings as Zak was, but he was willing to give her glimpses of another man from time to time.

They walked toward the house in silence, passing through fragrant gardens with bubbling fountains. He led her into the house through the terrace doors, and she found herself in a small but comfortably furnished room, a room that looked very masculine with its dark leather and wood paneling. But she barely noticed the furnishings. She uttered a small cry of surprise when she saw the large painting propped against a chair.

"I brought it out of storage to show you," he explained. "That was their wedding portrait."

Shivers ran through her, and she wrapped her arms about herself. It could have been a portrait of the two of them.

"They looked so happy," she murmured in disbelief.

The couple stood beside each other, with her golden head just barely touching his broad shoulder. His arm encircled her slim waist, and her fingers were entwined with his.

"They *were* happy," Jorlan said from behind her. "Their marriage was a rarity for its time. Most marriages then were made for political or dynastic reasons."

"But I'd always been told that theirs was, too—that he chose her to end the feuds between our families."

"I don't doubt that was part of it, but from what he wrote in his diary, he certainly wasn't unhappy about it. And neither was she. I thought Zak gave you a copy of her personal diary from that time."

"He did. I just haven't had time to read it yet." What she lacked wasn't time; it was courage. Now she was both more curious and more uneasy about it. The couple in the portrait seemed to mock all that she had believed about them.

"What did you want to discuss with me?" he asked neutrally.

She cast one last look at the portrait before resolutely turning her back on it. She wished that she hadn't seen it, especially not now.

"Is it your intention to marry me?" she asked, facing him squarely.

His shock was evident, and for a moment she felt relieved. Perhaps she'd misjudged his intentions, but then he nodded, his eyes locked on hers.

"I am not going to marry, Jorlan—not you or anyone," she said firmly. "There is too much I must do, more than a lifetime's work. Marriage would be too . . . distracting."

He just continued to stare at her, and she felt the tension rise in the quiet room.

"I wanted to tell you this now to be certain that my decision won't have any effect upon the Council's deliberations. You can't base any decisions you make as Chairman on our . . . situation."

"I can't?"

"No. If you wish to marry, surely you can find someone. And if our child is a boy, you can certainly see him as often as you want."

He rubbed his jaw, and his black eyes narrowed to slits. "Let me get this straight. You expect to keep the baby even if it's a boy."

"Well, of course. We're not on the island anymore, so there's no reason not to."

Anger flushed his face with dark red, and she backed away slightly, shocked at his reaction.

"Just what do you think I am, Amala—some prize animal you can use for stud and then ignore?"

"I don't understand what you're talking about."

He waved a hand angrily. "No, of course you don't. The technique used by the women was originally developed to breed better livestock. It was never intended to be used for people."

"Even so, I don't see what that has to do with this."

His anger grew again. "If you have a son, he's

mine. Naturally, you can have him from time to time."

She sank into a chair as her treacherous mind replayed that scene with Lev one more time. He was serious; she knew that.

He walked over and bent close to her, bracing his long arms on the chair as he stared down at her.

"Please explain to me how marriage will 'distract' you from your work."

She drew back as far as possible and looked up at him. "Well, that should be obvious."

"It isn't. I'm waiting for an explanation."

She looked down. "I don't want a whole brood of children. This will be the only one."

"You don't have to have a whole brood," he replied with infuriating calm. "Now let's talk about the real reason you're afraid of marriage."

"If we're married, we'll have children. That's what happens."

"That's what used to happen. We can prevent that now. I told you that before."

"But you'll control how many, won't you?"

"It seems to me that that decision should be a joint one, don't you think?"

"What I think is that you're not telling me the truth, Jorlan. I know you men have hated having no control over the population."

He backed off and sat down opposite her. "That was true for a time, but with no real wars anymore, it isn't important. We do lose some men in space from time to time, but not very often. You must have noticed that."

"I still don't believe you," she persisted, even though she was beginning to want to believe him.

"It's the truth. And it's also the truth that you don't want marriage because you're afraid of what you're already feeling."

His expression softened, and his voice became lower. "You'll get over that fear, Amala. I promise you."

She ignored that caressing tone. "I may not understand what's happening between us, but I know what it leads to—slavery."

"How can it? You're demanding that the laws be changed, and they will be."

She said nothing. He was right, and she hated having him be right.

"This morning I saw a woman who probably deserves to sit in the Chairman's seat more than I do. Now I see a woman who can't seem to think logically. I find this very confusing."

His eyes were lit with humor, and Amala found herself responding to it. "Well, I'm confused, too," she admitted with a smile.

"Come here," he said softly as he held his arms out to her. "Let's enjoy our confusion together."

She got up without even thinking—but then stopped just beyond his reach. "I think you know exactly what you're doing."

"Then you're giving me entirely too much

credit, because I don't. This is new to me, too."

"But you said there were women on Bethusa."

"There were, but this is different." He finished the sentence by leaning forward and grasping her arms, then drawing her down onto his lap.

Sensation after sensation washed over her as his mouth found hers and his tongue began a delicate probe. She barely recognized her own body as his hands moved over her. Liquid fire coursed through her. A voice that couldn't be hers moaned, and he answered with a deep groan.

His mouth left hers reluctantly and began to brush softly against her throat. She was totally aware of his hard body against her softness, of a just barely leashed control in him.

How could women have denied themselves this for all these years? She wondered if he could possibly be feeling what she felt and wanted to ask him, but his mouth had moved back to hers again and all that came from her throat was another moan.

Finally, with another groan, he raised his head and leaned it against the chair back as he traced her mouth with a fingertip.

"If I asked you to stay with me tonight, you would, wouldn't you?" he asked in a low, hoarse voice.

She hesitated. There was no point denying that she wanted to, but how could she explain it to Felis and Shatra? It would seem like a betrayal. She told him that, slowly and hesitantly, and to her very great relief, he nodded.

"I can be satisfied for now with knowing that you want to." Then he threw back his head and laughed.

"These negotiations are going to move very quickly. I can guarantee you that."

Chapter Nine

Despite Jorlan's promise, the negotiations seemed to move very slowly. Amala returned to Savleen, but she flew down to meet with the Council on two more occasions. Both times she left feeling hopeful, then descended into pessimism even before she'd returned to the fortress.

The members still gave away nothing of their feelings on most issues. Sometimes their questions and comments infuriated her, but she maintained an outward calm even as she seethed inwardly. And she had learned quickly to speak their language—the language of logic rather than of emotions. If she was certain of nothing else, she knew she had gained their respect, and that was no small victory.

Felis and Shatra did not accompany her on

these occasions. The invitation had been for her only. When she'd complained to Zak about that blatant slight, he'd told her that while the Council might be willing to permit female representation, they weren't going to permit lower-class women. To do so would require permitting lower-class men to serve as well, and virtually none of the aristocratic rulers of Volas were willing to consider that.

When she pressed him about Jorlan's feelings on that subject, Zak told her to ask him herself. She wasn't sure she wanted to, since something in Zak's tone hinted at the possibility that the two friends had disagreed on this issue.

Felis and Shatra took the news with far more equanimity than Amala had. Although both of them pointed out that Amala hadn't needed their assistance at the first meeting and was clearly capable of facing the men on her own, Amala was sure that they had adopted an attitude of resignation insofar as abolishment of the class system was concerned. More than ever, she was determined to rid their society of such unfairness.

Zak, who by his own admission was a detail man, had been assigned the task of working out the details for the actual assimilation of the women into the all-male world. When pressed by Amala, he admitted that he'd volunteered for the assignment.

"A lot can get changed between the Council's decisions and the actual implementation. Those ministries often operate like little kingdoms," he told her. "I want to be sure it works as it should."

Amala, who was definitely not a detail person, was shocked to realize just how many problems the situation posed. One area in which she knew there was nearly unanimous agreement among the Council members was the ownership of property. But how could that be carried out? The women had no money with which to buy anything, not even food and clothing.

And there were so many other issues such as housing when they left Savleen, education of a practical kind that would enable them to live in a very different world—and the matter of protection.

The women's demands had been made public, so that men in the city and small towns and the farming communes all knew what changes were being proposed. Amala learned that Zak had managed to persuade the Council to set up a special vidcom channel through which all citizens could register their preferences regarding matters before the Council. The Council was in no way bound by these opinions, of course.

"They agreed to it to silence my nagging about a parliament like the one you proposed, but I make sure they at least hear what people say," Zak told her with his mischievous grin. "They call them my weather reports. If they're discussing farm policy, for example, they'll say,

'How's the weather out on the communes?'—and they don't mean the atmospheric conditions."

Amala was learning a lot from her brother, although she doubted that she would ever be as accepting as he was or as willing to compromise.

Amala and her cousin Gemma exchanged worried glances and left the room quietly. As she closed the door, Amala looked back one last time at the slight, gray-haired woman who sat in the corner in an old rocking chair with her head lowered.

Gemma wiped away the tears that rimmed her gray-blue eyes. "I'm sorry to be bothering you with this, Amala. I know you're very busy, but I just don't know what to do with Mother. You see how thin she is; she hardly eats anything. I think she really wants to die."

Amala took her cousin's arm. "You're not bothering me. She's my aunt, after all. Let's walk outside. Some fresh air might help."

The two women walked through the long corridors where snatches of conversations drifted on the night air, along with the scent of woodsmoke from fireplaces. Summer was drawing to a close up here in the mountains.

Amala was feeling very guilty for having ignored her aunt until now, even though she was busy. She'd been aware of the fact that the woman was among those who had not made the transition well, but she'd just assumed that sooner or later she and the others who clung to the goddess would come to their senses. Now she began to realize that might not happen—for her aunt, at least. Most of the others appeared to be adjusting.

"I talked to Zak several days ago," Gemma told her as they walked out into the courtyard. "He's been so kind. He had me talk by vidcom to a psychologist."

Amala nodded. Despite her concern, she was amused to hear the women use new terms like vidcom so casually. It was amazing how quickly they were all taking such wonders for granted. She herself already treated the airsled like nothing more than a flying version of the jepsa.

"Yes," she said, "I've met the man. He's on the Council and one of our strongest supporters, I think." He also makes me uncomfortable, she said to herself. He seems to be dissecting every word, every gesture.

"What did he say?" she asked as they strolled slowly through the gardens the men had created for them in one part of the courtyard.

"He called it post-traumatic stress and said it's happened to the men as well, after battles and following accidents in space or in the mines. He said it's very important for her to talk about her feelings and that I should let her know I understand those feelings. He even offered to come up here to talk to her himself, but I explained that she'd never be willing to talk to a man. She won't even talk to Zak, and she knows he's family."

"And she won't talk to you or me, either," Amala sighed. "I really thought that telling her about the memorial to Aleala would arouse her interest."

"I did, too—but nothing! It's so frustrating!" She paused to draw a shaky breath. "Zak says that if she doesn't begin to eat better, we'll have no choice but to put her in the hospital so they can feed her through her veins. That sounds horrible—and going to the hospital would kill her. I know it!"

Amala suspected sadly that was true. "Mother will be released from the hospital within a few days, and she's decided to come here. Zak wanted her to stay at his home, but she wants to be here with the rest of us. They've always gotten along well, so perhaps she can get her to talk."

Gemma nodded but with little enthusiasm. Amala was concerned about her cousin as well. She seemed so depressed. They'd never really been all that close, since Gemma too had spent most of her time in the worship of the goddess. Given Amala's well-known lack of interest in Aleala, the two women had had little to say to each other.

"Why did she desert us?" Gemma asked quietly. "We were happy there, and now it's all gone."

"I don't think she really deserted us, Gemma," Amala said gently. "I think this was part of her plan from the beginning. We needed time to become stronger, and the men needed time to grow gentler."

She thought about Zak's remark that the men would never have learned to be good fathers if the women had been around. And she knew they would never have stopped making war.

She told Gemma about Zak's remark and about the men on the Council whom she knew supported their demands.

"None of that would have happened if we hadn't gone to the island. I truly believe that it was all part of the goddess' plan for all of us."

Gemma smiled a little. "But you never believed in her."

Amala sighed. "I didn't exactly disbelieve, either. I just felt so imprisoned on the island, so locked into the past. Maybe I'm better able to believe in Aleala now because I think I understand her plan."

They had passed through the garden area and were now approaching the outer wall of the fortress. The view from the top was spectacular with one moon full and the other approaching fullness. Amala suggested they climb up there, but Gemma shook her head.

"I'd better get back to Mother. Perhaps she's had time to think about what you said and will want to talk. I know she listened."

The two women hugged each other, and Amala murmured some encouraging words, then Gemma slipped away into the darkness.

Amala picked her way through the crumbling

stone to the top of the old wall. Her mind was filled with problems: her aunt, the council—and Jorlan. There seemed nothing she could do about the first two but wait. Jorlan, however, was a different matter.

She wrapped her arms about herself as she stared up at the brilliant night sky. Those memories of that night at his house wouldn't go away. She could summon up all the feelings she'd had as though it were happening all over again. Even the shame she'd felt was nearly gone, because she now knew that what she'd felt was natural, not a base, primitive feeling to be cast aside.

She'd read Amala's personal diary. It was written in a style so vivid and alive with feeling that Amala had felt as though the woman herself were sitting there talking to her.

All the emotion that had been missing from her writings after the exodus were contained in those pages. She *had* loved Jorlan. She'd wanted no one else from the moment she met him. She'd gone to their marriage bed willingly, even eagerly, and she'd continued to love him all the while she was forging her plans. Time after time she wrote that she wasn't sure she could go through with it, even as she made more plans.

Now, finally, Amala knew she'd been right. There *had* been a deep, terrible pain in her ancestress' writings on the island, the pain of a love she'd never forgotten, perhaps had never given up.

Was love worth that pain? She knew that

what she felt for Jorlan was the beginning of love. Should she let it happen? Should she take that risk, when there was so much she had to do? In the end, might Jorlan not turn out to be just like his ancestor? From Amala's description of that long ago warrior, she could certainly see similarities that went well beneath the surface.

She sighed and lowered her head. Too many questions and no answers. And how she hated indecision!

As she turned slightly to start back down from the wall, something out there in the darkness caught her eye. She frowned and peered into the deep shadows beyond the wall.

The moonlight was reflecting off something just inside the woods that came within 100 meters or so of the wall. Her frown deepened. An airsled? It was difficult to tell, but she thought she saw the outline of one. How could there be an airsled out there? They all landed within the walls on the far side of the great courtyard.

She wondered if it could be a derelict, then quickly dismissed that thought. She'd been up here many times before, by day as well as by night, and she hadn't seen anything out there.

A feeling of uneasiness rippled through her as she started down from the wall. Perhaps she'd better go report this to Zak. She was about halfway down the pile of rubble when she heard the scream.

Or was it a scream? It was cut off abruptly, leaving only silence. Her uneasiness edged toward terror, then backed off again. It could have been a nightbird; she'd heard them before. She peered into the courtyard. In the area before her, where the men had created a garden for them, there were scattered low lights, but from her vantage point those lights did little more than cast the area around them into deeper shadow. She held her breath and listened carefully but could hear nothing. The thick stone walls of the buildings held all sounds of the women inside, and the men's quarters were too far away. The buildings in between were empty.

Finally, she proceeded the rest of the way to the courtyard and began to hurry through the garden area. The huge tubs that contained flowers and shrubs and even small trees had been arranged to provide privacy for those who wandered there, but now it seemed like a threatening maze to her.

Instead of taking the shorter path that would have led back to the women's quarters, Amala went the long way through the gardens toward the men's building.

She turned a corner, and suddenly there were two dark figures ahead of her. The light between them prevented her from seeing them well, but she knew they were male—and they weren't wearing the light tan uniforms of Zak's men.

She ran around the planter that separated them, but they were too fast for her. As the one in front lunged for her, she heard a male voice cry out triumphantly, "That's her!"

She sidestepped and managed to elude his

grasp, then started to run again, but she'd only gotten a few steps before she was seized from behind. As she tried to twist out of the man's grasp, she lost her footing and fell.

The fall momentarily stunned her, and before she could scream, the dark figure had started to throw himself on her. She drew up a knee and kicked with all her might, and he toppled over with a cry of pain.

The other man hesitated just long enough to permit her to scramble to her feet and scream. As her cry pierced the silence, two other shadowy figures appeared. The man she'd kicked started to get up with a groan, and as Amala took off again, she heard their voices.

"That's her!"

"Forget it! Let's get out of here!"

She ran around the side of a planter and tripped over its edge. As she was picking herself up again, another group of men appeared, this time in the familiar tan uniforms.

"Over there!" She pointed. "They tried to attack me. I think they have an airsled outside the wall."

All but one of the men took off in the direction she indicated. The one who remained behind helped her to her feet. Even though she knew him, his touch sent shivers through her.

"Are you all right, Lady Amala?" he asked anxiously.

She nodded. "But I thought I heard a scream earlier. They might have hurt someone else."

At that point they were interrupted by the

sound of running feet, and Zak appeared with several more men. She ran to him gratefully, and his touch soothed her. She repeated her story, and Zak sent the men off to look for another victim.

"Zak, I should go with them. If someone's been hurt, even your men might frighten her."

Without waiting for his reply, she ran off after the men. He hurriedly caught up to her.

The men carried bright flashlights as they began to search the narrow pathways between the abandoned buildings. Each time the beam revealed empty stone walls, Amala's concern lessened. She had nearly convinced herself that what she'd heard had indeed been a nightbird, when one of the men shouted.

"In here!"

Zak tried to restrain her, but she slipped out of his grasp and ran to the alleyway. Before she even turned the corner, she heard another scream, pitifully thin this time.

Gemma lay huddled against a wall, her dress in shreds and her face nearly unrecognizable. Her pale eyes stared wildly at the man who held the flashlight and was approaching her with what he intended to be words of reassurance. Amala pushed him aside.

"Get out of here! Call a nurse and get Felis and Shatra!"

She heard Zak repeat her order as she ran to Gemma. When she reached out to touch her cousin, she flinched and huddled even deeper into the corner, her eyes wild.

"Gemma, it's Amala. These men won't hurt you, and the others are gone." She was shaking inside but managed to keep her voice calm.

Gemma began to sob, and Amala asked her where she was hurt. She could see the scratches and bruises on her face and arms. She tore off her shawl and wrapped it around her cousin's shaking shoulders.

"They . . . hurt me!" Gemma cried as her tremors became worse.

"But where are you hurt besides your face and arm?" Amala asked gently.

She heard the voices of Felis and Shatra and Zak behind her as her cousin sobbed again and moved a shaking hand down across her stomach. "There. They . . . they . . ."

By the time Felis and Shatra knelt beside her, Gemma had mercifully passed out.

"She should go to the hospital, Amala," Zak said sternly.

"The nurses can take care of her," Amala replied. "Besides, she refuses to go anywhere there are men, and she'd never let one touch her after . . ."

She drew her cloak around her more tightly, even though Zak's quarters were comfortably warm. Then she looked up at him, her blue eyes wet with tears.

"They thought she was me, Zak! In the dark there's a strong enough resemblance, especially the hair."

"Why should you think they were after you?"

"Because the ones who grabbed me said, 'That's her,' and they said it again when the other two appeared. I was the one they were after."

Zakton's frown deepened. They'd gotten away. By the time his men had climbed the wall, their sled was lifting off into the darkness with no lights and therefore no way to identify it.

Amala hunched deeper into her cloak and sipped the tea he'd made for her. He ran a shaky hand through his tawny hair as he watched her, guiltily glad that their cousin had been the victim and not her.

He was angry—but with himself, not his men. When they'd first arrived, guards had been posted on the walls at night, but as the weeks had passed and there'd been no incidents, he'd removed them, wanting to prevent the place from looking like the prison Felis had at first believed it to be. He'd also decreased the number of men at the fortress, mostly as a way of preventing just such an incident. The only ones who remained were men he deemed totally trustworthy.

"Amala, I feel so damned bad about this."

"Don't blame yourself, Zak. We all became careless. After all, I felt safe enough to go out there and climb up the wall alone."

She stood up slowly, wincing as her strained muscles protested. Zak started toward her, but she put out a hand to ward him off.

"I'm all right—truly. I'm just sore, and I'll have a few bruises. I want to get back to Gemma."

Two men walked her back to the women's quarters, where there were now two more guarding the entrance. She glanced out toward the wall and saw another figure there.

"We've got guards on the walls, too," the one man reassured her. "The women are safe now, Lady Amala. Please make sure they understand that."

The other man spoke up hesitantly. "We're really sorry about what happened. We don't want the women to think we're all like that."

Touched by their concern, Amala assured them that the women understood that.

Aching in body and spirit, she walked into the main room to find it filled with women standing around in small groups. She wanted to talk to them and reassure them, but she hurried past and headed for Gemma's quarters. Before she got there, she met Felis and Shatra.

"Gemma is sleeping," Felis told her. "They gave her some medicine the doctor brought."

"How badly is she hurt?" Amala asked, leaning tiredly against the wall.

"She's bleeding a little, but the nurses say she'll be all right."

"In body, anyway," Shatra stated.

"It was me they were after."

Both women nodded. "Gemma said they called her your name when they grabbed her."

"What about my aunt?" Amala asked, silently cursing herself for not having thought about her immediately.

"She doesn't know yet," Felis stated, "but she'll have to be told. It will be days before Gemma's face heals."

Then Felis put a hand on Amala's arm. "Don't blame yourself for this."

"I remember worrying about the men's reaction to me when we first left the island. I knew there would be some who might hate me for my resemblance to her, but then I forgot about it."

"It isn't really you they hate," Shatra said. "It's what you represent. They see us as a threat to them."

"Zak says they'll be caught and killed," Felis stated.

Amala shook her head. "But how many more of them are out there? Those two can't be the only ones."

"We're staying here, and we're going to provide for our own safety," Shatra stated defiantly. "We've decided tonight to post our own guards. No one is willing to leave now."

Felis nodded. "She's right. And many of the women want the men to leave the fortress completely."

Amala just nodded and made her way slowly to her rooms. What could she do? She understood how the women felt, and she had no words to change their minds. What had happened to Gemma had to be the worst crime men could perpetrate against women—maybe even worse than murder, because this crime had no ending.

"They even want us to leave, Jor. Amala said she'd try to persuade them to rethink their decision, but I'm not hopeful."

Zakton had difficulty meeting his friend's eyes, even on the screen. Jor looked ready to kill, which was just how Zak himself felt.

"You're not leaving. If they insist, then we'll just have to set up camp outside the walls. And I'm coming to get Amala. I won't have her in the midst of this. She needs to be where she's safe."

"She won't leave, Jor. I just came back from talking to her. I even told her that if we make it public that she's left Savleen, it should discourage them from returning or others from trying the same thing. In spite of what I told them, this place isn't that easy to guard with those walls in such shape. I think she knows that, too, but she won't leave."

"She's leaving—willingly or not!" Jorlan's face was set with cold determination.

"Jor, I agree that she should go for a while, but you can't just come up here and drag her away. The women are upset enough as it is."

"Then come up with a way that I can get her out of there quietly, because I'm taking her tonight!"

Zakton slumped in his chair and drummed his fingers restlessly on the tabletop. Then he suddenly straightened up. "I've just thought of something. It might work, but are you prepared to deal with her afterwards?"

Jorlan nodded, and Zak described his plan.

Several hours later, Jorlan landed in the courtyard. One moon had already set, and the night was at its darkest. He brought a government sled of the type the women were accustomed to seeing come and go from the fortress. Zak had told him that there were now Semlian guards posted at the entrance to the women's quarters and on the roof as well.

He brought the sled to a halt at a point far from the women's quarters but close to the building that housed the men, turning it so that he could use it as cover to enter the men's quarters unobserved by the guards on the roof. Zak was waiting for him inside.

The two men hurried through the building to the cellars. Zak carried an infrared flashlight, and Jorlan had a blanket under his arm.

"I discovered the tunnels years ago when I used to come up here regularly. I don't think anyone else even knows of their existence, since the entrances are all concealed. It may take us a few tries, but I know that one of them comes up in the building the women are using—and if I remember correctly, it comes up not far from her quarters."

"Even if it doesn't, there shouldn't be anyone about at this hour," Jorlan said, "and they won't have any guards inside the building."

"If they do, we're really in trouble," Zak replied darkly.

Both men had a keen sense of direction, and after a short time they came to a heavy door that they felt certain was the one they sought. But they stopped as Zak's light picked out a neatly stacked pile of bundles.

"What's that?" Jor asked in a whisper.

Zak leaned down to examine them. "I don't remember seeing anything in here years ago. If I had, I'd have opened it."

He handed Jorlan the light and withdrew a small knife from his belt to slit the string on the top bundle.

"That wrapping looks like the cloth the women wove on the island," Jorlan remarked.

Zak ripped open the cloth and reached in to pull out a fine, powdery substance. He sniffed at it, then held it up to Jorlan.

"Some kind of herbs," Jorlan said.

"That's what it smells like. They must have discovered the tunnel themselves and decided to use it for storage, maybe because of the cold."

"Then we've got to be even more careful if they already know about the tunnels," Jorlan stated, frowning at the door. "How much noise will that make when we open it, and where does it open to?"

Zakton took the bundle he'd opened and moved it to the back of the pile. "I don't think it'll make any noise. I remember them all being as silent as the one we came through. The

Hevasi built this place well. And it opens into a storage room. I don't think they'd be using it for anything. There's a staircase a few meters down the hall to the left, and Amala's rooms are up one flight, just off that stairwell."

"Let's go, then." Jorlan handed the light back to Zakton and reached for the heavy iron handle.

Luck was with them. The door opened with only the slightest protest, and the room beyond was empty. Even the hallway was silent and deserted. There were no locks on the individual rooms, so gaining entrance to Amala's quarters posed no problem.

The two men crept through the small sitting room into her bedroom, where the pale light from outside reflected off a golden head. Jorlan paused for only a moment before withdrawing a small packet from his pocket and tearing it open. The doctor had guaranteed him that the drug posed no health risk to Amala or the baby, but he still hesitated before approaching her bed and quickly pressing it against her face. She never moved.

Twenty minutes later, Jorlan deposited his blanket-wrapped burden in the passenger seat of the sled and strapped her in. He turned to Zakton before climbing in himself.

"As far as she's concerned, you had nothing to do with this. I just showed up here and pulled rank on you. There's no point in having her angry with both of us."

Zakton nodded distractedly, then spoke up as

Jorlan was about to climb into the sled. "Jor, wait! Those bundles worry me. What if they're not just herbs for cooking? I've been in the kitchen, and they keep herbs there. I think they could be hiding them for some reason."

Jorlan was uninterested in such speculation now. He wanted only to get Amala away. "We can discuss it later," he said and closed the door.

But as he headed back to the city, Zakton's urgent tone stayed with him, and he too began to wonder about the bundles. Zak could be right, but what could they want to hide?

Then abruptly he recalled Amala's having said once that the women had a weapon to use against the men. Herbs as a weapon?

He was over the city and nearly home when a possibility struck him.

When they left for the island, the women had left behind instructions regarding the transfers —and a warning! They'd claimed to have poison they would take if the men ever tried to grab them during the transfers. It was known that there had been poisonous herbs on the island; centuries ago, they'd been gathered for various evil purposes.

Was poison the weapon they held over the men? Would they actually threaten mass suicide if they didn't get the reforms they wanted?

Jorlan stared at the fine golden hair that spilled out of the top of the blanket, and all his old beliefs about the basic emotional instability of females came rushing back.

And he remembered the cold determination on her face when she'd stated that the women would never go back to the old ways.

"She's fine," Jorlan said the moment Zak's worried face appeared on the screen. "I had the doctor here to check her, and he said she'll probably sleep for another three or four hours. She's going to have a headache when she awakens, but I doubt that'll stop her from giving *me* one."

Both men laughed at that, then Jorlan turned serious. He told Zak his thoughts about the herbs, and Zak's face drained of color.

"I can't believe they'd do that," Zak said, but his tone held just a hint of uncertainty.

"Neither can I, but can we afford to take that chance? I think we'd better get those herbs—now!"

When the screen had gone blank, he got up tiredly and went to her room, a small room off the master suite that had once been used by servants. It wasn't luxurious, but he wanted to keep her close by until she awoke. After that, he'd be happy to put as much distance between them as possible. She definitely was not going to be happy, and he knew he wasn't helping his cause, but he had no regrets.

He hadn't bothered to darken the window, and a shaft of light from outside spilled over her face. Her golden hair seemed almost luminescent. Although he'd had every intention of going to bed himself, he drew up a chair and sat down to watch her.

The incident at Savleen had forced him to think about her future. It simply hadn't occurred to him that she might engender such hatred, and yet he knew, sadly, that he should have thought of that. How was he to convince her that she might have to face that anger for the rest of her life? And how would she react to such knowledge—by locking herself up in Zak's compound?

No, in all likelihood she would react by ignoring it and tempting fate. After all, she'd ignored her own safety by driving across the island through that inferno without any good reason, as far as he could see.

As he sat there watching her still form, Jorlan began to understand both the pleasures and frustrations of having one's life inextricably linked to that of another person.

"Felis, wake up!"

Felis opened her eyes reluctantly. Then, when she saw Shatra beside her bed, she sat up quickly. "What is it?"

"Amala's gone! I think Jorlan took her away!"

"What?" Felis shook her head. "How could he? What about the guards?"

"He didn't come past them. I think he used the tunnel."

"The tunnel?" Felis blinked. "You mean where we hid the herbs?"

Shatra nodded. "I found footprints in the

dust that definitely weren't ours, and someone slit open one of the bales, then tried to hide it."

"But how do you know she's gone? Maybe she just went to see Zak."

"That's not likely at this hour." Then she explained that one of the guards on the roof had seen a sled arrive, then leave a short time later. The woman hadn't been sure that it was Jorlan, but few other men were that big—and he was carrying something large enough to be a person. They'd also caught a glimpse of Zakton with him before he left.

Felis lept out of bed and started to dress. "I'm going to see Zak—now!"

"Good! I'm going to bring the herbs up to my rooms until we can find another hiding place."

Felis ran through the dark, silent corridors, passing the Semlian guards at the entrance without a word, and burst into the courtyard where a nervous male guard raised his weapon before seeing who it was.

"I must speak to Za . . . Lord Zakton right now!" Without waiting for a reply, she started across the courtyard. One of the guards caught up with her quickly and began to protest about the lateness of the hour, but after seeing the determined look on her face, he led her inside the men's quarters.

They both stopped in surprise at the entrance to Zakton's office. He was there, just getting up from the vidcom. He looked tired and worried, but he didn't seem surprised to see her. He gave her a smile and waved the guard away as the man explained Felis' insistence upon seeing him.

"Amala's gone," she said without preamble. "Jorlan took her, didn't he?"

Zakton ran a hand through his thick, blond hair. "Yes. She's in danger here, Felis. All the women will be safer once it's known that she's no longer here, and believe me, no one will even try to get her at Jor's home."

"She couldn't have gone willingly."

Zakton shook his head. "I tried to persuade her earlier, but she wouldn't listen to me. He drugged her, but it was safe. I just spoke with him, and the doctor has checked her."

He stared at Felis' angry, flushed face and wanted very much to ask her about those herbs. The thought that this vibrant, lovely woman and his beloved sister might take poison filled him with a cold, terrible dread. But he didn't ask, because he needed time to get the herbs out of the tunnel. Then they could be analyzed.

Felis wasn't even thinking about the herbs at this point. She was too angry. "Zak, how dare you have any part in this? Jorlan doesn't surprise me—but you? Here we are, negotiating for rights you claim to believe in, and you let something like this happen!"

Before he could even begin to defend himself, she went on. "And do you have any idea what this will do to the women? They're already upset and distrustful."

"Don't be so hard on Jor," Zakton said placatingly. "He isn't rational where she's concerned, and he never will be."

"That's no excuse!" Felis folded her arms across her chest and gave him a grim smile. "I wouldn't want to be in his place when she wakes up. He's going to regret it."

"Well, that's his problem for now. What are we going to do about the women? I agree with you that this is going to make matters worse."

"What are *we* going to do?" she echoed. "Do you think you're going to draw me into this?"

"You already are in it," Zak pointed out. "I was thinking that perhaps we could make up a story the women would believe. They all know she's pregnant and that she was attacked, too. Maybe we could say that she became ill and had to be taken to the hospital. That would quiet things down for a few days at any rate."

Felis glared at him. She wanted to scream out to everyone and tell them all about this outrage. But what would that accomplish? Finally, she nodded.

"All right. The only other ones who know she's gone and how she left are the Semlians, and if Shatra tells them to keep quiet, they will. But we'll only go along with this if Amala agrees."

Zak smiled. "Once she's finished giving Jor a tongue-lashing, I think she'll agree. Like you, she'll put the welfare of the women first."

Felis shook her head. "I think that Amala and

Jorlan are headed for disaster."

Zak chuckled. "A lifetime of it is my guess."

Felis started to protest that Amala would never marry Jorlan, but the words stayed in her throat. In some way she couldn't begin to comprehend, she knew they belonged together.

She nodded with a hint of a smile. Then she forgot all about them and everything else as Zak reached out tentatively to smooth her sleep-tousled hair. She raised her arm, half-intending to push him away, but he took her hand and brought it to his lips. His blue eyes never left hers as he brushed his mouth across the back of her hand.

She held her breath until he released it, then she turned quickly and left his office. He called out to say that he would let her know as soon as Amala awakened.

At that moment, it was difficult for her to recall why she had to talk to Amala.

Amala awoke to feel her head throbbing painfully. Then she became aware of her strange surroundings as well as deep, regular breathing somewhere nearby. She turned toward the sound and groaned as even that slight movement made the headache worse. By the time she saw him sprawled in a chair, his eyelids were already fluttering open.

He smiled at her, and for a moment, she actually started to return the smile. Then, as the situation began to dawn on her, she frowned.

She'd been kidnapped and brought to his house. He must have drugged her; that was the reason for the headache. But how did he manage to steal her away from Savleen?

"Did Zak agree to this?" she asked, effectively cutting off whatever he might have been about to say.

"I didn't ask for his agreement."

That wasn't really an answer, but she was disinclined to pursue it at the moment. She sat up in bed and pressed her fingers to her temples.

"Lie down," he said gently. "The headache will go away soon."

She ignored him. "I want to go back to Savleen—now! It's illegal to hold someone against their will."

He sat down on the edge of the narrow bed, and she moved as far from him as she could. "National security supercedes all other laws," he replied matter-of-factly.

"National security?" Her voice rose, but dropped quickly. It hurt too much to shout.

"As the representative of the women, you're very important to our people right now," he continued in the same tone.

"This is the worst abuse of power I've ever heard of," she cried. "How dare you?"

He shrugged. "You said you've studied our laws. Therefore, you know that it's within the Council's right to take any action it deems essential for the national security."

She glared at him, although even frowning

hurt at this point. "Jorlan, I need to be at Savleen now, and I do not appreciate being dragged away just to calm your fears about the baby. *That's* why I'm here. National security indeed!"

He got up and turned away from her. "It isn't just the baby," he muttered.

She lay down again, and the headache became nearly bearable. Shouting at him obviously wasn't going to do either of them any good. "Jorlan," she said in a deliberately reasonable tone, "don't you see what this will do to the women? You're only making it worse."

"Then you can tell them you left voluntarily."

"But they must know already that I didn't. How did you get me here?"

He told her. He wanted desperately to ask about those herbs, but he knew she'd never tell him the truth now. He'd have to wait until Zak got them and had them analyzed.

When he had finished, she closed her eyes, and for a moment he thought she'd gone back to sleep. But then she sighed.

"All right, I'll say that I left to protect them, but I want to stay at Zak's."

She opened her eyes again and could see that he was about to protest, so she closed them again. "Please let me go back to sleep."

It was late morning by the time she awoke again. The headache was gone, and she was ravenous. He'd left a robe for her, so she put it on, noting that it must be one of his, and went to find some food. A Feloth she encountered directed her to the terrace where she found Jorlan, eating and reading what appeared to be a very old book.

"How are you feeling?" he asked as his dark eyes searched hers.

"I'm fine, no thanks to you."

"You know you're safer here, and the others are safer if you're gone."

"You may be right, but I prefer to do my own thinking."

"Even if you're not doing a very good job of it?" he asked with a smile.

But she barely heard him, since she was staring at the book he'd set aside.

"You can read it if you wish," he said, pushing it toward her.

She picked it up and read the gold lettering on the binding. "This is the original? All of it?"

He nodded. "Including the parts that have been kept private. But it can't leave here."

She looked from the old diary to him and back again, then opened it to flip through a few pages. The great warrior had a surprisingly neat handwriting, far neater than his wife's. Then his final words registered.

"Is this your way of bribing me to stay here?"

He nodded without hesitation as he handed her the bowl of fruit.

"It just might be worth it," she murmured,

still flipping through the pages carefully.

"It will be," he promised.

Reluctantly, she set the journal aside and began to eat. He told her about the plan that Zakton and Felis had concocted and said that Felis had grudgingly accepted his word that she agreed with it.

"But she doesn't trust me, so you'd better speak with her yourself."

"Felis is very bright," Amala said, "and she's a perfect example of why the class system has to be eliminated. She deserves better than to live out her life in some terrible little mining village."

"First of all, it's my mining village you're talking about, and it isn't so terrible. She'd live better there than she did on the island. And secondly, I doubt that's what fate has in store for her."

"What do you mean?"

"Maybe you should ask your brother that question."

Amala stared at him, but what she was seeing were those memories of the two of them together. A smile grew slowly. What could be better? Her brother and her best friend. Then the smile died away.

"They can't marry unless the laws are changed."

"As I recall, that's one of your nonnegotiable demands."

"Has the Council agreed to it?"

"Officially, no—but unofficially, I think they will, at least as far as marriage is concerned. Zak has made a good case. He says it would be a painless concession, since no man of a Great Family would ever marry beneath him in any event."

"But then . . ."

Jorlan smiled. "Zak is very smart, too."

Amala laughed, the first true laughter to come from her in quite a while. She hadn't thought it possible to love her brother anymore than she already did.

"So you find the thought of marriage between the two of them pleasant?" he inquired casually.

"Of course, if that's what they want." And she saw the trap just as he sprung it.

"So marriage is fine for Felis—but not for you."

"No."

"Somehow, that doesn't sound very logical to me."

She got up from the table and picked up the diary. "If you want logic, go talk to your computer. Zak tells me they're perfectly logical."

Amala discovered a quiet, shaded spot in the garden and began to read the diary. There were certainly other matters that had a claim upon her attention, but for the moment she was content to delve into the past.

Jorlan had begun the journal when he was 14, prodded by his father, who told him that "all great men record their thoughts in order to learn from them later in life." Whether the promise of greatness was already upon the boy or whether his father merely had high hopes, she couldn't at first begin to guess.

The early entries were those of a boy who chafed at the long hours he was forced to spend in study at the Volas Military Academy, the precursor, Amala assumed, of the current Space Academy. He liked math and science well enough, but he thoroughly detested literature and the arts. "Father says I must learn them as well, but they are clearly inferior subjects fit only for girls."

He did not, however, seem unhappy with the apparently quite severe discipline of the school, although from time to time he did get into trouble, being very fond of practical jokes.

She was in the midst of a rather charmingly rendered tale of mischief when the other Jorlan appeared. Because she was so engrossed in the diary, she at first believed this ancient diary to be his, or perhaps she thought he was his ancestor come to life. Whatever the case, for one brief moment, past and present merged.

"I commend you on your thoroughness," he said drily. "You apparently haven't given into the temptation to turn to the end."

"Is this the only journal he kept?" It was a very large book, but she knew he had lived a long life.

"No, but the others were written for public

consumption—battlefield diaries and other writings. This one he kept for his private thoughts, intended only for the family."

She wondered if he himself kept such a journal but felt it improper to ask.

"The Council will be meeting within the hour, and they request that you attend."

So she accompanied him to the Council building, dressed this time in one of the gowns she'd left behind at his mountain home that he'd been thoughtful enough to have brought here. He didn't tell her the purpose of the meeting, but she assumed it had to do with the attack upon Gemma.

Her assumption proved to be correct. Each member of the Council in turn condemned the rape, and several inquired after her cousin's welfare.

"Her body will heal, but her spirit may not," Amala told them. "She was already suffering because of her mother's withdrawal and her belief that the goddess had turned her back."

One of the older men, whom Amala had reason to believe was not an ally, turned to Jorlan. "I propose that we authorize now the expenditure of funds to build the women's center dedicated to Aleala that Lady Amala has requested."

The motion carried unanimously. Amala was surprised, since this was the first time they'd taken any action in her presence.

"Thank you on behalf of the women. I'm sure

they will be very pleased."

Another man, who'd said little at previous meetings, expressed his concern for the women once they left Savleen. "We need not be concerned about the welfare of Great Family women, of course, but some guarantees of safety beyond the usual constabulary must be made for the others."

Amala remained prudently silent, refraining from mentioning that at this point the women were adamant about remaining at the fortress.

"I've already given some thought to that and had intended to discuss it with Lady Amala to get her opinion," Jorlan stated, "but I will give you all my thoughts now. I believe that what we need is some sort of special constabulary to deal with any complaints of abuse or harassment of the women. It seems to me that the Semlians might serve this purpose well, and their leader could report directly to the Council for the time being."

Once again, Amala was surprised and pleased. She said so and expressed the opinion that the Semlians would be very willing to assume such a role. This motion, too, carried unanimously.

Jorlan then informed her that the Council would continue their discussions about other matters, all of which he hoped would be resolved within the next few days. From the look he gave the other members, Amala guessed that would happen.

She thanked the members and left the meeting to be driven back to Jorlan's residence by one of his aides. The young man offered to take her back by sled or to drive her through the city if she so wished. Touched by his thoughtfulness, which she assumed to be Jorlan's doing, she accepted.

Chapter Ten

AMALA HAD SCARCELY BEGUN TO READ THE DIARY again when both Jorlan and Zakton appeared. After her drive through the city, she'd spoken to Felis and Shatra. Both were very excited by her news, and Shatra said she was sure the Semlians would be happy to assume this important responsibility. All three women felt that such guarantees would go far to dispel the women's fears.

When Jorlan and Zakton arrived, she told them about her conversation with Felis and Shatra.

"I have decided to go up to Savleen to speak with the women myself," Jorlan stated. "Zak will be returning, and naturally I'd like you to accompany me."

"But I'm supposed to be in the hospital," she reminded him.

He frowned. "I'd forgotten that. Well, I want to get this over with, so just try to look sick."

Amala turned questioningly to Zakton, who chuckled. "Jor is facing this with about as much enthusiasm as he once faced poetry reading in school."

Jorlan turned away. "I suppose I'd better dress the part. I'll be ready in a few minutes."

Amala stared after him with a smile. "Why is he afraid to speak to them?"

"I think Jor finds women rather difficult to deal with, although I can't imagine why. I'm going to enjoy this."

Word had been sent to Savleen, and by the time they arrived, virtually all the women were assembled in the great courtyard. Amala saw to her surprise that even some of the more religious women were there, though her aunt was not among them.

The women were clearly pleased to see her, and she already knew that most of them regarded Zakton with fondness or at least with trust. But she saw the wary looks given to the man at her side. His great size and his elaborate uniform, complete with sword, didn't aid his cause—and neither did the slight scowl he wore.

But if he was uneasy, it didn't affect his speech. His delivery was rather abrupt, but the words were well-chosen. He expressed his sorrow and anger over what had happened. He pled for their understanding that not all men were such monsters, although he understood how they might not believe that again. He assured them that their basic rights as citizens would be guaranteed, although some of what they sought might not be accomplished quickly.

Amala watched the women as he spoke, paying particular attention to those whose skepticism regarding men was well-known. They were attentive to his every word and even nodded in satisfaction from time to time.

When he had finished, the Semlians scattered through the crowd began to applaud, and others joined in until the stone walls rang with the sound. Jorlan was clearly pleased with himself, but after a few moments, he glanced at her and then held up his hands to still the gathering.

"There is one more thing I wish to tell you. Perhaps Lady Amala will forgive me for not having told her first, but this is a victory for all of you. The Council has voted unanimously to invite Lady Amala to become a member, with all rights and privileges."

He glanced at her again and smiled. "Although she will have only one vote, I can assure you that hers will be a very powerful voice. On issues directly affecting women, she has been given the power of veto."

Amala was stunned. She barely heard the applause and cries of delight. She had expected at least one seat to be given to the women, but never had she dreamed they would grant her such power. Even in the midst of her shock, she was wondering just how far she could stretch those "issues directly affecting women."

The women all began to crowd around her, congratulating her and inquiring after her health. She could only hope that her shock would be interpreted as sickness.

Felis finally made her way through the crowd to hug Amala. "I keep thinking about that old saying that out of evil always comes some good."

Amala nodded and inquired after Gemma and her aunt. Gemma's mother had been told that her daughter had a highly contagious sickness and must stay away from her for a few days. Her wounds would take much longer to heal, but since Amala's mother was due to arrive at Savleen the next day, they all hoped she would be able to deal with her sister.

Felis told her that Gemma was as well as could be expected, and they both turned to find Jorlan once again at her side.

"Will your cousin see me?" he asked. "I'd like to speak to her."

Amala looked doubtful. Gemma hadn't even been willing to see Zakton, and she knew and liked him, but Felis suggested they go ask her.

It took some persuading, but Gemma agreed to see both men. Amala was proud of her cousin's bravery and told her so. Then they returned to the courtyard and led Jorlan and

Zakton to Gemma's room.

Amala had very nearly exhausted her capacity for surprise, but she discovered a reserve supply as she watched Jorlan speak with her cousin. His anger over what had happened to her was quiet but very evident. He repeated what Amala had already told her about the special constabulary for women and the women's center.

"Right now, you must be feeling very ugly, maybe even ashamed, but you're a very beautiful woman and one day you'll put this behind you."

As they left, Gemma actually smiled at Jorlan and put out her hand. He bent over it and kissed it, and Amala's last glimpse of her cousin was that of a woman who just might have found hope again.

Zakton and Felis stayed behind to talk some more to Gemma, and as soon as they were alone in the hallway, Amala turned to Jorlan.

"I . . . I don't know what to say to you. You gave her hope. You gave them all hope. How could you have been afraid to come up here?"

"I'm glad it's over. Now, are you going to come back with me willingly, or do you plan to undo all this by putting up a fight?"

"Oh, I'll come back with you. I'm very curious about this veto power, and of course I want to finish the diary."

Jorlan groaned. The veto power had been his suggestion, but he'd extracted a promise from

Zak that she would never know that. She had too damned much power over him as it was.

He walked out into the bright sunlight of the courtyard, where most of the women stood about in animated groups.

The past is done with, he thought. For better or worse, we're moving into the future. Then he glanced at the golden head beside him and began to worry anew.

Amala awoke to a scream, then realized it was hers. The nightmare came back in all its horror—dark, shadowy figures chasing her across an endless courtyard. Her legs had seemed weighted down, unable to move. "That's her!" echoed endlessly through her brain.

Then a dark, shadowy figure was there in her room. She cried out again, still too caught in her dream to recognize him. He bent over her, and she pushed at his bare chest.

"Amala, it's me! You were having a nightmare." He resisted her feeble attempts to push him away and wrapped his arms about her.

The nightmare began to fade. She shuddered. "I dreamed that those men were chasing me again." She drew in a ragged breath.

"I should be having good dreams now."

He smoothed the hair from her brow. "Seeing Gemma probably brought it on. Would you like some mulled wine?"

She nodded, and he left the room. She sat there, willing her body to calmness again. She was glad he was there, and it took a few moments for her to consider the implications of that. She was glad *he* was there, not just someone she knew and trusted. She thought about last night, when she'd awakened to find him asleep in the chair near her bed. She thought about that smile. She thought about how wonderful he'd been at Savleen. She thought about the wonderful evening they'd spent, discussing their society's future.

Her thoughts were interrupted as he returned with two goblets of wine. It was a different kind, warm and smoky and richer in flavor. She sipped it slowly as he once more sat down on the edge of her bed.

He hadn't bothered to put on a robe. He wore only the briefest of shorts, and his body stood out starkly against the white of the bed linens. But this time she didn't move away.

"This is very good," she murmured as she sipped some more of the wine.

"It is, but it's also strong. That's why I didn't give you much."

"I'm sorry I woke you."

"Would you be sorrier if I weren't here?" he asked in a quiet, serious tone.

She shook her head. "I'm glad you are. Very glad."

He took the goblet from her and set it beside his on the table. Then he curved a hand around her head and lowered his mouth to hers. His lips tasted of the wine as they moved with persuasive gentleness over hers. She lifted both arms and wrapped her hands around his neck as she arched toward him. He drew in a sharp breath, then groaned as he slowly bore her back against the pillows.

The nightmare was left behind, and she seemed to be moving into a dream, a dream where she was surrounded by a big, hard body that trembled as much as her own. He trailed kisses across her face, along her neck and throat and down into the deep vee of her nightshirt. His hands molded themselves to her with a gentle fire.

A longing was growing in her, burning away all reason, driving out all fear. She felt heavy, languorous. She wanted.

Then he drew away from her and sat up again. "Amala, I know you don't understand what's happening, but I have to stop now while I still can."

She nodded, if only because she could hear the anguish in his voice. He took her outstretched hand for a moment, then got up and left the room.

She lay back against the pillows, glorying in these strange, new feelings, but she still wanted. The heaviness, the need, was still there. Somehow she was out of bed before she knew she'd made a decision. She walked down the silent hallway and paused only once, when she reached his closed door, but her hand lifted itself to knock before her feet could carry her back to her room. She opened the door as soon as she heard him say her name, his muffled voice sounding worried.

He sat up in the big bed, staring at her, but she spoke before he could say anything.

"I want to be here—with you."

"Are you sure?"

"Yes." Then she frowned as a thought occurred to her. "Could this harm the baby?"

"No. I'll be careful."

Swiftly, he was out of the bed and across the big room and lifting her into his arms. She felt the tremors still running through his body and somehow that calmed her.

He laid her on the bed, then drew the nightshirt over her head and quickly rid himself of his shorts. She made a small sound of surprise when she saw him. He bent to kiss her and smiled.

"I promised I'd be careful."

And he was. Time lost all meaning for them both as he led her into a new and wondrous world, and she brought to him what he'd never known could exist. Outside, the night grayed toward dawn as they discovered each other, slept and awoke to make new discoveries. What began with urgency moved on to slow tenderness.

Once, when he slept, she lay there wrapped in his arms and stared at him, not quite able to believe what was happening. And later, as she slept, he watched her, knowing only that he could never let her go, that they were two parts of a single whole.

Sunlight was pouring into the room when Shebba came as usual to wake him. She stared at the entwined bodies on the bed, started to approach them, then dropped to all fours and scurried off to discuss this strangeness with her family.

Jorlan paced back and forth on the walkway suspended over the gigantic work area. Below him, the starship he'd helped to design was swarming with workers. There was no reason he needed to be here on Ethera, and indeed his arrival had surprised the Maintenance Chief, who even now stood near the bow of the starship staring up at him with a puzzled frown.

He was here because he needed to be anywhere but *there,* where she was. He'd left her just after they'd breakfasted together, telling her that he had some things to check on up here and might not be back until the next day.

He stopped his pacing and leaned against the railing, unaware of the fact that his presence made both the Chief and the workers nervous. This ship had been virtually his home for the past seven years, and he'd expected that to continue for at least the next five—until it was replaced by the new one he was even now working on or until he was forced to decide about the Chairmanship.

If he'd been asked why he chose to risk his life

in space, he would have said simply, "Space is where I belong." Up until now, he'd never questioned that. Up until now, there were many things he'd never questioned.

Born to great wealth and power and blessed with intelligence and the innate qualities that make for leadership, Jorlan had never questioned that he was master of his own destiny. Even as a child he'd known that. His father had believed that raising a son meant letting him try and fail, allowing him to test his own limits.

Now he was trying to face the certainty that his destiny lay in the delicate hands of one fragile woman, and to him, she would always be fragile. The great strength he had seen in her was something she put on and then discarded, like an ancient suit of armor.

Last night with her had been . . . Even in his mind, he could not put words to it; he could only feel it. He stared at the starship, remembering the day he'd come up here to take command. What he'd felt at that moment—the best moment of his life, he'd believed—was insignificant by comparison with his feelings last night when she'd suddenly appeared in his bedroom.

But the analogy ended abruptly right there. The ship had been his to command; Amala was not and never would be. He realized now that Jorlan's mistake all those years ago had not been his failure to control his wife—but his attempts to do so.

"We hold love by letting go." The phrase came back to him from somewhere. Probably the poetry he'd been force-fed in school. He winced as he thought about the things he'd said to her last night; surely the reality wasn't as soppy as he was remembering.

Then he recalled where he'd read that phrase —in Amala's diary.

"Is something troubling you?" Felis asked as she peered closely at Amala.

Amala turned away briefly so her friend wouldn't see the flush that she felt creeping through her fair skin. "No, of course not. I'm probably just a bit dazed by all that's happened."

Felis laughed. "So am I. Zak's been talking to individual Council members, and he's sure that everything will be settled when they meet day after tomorrow. He says he can't talk details, but he feels that we'll get a lot more than he'd expected us to get."

"He said the same thing to me."

They were standing in the middle of the courtyard at the edge of the garden area. Both women remained silent for a moment, then Felis said in a strange tone.

"This place will probably be deserted again before winter comes."

"Yes, I think so," Amala replied, then cast a sharp glance at her friend. "You're not happy about that."

This time it was Felis who turned away. "No, though I know I should be."

"But Felis, you won't have to go back to your family. You can stay with me. I already told you that."

Felis smiled sadly and shook her head. "I appreciate the offer, but I think I'll probably go to one of the women's residences they plan to set up. I want to study engineering, if I can."

"But why should you choose to go to a residence when you can stay with me?"

When Amala saw the look in Felis' eyes, she thought she knew the answer, but she waited, hoping Felis would say it first. She didn't, and Amala finally said it for her.

"It's because of Zak, isn't it? You don't want to stay with me because he'll be there."

"That's not true," Felis protested, a bit too quickly. "You know I like Zak."

"And that's just the problem."

"Besides," Felis hurried on, ignoring Amala's remark, "I don't think you'll be there very long. You'll marry Jorlan."

"Well, I'm glad you have that all figured out," Amala said drily. "*I* certainly don't."

"You belong together."

"So he says," she muttered. "He says a lot of things like that."

"He's not so bad," Felis went on. "I'm revising my opinion of him after yesterday. Of course, he's not at all like Zak, but neither is he the monster I thought he was."

"That's a wonderful recommendation for a husband."

At that moment, both women spotted Zakton and Lady Mava approaching them. Amala hadn't yet seen her mother, since she'd been closeted with her sister. As she waited nervously to learn how she'd fared, she couldn't help noticing the ease with which mother and son talked.

Amala kissed her mother and inquired about her aunt. She also thought her mother looked ten years younger than she had before their flight from the island.

"She talked a little bit. I decided to keep up the story that Gemma has a contagious illness because she seemed to have accepted it. Gemma has agreed to go to the hospital to receive treatments that will heal her face quickly. Even though Ester will have to be told at some point, it would be easier if she doesn't see the damage."

"Mother, I think you're a miracle worker," Amala said, hugging her.

Lady Mava shook her head. "From what I've heard, you are the true miracle worker—you and Zak and Jorlan. He's quite nice, by the way. Not at all like his namesake, I daresay."

"You've met him?"

"Yes, he came to visit me in the hospital the other day. He's terribly big, though. I do hope that baby of his isn't going to take after him. Large babies can be difficult."

Amala didn't care about that at the moment. "Why did he come to see you?"

"Well why not? He's Zak's best friend and the father of my grandchild." Then she turned to Felis, who stood quietly on the edge of the family group.

"Felis, dear, Zak tells me that you will be coming to stay with us, too. I've been hearing such wonderful things about you."

Amala exchanged glances with her brother as their mother chattered on. She couldn't tell at this point if her mother was merely being polite or was wholly sincere. Lady Mava was a very diplomatic woman. Amala whispered to Zak that she needed to speak with him privately, and they left the other two.

As soon as they were alone in a corner of the garden, she gave her brother a steady look. "I want to know your intentions regarding Felis."

Zak grinned. "Oh? I always thought that was a question for the head of the family to be asking."

"Don't try to sidestep the issue, Zak. Jorlan told me how you maneuvered the Council into dropping the laws against inter-class marriage."

"Jor was under an oath not to talk about Council deliberations. Just how did you get that out of him?" He grinned at her challengingly.

Once again, she turned away to avoid having someone see her suddenly rosy face, but Zak was perhaps more perceptive or more knowledgeable than Felis had been.

"So it's like that, is it?" He chuckled. "He might at least have come to me to ask for your hand in marriage first. What kind of example are you two setting? And where is he, by the way? Under the circumstances, I'd have thought he'd be unwilling to let you out of his sight."

"He had to go up to Ethera, something to do with his ship. He may not be back until tomorrow." And she wasn't displeased about that, although she didn't say so.

"So he ran away. Poor Jor. This is rough on him. Unhinged by a woman."

"He didn't run away. He had business up there."

Zak leaned toward her, grinning. "Hah! He has no more business up there than I do at the moment. He's scared."

She frowned, thinking about his distracted behavior this morning. She'd been rather upset, because he'd seemed to have already set last night behind him. She had just assumed that was the way men were.

"Do you really think so?"

Zak nodded. "And since he broke his oath, I'm going to break mine as well. Would you like to know how he managed to get that veto power for you?"

"I assumed that was your idea."

"No, although it's a great idea. The Council wouldn't hear of having anyone but Great Family women on the council, and Jor knew you would never accept that restriction, so he came up with the idea of your having veto power over women's issues. The only way he could get the more conservative members to go along with it was to explain that since you'll be his wife, he'll be able to keep the situation under control."

"Wh . . . what?" Amala spluttered. "How could he? I'll . . ." She clenched her fists. "If he knows what's good for him, he'll just get on that ship of his and disappear."

"That might be a little bit difficult to do, since the ship's in the repair bay."

"That does it! I will *not* marry him!"

"Does that mean you were considering it?" Zak asked with a smile.

"I was, but now I'm not. And you still haven't answered my question about Felis."

"I'm . . . very fond of her."

"Like a sister, you mean?"

"She's not my sister."

"Zak?" she said threateningly.

He backed off in mock fear. "Save your anger for Jor. I care a lot for Felis, but I need to see how she gets along with Lev. And we also have to talk about what marriage to me would mean for her. She just won't be accepted by some people, Amala. Abolishing a law doesn't necessarily change everyone's minds."

"Felis is strong, and she has me. I won't let anyone be unkind to her."

"Neither would I, but we can't protect her from everyone."

"Have you talked to Mother about this?"

Amala asked, recalling her mother's changed behavior toward Felis.

"Well, I hinted at it, but she knows nothing yet about the change in the laws."

"Mother will definitely have to be eased into this. I think she already had several candidates in mind for you."

"It might help my cause if she saw at least one of her children happily married to an appropriate mate."

"Bribery will get you nowhere, Brother."

Early that evening, Amala watched Felis playing with her little nephew, showing a lot more skill with the freba than Amala herself had. Amala, Zak, their mother and Felis had all flown down to the city to have dinner at Zak's home. She hadn't bothered to leave word at Jorlan's about her plans. If he came home, he could find her, but she hoped he wouldn't come back yet. She needed to calm herself a bit first.

"He's such a sweet child," Lady Mava said as she watched her grandson.

"How could he be otherwise with Zak as a father? He seems to like Felis, too."

She spoke casually, but she held her breath as she waited for a reply. However, her mother obviously had other things on her mind at the moment.

"Dear, I know I have no right to pry, but are you going to marry Jorlan? It would certainly be an excellent match, don't you think?"

Actually, thought Amala, it might be more of a collision. "I don't know yet. We have some things to discuss."

"Well, I hope you will. Zak certainly doesn't seem interested in marriage."

"Ummm," Amala replied. Zak could deal with this himself.

A short time later, she took her leave. Zak was flying his mother and Felis back to Savleen, and she insisted upon flying herself back to Jorlan's —not because she wanted to see him, but because she wanted to read more of that diary. She might not have another opportunity.

The skies were crowded, but she had no problems. Piloting an airsled had become second nature to her. When she reached Jorlan's compound, she found, to her pleasure, that he hadn't returned.

She settled down in the small sitting room of her suite with the old diary. Since it was entirely possible that she wouldn't be remaining here after he returned, she reluctantly did what he'd commended her for not doing. She turned to a place near the end. Then, after reading a few lines with increasing disbelief, she flipped backwards to the time just before their marriage.

There were sections she was able to skip, because even in this personal account he wrote about matters of no interest to her at the moment—wars and struggles within the Council. But what lay between those parts held her in thrall.

He *had* loved his wife, and at times, it was clear that he'd even understood her quest for rights and freedom. He was a prisoner of his time, though; he accepted things as they were, when he might have used his enormous power to effect change.

She paused for a moment, thinking about the present Jorlan. He too had enormous power, but unlike his ancestor he'd used that power to transform their society. She knew that both she and Zak had played major roles, but she also knew that without Jorlan they could never have achieved anything.

She returned to the diary, and there were tears in her eyes as she read the pages he'd written after Amala had gone off to the island. At times, he sounded nearly deranged. Perhaps he had been; that could account for the disaster at Savleen.

And then she read the final entries. She knew that he'd lived a long life, and his slightly unsteady handwriting at the end showed that. But his mind had recovered. In the years between his wife's departure and the end of his life, every entry showed a terrible sadness, but there was no further mention of her. The parallels between this diary and Amala's were striking in that regard.

The final entry was difficult to read; his handwriting had deteriorated badly. Perhaps he knew even as he wrote that it would be the last entry because he finally wrote of her again.

"I have lived too long without her, without the best part of me, and I would gladly give up all that I have accomplished to have her back beside me. She was the best of me. One day, if the old goddess permits it and women return, it is my hope that men can learn from my mistakes."

The heavy diary fell from her lap onto the thick carpeting with a soft thud as her eyes fluttered open. Once more, she was caught between the past and present as she stared at the man who stood there before her, his dark gaze flicking from the diary to her.

"I cheated," she admitted when she had oriented herself. "I read the final entries."

Then she frowned. "I wasn't expecting you to return tonight."

"You sound disappointed," he remarked neutrally as he picked up the journal.

"Perhaps I am," she agreed, engaged in a silent debate with herself about discussing this now. What she really wanted was to go back to the bed they'd shared last night.

"It wasn't necessary for me to go up there today," he said in a distracted tone.

"I know that. Zak told me."

"And he also told you that I ran away because I was scared."

"Oh! Then you talked to him?"

He smiled. "No, but he knows me, even though I wish he'd keep his knowledge to himself."

"So you *were* scared!"

"No, I *am* scared. It hasn't stopped." He indicated the diary he still held. "Well, what do you think of him now?"

"I think he was as unhappy as she was, and they were both caught in their time. But he could have changed it, and he didn't."

He nodded.

"You *have* changed things, Jorlan. Is that why you're scared?"

He was silent for a long moment, then nodded. "I was standing up there today, staring at my ship and wondering what kind of world it will be when our son goes off on his first starship."

Amala decided this was not the time to suggest that the son they didn't yet have might decide to choose another career. She'd learned that in those rare moments when this man was willing to reveal his private thoughts and feelings, it was best not to interrupt him.

He looked down at the diary again. "But I don't want to come to the end of my life with the regrets he had."

"You won't," she said softly.

He seemed not to have heard her for a moment, then suddenly jerked his attention away from the diary. "What do you mean?"

"I'll make sure you don't regret it—that is, as long as you don't try to control my power on the Council."

"You and Zak must have had quite a conver-

sation. So he told you about that, too?"
She nodded.
"It was the only way I could get them to agree."
"I know that now, but at the time I would have been happy to see you fly off on that starship of yours."
"But it won't work if you don't marry me," he pointed out.
"Yes, I can see that. Either I marry you or the Council might take away my power, is that it?"
He said nothing as his dark eyes searched hers, trying to determine if she were serious. Then he shook his head.
"I won't let them do that."
"Good, because no one should be forced into marriage." Then she got up and took his hand. "Of course, I could be *talked* into it."
He stared at her until his somber mood suddenly vanished beneath a smile. She returned it and spoke in a teasing tone.
"You were rather good at talking last night, as I recall."
He swept her up into his arms and started for the bedroom. "But I'm much better at other things, wouldn't you agree?"
And he was. She'd wondered if it could be this good again, and it was even better. He knew her now, and she was beginning to know him as well. There was less urgency, too, and more time to touch each other's feelings. Their bodies flowed against each other and melted into one.

They fell asleep still joined in love and in their dreams.

Beyond the walls of the compound, the world was poised to change forever.

EPILOGUE

"I'M STILL NOT SURE I LIKE THIS," JORLAN MUTtered.

"And you never will be, either, but don't let her know that," Amala whispered.

Zak's voice came as a low murmur in her other ear. "She already knows. She says he's too old to change, but she loves him anyway."

They sat with the other Council members in seats of honor on the dais. The large audience was spread out below them on the field. As the speaker's voice droned on, Amala's eyes swept over the front rows of identical cream-colored uniforms. The graduating class was seated on the platform behind her, but the undergraduates were assigned to the first rows in the field.

Her roving gaze found Tevi. His auburn hair glistened in the sun, and even from here she thought she could see those mischievous blue eyes. She smiled and let her gaze move on to Felis, his mother, who sat in the first row behind the academy students. Her own auburn hair now held a tinge of gray.

Amala smiled again at Tek, the near-perfect image of his father. Sometimes she wondered if she'd had anything to do with him. Next year he too would be a student here.

Beside Tek was Lev, still sporting his tawny beard. He'd just returned from some unpronounceable star system, and she could still recall the wistful looks on the faces of his father and uncle as he described his voyage.

The speaker finally droned off to silence, and Jorlan got up to say a few words as Council Chairman. She smiled her love at him as he walked to the podium in the midst of a hushed silence. He still hated speeches, yet he never failed to rouse his audience.

He has already passed into legend, she thought. He could read the Citizen Directory, and they would still hang on his every word. If his ancestor had been characterized as their greatest warrior, this man was indisputably their greatest Chairman.

When he had finished his remarks, he waited at the podium as the Cadet First Captain, the leader of the graduating class, came down from the rows behind him. Father and daughter embraced to cheers and applause. Zak leaned over to her, grinning.

"It's times like this that make him worth living with, right?"

She laughed, amused as always at Zak's habit of speaking her thoughts before she herself did.

Glea's voice was firm and clear, even though she'd been a tangle of nerves only a few hours ago. Amala stared at her daughter with a pride and love that threatened to burst forth any moment. She was tall, almost as tall as her namesake, but she had her mother's golden hair and blue eyes.

Jorlan had returned to his seat beside her, and when she cast him a sidelong glance, she saw moisture in the corner of his eye. He would deny it, of course, if she ever mentioned it. And she wouldn't mention it for that reason. Glea's speech was drawing to a close.

"That's what I hope the world of the future will hold for us, but I'd like to finish by paying tribute to the two people who are most responsible for the world of the present and for my being here today."

Glea turned to them, smiling, and the applause grew to deafening proportions as she came over and drew her parents to their feet.

Amala stood there in the bright sunlight and stared off into the heavens. Glea would soon be out there, and it looked so very big.

For just a moment, she too wasn't sure she liked it. But she would never tell Jorlan that.